TEXAS

Orly Mann Racing Series

Ken Stuckey

Xulon
PRESS

Dedication

This book is dedicated to the hard working folks of the National Fellowship of Raceway Ministries. I am much impressed by their vision and their desire to serve as they minister across the United States in the racing world. You might find them at the bullring outside Amarillo or the road course in New York or even the Indianapolis Motor Speedway. Wherever you find them, rest assured that they will be doing their best to bring blessings to the race fan. They are a great group of people.

Nobody writes a book by themselves, at least not me. Thanks Ging, Sam and Steph, and Katie for your constant encouragement and willingness to put up with Dad's crankiness as he works with deadlines. Emery James, may you grow up to be a good man just like your Papa. Grandpa loves you.

Author's Note

I have been involved with Stock Car racing most of my adult life. I love the sound of an open exhaust resonating beneath a full-bodied race car. Through the years it has been my pleasure to visit a good number of racetracks on the NASCAR circuit. Each track is unique and has its own personality.

Las Vegas is clean, and every time you go, they have built something new or changed something.

Bristol is an experience, especially when you stand down low in the grandstands at turn one. The cars seem almost vertical on the banking, and you can see the driver working the wheel as he tries to keep it off the fence.

Talladega is fast and mean, and boy do they run close. Talk about spectacular. I often hear people say, "I could do that." Then they watch the pack go screaming by at two hundred plus and suddenly it doesn't look so easy. Especially when you realize that the cars are literally bobbing and weaving, and the slightest error or miscalculation is going to be catastrophic.

Atlanta takes precision. I watched Kenseth run lap

after lap, literally pulling flecks of paint off the turn four wall. Then a tire let go and there was that familiar sound of grinding sheet metal punctuated with the smell of hot oil and tire smoke. Blam! That quick.

My home track is Sear's Point. Yeah, I know they call it Infineon today, but to me, it will always be Sears. There is nothing finer that watching a skilled driver hustle a 3800 pound car through the esses, setting somebody up for a pass through turn Ten. Racin' is rubbin' don'tcha know.

Yes each track is unique, but in my mind there is one that stands head and shoulders above the rest, and that is Texas Motor Speedway. Eddie Gossage, the guy in charge, knows how to promote and to entertain. He listens to the fans and if it ain't right…he fixes it. The place is big, sprawling big. It is clean and well run. Everything a race fan could need is available. The campgrounds are great, with showers and even a general store. Generally speaking there isn't a bad seat in the house. The track itself is fast and provides great racing. The place has character. And dear reader, it is the setting for this Orly Mann adventure. Enjoy.

Prologue

*"I tell you. If it ain't one thing
it is something else."*

Henry (Bear) Erickson

The black dog watched Bear intently from his bed in the corner of the cluttered office. Bear was pacing the floor as he talked on the phone, and the dog tracked his movements with his head up and his ears pricked forward like antennae. From the dog's perspective, it was getting close to quitting time and supper was just around the corner. Of course lately they had been staying pretty late and eating supper right here in Bear's office. But being a dog, you never know, maybe this was a precursor to heading home.

Finally Bear stopped pacing and collapsed into the chair behind the desk. As soon as he did, the dog was up and across the room to lay his head into Bear's lap with a look in his deep brown eyes that said, "Well, Boss, what's it going to be? We staying or going?"

"Yes, Rosie, I know." Bear leaned back in his chair and absent-mindedly scratched the black dog behind the ears with one hand while he cradled the phone with the other.

"Later tonight, then. Okay, do you want me to come and sit with you?" Bear nodded as if he was talking to a lady across from his desk. "Yes I know these things happen. Just one of those things, I guess. I feel for him. Wasn't his fault. Like I said, he just stepped back at the wrong time and got his feet tangled in a floor jack and down he went. I didn't realize how bad he was hurt till he started groaning. 'Course we called 911 right away... well, you know the rest."

Bear pushed the dog away and stood up from his chair wishing the conversation was over. He had nothing against Rosie, but if she didn't want him to come to the hospital, he had other things that had to get done. He walked over to the big plate glass window that took up almost one whole wall of his office and looked down on the busy shop.

It was a beautiful facility. The place was large and over a hundred employees were hustling around with a specific purpose. Everybody was busy. Nobody was standing around wasting time. Bear could see that the lights were still on in the motor shop at one end of the building. That was good. They needed those guys to step it up some. Show me a crew chief that doesn't want more power out of his motors. Of course he had no complaints. They only broke two motors all year (so far) and that was pretty doggone good. But then again, they still had three races to go, and of course anything could happen.

He mentally counted how many cars were under construction in the fabrication area of the shop. Eleven.

Six were decaled and painted in the Blue Saber colors. Bear could see the big #11 on the doors and roof. Five were decked out in the Speed King yellow and orange with the purple highlights and the number #37.

It was getting close to quitting time, but a few guys were putting the finishing touches on one of the Speed King Chevrolets. Two big, eighteen-wheeled haulers were backed up to the big doors at the end of the building. Another small group of men were walking up and down the loading ramps as they moved equipment into the big trailers. *Getting ready to hit the road for Texas,* Bear thought to himself. *This here is Tuesday and they will be heading out Wednesday night for the trip. It seemed like those Haulers hardly stopped anymore.*

Bear watched with a critical eye as a mechanic slithered into the car head first with only his hips and legs hanging out the window. *Probably adjusting a seat bracket or something.*

He mentally shifted gears and got back into the conversation.

"Okay Rosie, you call me when the surgery is done. It don't matter what time it is. You got my cell number so just let me know how it goes. You know everybody here is praying for him. I'm sorry this happened. All right then, I'll talk to you later."

Bear started to click the phone off, then stopped dead in his tracks. "Really, well when did they show up? Man, they don't miss a trick. Well, don't tell them anything but the truth. I'm sure they will be calling me here shortly."

Bear walked back to his desk and sat down. He put his head into his hands and leaned over the desk. *Why*

*oh why Lord? Especially now, this week? We are sitting
second and fourth in the championship standings with
three races left in the season. This accident just couldn't
have happened at a worse time.*

The black dog took up a station next to Bear's thigh
once again and patiently put his head on his knee. Brad
Gillespie was Rosie's husband. He was also the crew
chief for the Blue Saber Chevrolet, driven by T.K.
Kittridge, which was the other Orly Mann team car. It
was a fluke accident. Late this afternoon Brad had his
head buried beneath the hood of the car working on
a shock bracket. He backed up to grab a wrench out
of the toolbox. Somehow he got his feet tangled up
in a floor jack and took a fall. He fell awkwardly, and
in the process, he wedged his foot under something,
fracturing his ankle, banging his head on the concrete
and breaking a bone in his face. At first it didn't seem
serious, but when he didn't get up, everybody realized
he was hurt and unconscious.

The ankle injury turned out to be a 'severe frac-
ture', as the doctor said, and he was getting ready to
undergo surgery to have some pins and screws put in.
The facial injury created a lot of swelling, but so far it
was minimal. On the surface it was just one of those
unfortunate accidents that happen in a busy shop with
nearly a hundred employees. It could have happened to
anybody. Bear had a bad elbow himself from tripping
over something in the shop years ago. But this was a
bad thing for the Orly Mann Team. A really bad thing.

Brad did for T.K. what Bear did for Orly. That
meant that he was top dog in charge of making the
car ready to race. It had to be ready to go when it was

off-loaded from the Hauler. There was no extra time in the busy weekend to lollygag fixing the car with something that should have been done at the shop. Brad also had to co-ordinate getting all the parts and pieces they might need in the course of the weekend to the track. Then once he was at the track, the most important part of his job was to fine-tune the car to make it go as fast as it possibly could. He also had to be smart enough to make the proper adjustments on the car through the course of a race.

The crew chief worked closely with the driver, but he was also in charge of coordinating the efforts of the fabricators and mechanics that built the cars back at the shop. He had to know every aspect of the car inside and out. Then he had to know the driver's preferences in terms of handling and driving style. At the same time, he walked the delicate tightrope of trying to get the best out of the characteristics of the car itself. In other words, the crew chief had to talk the driver into working with what the car would give him while tweaking the car to get the best it had so the driver could go fast.

It wasn't an easy job. It took patience and combined the listening skills of a good therapist along with the mechanical wisdom of a topnotch, experienced engineer.

A good race team was a blend of personalities. Chemistry, they called it. Some of those personalities could be volatile. Racing was a competitive sport and most people weren't in the business to run second. Most of all it took experience. Good crew chiefs weren't easy to come by, and the really good ones were already working. You didn't just put a help-wanted ad in

NASCAR Scene or one of the other trade publications, or post it on the Net and expect somebody to come out of the woodwork.

Then you throw into the mix handling the race weekend itself with all the media pressure and coordinating the pit crew and calling the race and ... it was a tough job.

Bear groaned into his hands again. "Oh mercy" he said out loud.

He got up and walked over to the window again. He stood with his hands in his pockets and surveyed the shop. Bear could see that the lights were going off in the motor shop at the far end of the building as the engine guys shut the place down for the night.

The Orly Mann Team, of which Bear was half owner, had two cars in the Chase for the Cup, which was pretty amazing considering that they were essentially the equivalent of a mom and pop organization. Well, they used to be, anyway. That is not to say they weren't professional. Bear and Orly prided themselves on quality and their level of performance showed that. The shop was state of the art. They had a seven-post shaker and virtually every piece of equipment they needed to be competitive, including state of the art computers and complete tech setups.

Orly was always a threat to win every race he entered. It was just that it was extremely hard to compete against the big multi-car teams and all their resources. Multi-car teams had the advantage of more testing dates and ultimately shared information with each other among their own teams. They also had the incredible resources that came from having multiple big name sponsors.

That was why Bear and Orly jumped on the opportunity to run a second car. The company that bought the Blue Saber Manufacturing Company also bought out the Speed King Oil Additives Corporation. Speed King had been the primary sponsor of Bear and Orly throughout their whole racing career. Harry Hornbrook and Speed King started with them in the early dirt track days and stuck with them through thick and thin. When Bear and Orly stepped up to the Cup level, Speed King went with them.

Harry was an astute businessman and worked hard to build the company into a national icon. It still was. In the process, Orly won two Cup championships, which was an amazing feat. When Harry died, he left the company to his daughter, Hildy. She ran it for a year with great success. Bear was glad for that because it meant that Speed King was able to maintain full sponsorship of the team, and that gave them the ability to put the focus on racing instead of promoting for a new sponsor.

But then came the offer from the same company that bought the Blue Saber Company to buy out. It only made logical sense to sell. For a while Bear and Orly thought they might have to do the sponsor search thing but that wasn't the case. Blue Saber manufactured car care products like finish coats, wax and other auto detail chemicals. It was a no-brainer for them to sponsor a Cup car. The owners not only maintained the connection between Speed King and the Orly Mann team, but they upped the ante and offered Bear and Orly the opportunity to run a second team under the Blue Saber banner.

That too was a no-brainer. Several men on the board

owned smaller companies of their own and wanted to connect with the Orly Mann Team as well. People like the Eilersen family that owned Classic Manufacturing saw the advertising advantage of having their company name on Orly's car and were willing to invest their promotional dollars accordingly. It was good for everyone involved.

It also gave Bear and Orly the opportunity to offer a ride to T.K. Kittridge, which considering the history, wasn't an easy decision. T.K. brought a wealth of open wheel and dirt car experience into Cup racing but the truth was his first and second years on the circuit were disasters. He was a wild man and he and Orly, along with several other drivers, had several fender banging, paint swapping dustups before he settled down. Orly always said that T.K. had more natural talent than anyone he had ever seen. Bear said he was the only guy he ever saw that could go into a corner "three wide all by his self."

When the original Blue Saber team went belly up, T.K. was out of a ride. Orly was for hiring him right away, but Bear wasn't so sure. Ultimately Bear agreed and Orly's assessment was right. It was a good match. T.K. came willingly with a changed attitude and a desire to win races.

Under Orly's careful tutelage, T.K. matured. Some years ago NASCAR instituted what they called the Chase for the Cup. It was sort of like a playoff championship. After the first twenty-six races, the top twelve drivers in the points were put in a separate category with a different point structure to compete in the last ten races of the season. It was only the top twelve that had a shot at the championship.

The grueling Cup schedule was thirty-six races long. If a driver and a team were going to make a championship run, they had to be in the top twelve in points at the end of the first twenty six races. Every race counted and every finishing position was extremely important. Patience was the key. Take what the circumstances would give you and don't do something foolish that would cost you spots and ultimately points.

It was a testimony to T.K.'s willingness to learn that he entered the Chase for the Cup in a solid seventh position. He had even pulled off a surprise win at Loudan New Hampshire in the first of the last ten races for the championship. Now with three races left, he had moved up three spots to fourth in the points. But now Bear had a train wreck on his hands. Well that wasn't exactly true. A train wreck was a total disaster, and Bear had some options in regard to who would take over Brad's responsibilities for the rest of the season.

- *O* -

In the meantime, Orly Mann hadn't been doing too bad himself. He entered the Chase in the fifth spot, but after six out of the ten races was sitting in second just a handful of points behind the leader. Problem was the third place guy was breathing down his neck, and T.K. wasn't all that far behind in fourth. With three races left, the championship was up for grabs.

There was a big part of Bear that wished he could just sweep all the other stuff out the door and put his total, full focus on Orly's championship run like they used to do in the old days.

"Never happen," Bear muttered out loud to himself.

Just then his cell phone rang. Bear looked at the phone then pushed the button to answer.

"'Lo, Orly Mann, what are you doing? I wish I was rich and famous so I could take the week off in the Napa Valley while my tired old decrepit partner works hisself to the bone giving me the best race cars in the world so I could win the Texas race and the entire champeeenship."

Indeed Orly and Hildy were in the Napa Valley. They had just arrived at some very dear friends' house and were getting settled in for the night when Orly got Bear's call. It was a much needed break for Orly, but it was also a working holiday. He and T.K. would be testing a Pontiac Riley Daytona prototype car on the road course at Infineon Raceway tomorrow. (Infineon used to be called Sear's Point before the sponsor bought the naming rights.)

Orly was an excellent road racer, although it had been a couple of years since he had driven a prototype car. This would be T.K's first experience. They were scheduled to compete along with an Italian formula one hotshoe in the Rolex 24 Hour Race, which kicked off Speedweek at Daytona next February. It was an interesting change of pace for a Cup driver, and Orly was looking forward to the experience, that plus the fact it took him out of Charlotte and gave he and Hildy a chance to get away from the constant media crush that followed the drivers involved in the Chase. Orly knew it wouldn't be long before the Nascarazzi tracked them down, though. That was why they were staying at their friends' place. Some well-meaning waiter or room clerk wouldn't be able to drop a call and earn a few bucks in the process.

Orly laughed out loud. "Hey Henry, what's going on? I can't be gone ten minutes before you're bugging me already."

"Yeah, well I'm just getting started, so hang on." It was good-natured banter between friends that respected each other and had a good history together. The truth was that they loved each other like brothers. And also like brothers, they often disagreed on certain things.

"Uh, we had a little problem at the shop. Seems like Brad went and tripped over a jack and broke his ankle. Pretty serious break, actually. They are going to operate tonight and put a bunch of screws and things in, I guess. He's going to be down for at least two weeks and then is looking at some serious rehab." Bear, whose given name was Henry Erickson, paused and cleared his throat.

"What it means is I don't have a crew chief for T.K. and I need some advice."

"I'm sorry to hear that. Does mess things up a bit. What are you thinking? Anything we can do for Brad and Rosie?"

"No. I got that part covered. But, well, I was thinking Paolo is the natural choice to run the show for the last three races. He can do the job. He's been the car chief all year for you and done pretty much what he has been asked to do. No, that ain't right. He has done more than he has been asked to and in fact, has come up with some great ideas of his own."

"No doubt about that," Orly agreed.

"He lacks a little confidence, but he knows and I know he can do it. It would put him in a position to give orders rather than just take them. He gets along very well with the rest of the Blue Saber team. They trust him, I think, and probably would support him. Depends on T.K.'s reaction. I have trusted Paolo about everything I can. He's smart."

"True," said Orly.

Bear continued. "I can't oversee both cars, you know that, but I think we could put Doug with him and they would do a good job. He is familiar with the setup they use and I am sure he could call the race pretty good." Bear paused again and took a breath.

"Now Orly, that sounds good on the surface but you know as well as I do that there is no love lost between Paolo and T.K. Especially since T.K. has been dating Alicia. I don't know how those two guys would mesh without Brad in between them. Both of them are opinionated and have pretty good tempers. I do my best not to get involved in these young people's lives. They are adults, you know, but this is something we need to think about. That's why I bugged you. What do you think?"

"Well, what comes to mind first thing is that we need to see the big picture right now. Both Paolo and T.K. call themselves professionals. We got three very important races in front of us and there is a lot at stake here. They both make good money. They have got to be able to put their personal differences aside, at least for the next few weeks, and get the job done. We could remind them that this is just for three races, and we are working under the so-called tyranny of the urgent, so to speak. We can't afford to let their feelings affect how the team functions. That is number one. But I'm a realist like you and I am not sure they can do that. Do we have any other options?"

"Well, not really. I mean we have a couple of other guys that maybe could do the job but it would be a major stretch for them and the team. This is the best call I think."

"Yeah I agree. Have you told T.K. and Paolo yet?"

"No, T.K. is out there with you and I was hoping you might take him aside and have a heart to heart with him. He listens to you pretty good." Bear got up and walked around the desk. "Paolo and Doug aren't here right now. They are already in Texas doing a publicity thing for the western wear company that is coming on board with us for the Texas race. I wanted to talk to you, then I would give him a call."

"All right then," said Orly. "I will talk to T.K. tomorrow. I might have Hildy put in a word. He respects her and she treats him like a little brother."

Orly stretched his arms and yawned. "On a different note, there, mighty crew chief, what are you thinking for Texas? The setup we ran for Atlanta was pretty good. I think if I would have had five more laps I might have got around the #18 car for the win."

Texas. The thought of Texas Motor Speedway made Bear smile. He loved that place. The Great American Speedway, they called it, and indeed it was. It was a great track and the crown jewel in the Speedway Motorsports Incorporated portfolio. SMI was owned and controlled by a man named Bruton Smith. Smith owned the place along with Atlanta, Bristol, Infineon,

Las Vegas, Charlotte and Kentucky. A few years back, he bought the New Hampshire track from the Bahre family and Bear was pleased to see what he was doing with that place. Smith believed in treating the fans and the competitors with respect and dignity. They got what they paid for.

Eddie Gossage was the CEO of Texas, and he was uniquely talented in not only carrying out Smith's vision but adding his own spin as well. Eddie G., as everybody called him, had been with the racetrack since it was nothing but a dirt field. The first couple of years were less than stellar. But once Eddie G. worked the track through the teething cycle, it had been nothing but spectacular. He poured his energy and talents into the place and it showed. It was a good place to race. Bear always said that Eddie G. had the marvelous gift of hospitality and he worked overtime to make the competitors and fans welcome.

"Well I'm making some subtle, minor changes...but I'm not telling you in case this phone is tapped."

Orly laughed.

"Hey listen," Bear said. "On another note. I got a call from Dr. Miller at Texas Alliance of Raceway Ministries (TxARM) and he asked for a favor. He seldom asks, but when he does, it's something important. Seems like they have a kid that lives in the area that is suffering from some form of disease, the name of which I can't remember. At any rate, it's bad. What they want to do is let him park in the motorhome lot next to us and kind of follow us around all weekend. Eddie G. has given them the proper passes and setup the use of a motorhome for the weekend. It appears that the kid has specifically requested that he be able to hang out with our teams."

"Is this kind of like the Make A Wish thing?" Orly asked.

"Yeah, I guess so, but it's a private deal. Seems like the local folks at TxArm worked to put it all together."

"Well I got no problem with it as long as it doesn't turn into a media circus and become a distraction for us."

"Well that is what I told Roger. I told him we would work with him and his crew. They are a good bunch. We all know that." Bear leaned back in his chair and put his feet on the mahogany desk. "So you really think that is the best move to make Paolo the crew chief?"

"Yes it is, Bear. You know it is. I don't think we have another choice."

"Yup, you're right. Hey listen, Rosie said there was a media guy at the hospital already asking questions about what we were going to do and whatnot. I am sure they will track you down in the morning, but I think the best thing is to just keep it under our hat until we get the details sorted out."

"Yeah, I agree. I'll see you at the track on Thursday night."

Bear clicked off his cell and watched the phone on his desk light up. Yeah, the media was hot on the trail. This was a big story and they would be demanding answers. Well, tomorrow would be soon enough.

The black dog got up and stretched, then sat down and licked his lips with a look on his face that said, "Well are we going home or what?"

"Yeah, let's get out of here, Black Dog. Time to go

home and eat. Let me tell you something, Dog. Just about when you got everything figured out is just about the time something goes sideways. Yup, that's a fact."

- O -

In the meantime, William Williams sat behind his desk and contemplated the expanse of his auto dealership. He was a big, beefy man with a somewhat pretentious handlebar mustache.

He looked down on the expanse of his car lot. In past days it used to be rows and rows of shiny new models but now was mostly empty asphalt. His stock had dwindled to just a handful of cars which weren't even the best sellers. He looked down at the laptop in front of him and surveyed the sales sheets once again. he thought to himself. No sales meant no ability to buy new stock. No stock meant no new sales. It was a vicious circle and the creditors were starting to catch up.

It isn't my fault, he reasoned. *It's the manufacturer. If they made a decent product, it might be a little easier to sell. Been telling them that for years, but now they have me locked in a box. They have been trying to get rid of me for years and now they have me on a cash only basis.*

It took money to make money, that was a fact, and money was in pretty short supply right now.

Of course he wasn't willing to take into account that he had the reputation of being the most crooked dealer in the southwestern United States. He worked with every sleazy finance company that gave credit to anybody and charged the most exorbitant rates. Part of the deal, naturally, was that they would kick back (under the table) a piece of the action to him. That wasn't his fault either. individuals just didn't understand that he had to make a living and a fellow had to do what he needed to do. If somebody signed one of those contracts, it wasn't his concern. The customer has an obligation to be aware of what he is doing. That's what he tried to tell the judge before they slapped him in jail, anyway.

Despite his stupid lawyer's protestations, they gave him six months for just trying to make folks pay him what they owed him. Something about illegally repossessing cars. Then he had to pay fines and give restitution to some of those losers. Fortunately because of the over-crowded conditions in the minimum security jail facility, he got out in two and a half months. Good thing because he was starting to go crazy in that joint. It wasn't the first time he had been in the slammer but doing time was easier when you were younger. Fortunately, he was able to hold onto the dealership, but now he was in big financial trouble. He needed cash and he needed it right now.

The kid had money. He knew he did, and in fact, he was probably going to make a lot more if he won the championship this year. Most of that money was his. The kid owed it to him whether he was willing to admit it or not...and he meant to get it. Plain and simple. There was a blue sky just over the horizon.

He pushed the intercom button. "Hey Pedro, tell the boys in the shop to give the motor home the once over and gas it up. I am headed to Texas on Wednesday morning. I got business to take care of."

Chapter One

"*When you drive lightweight, fragile G.T.
prototypes, you drive with a different attitude
towards the machinery. 'Well pip, pip, we turn here.'
Those stock car guys go tearing through the esses,
and if there's asphalt under the car, OK. Dirt,
that's OK, too. Who cares!*"

Rocky Moran

Orly stepped out onto the porch and quietly closed the door behind him. He set his helmet bag down and took a deep lungful of the early morning air, extended his arms and stretched like a cat in the warmth of the sun.

Yeah, thought Orly, *just another late fall, perfect day in Northern California. Napa Valley never looked better. The sun is bright, the air is cool and all is right with the world.*

The leaves on the grapevines and trees were turning a bright yellow orange. Orly walked out on the porch and headed down the circular driveway to what was politely referred to as the "the barn". It was sort of shaped like a barn, but in truth, it was the fulfillment of every "car guy's" dream. It was a very large, functional garage with a full set of workbenches, two hoists and two of the biggest Craftsmen rolling toolboxes ever made. The front sliding doors of the building were open, letting in the early morning sunlight.

Orly paused to admire the dark blue '07 Corvette parked next to a very rare mid-engine de Tomaso Pantera. Back in the corner was a '56 Chevy Bel Air set up for the drag strip. Next to that was a beautiful, fully restored, blood red '69 Chevy Camaro. Parked in the center was a dark blue '32 Ford roadster with a man up to his elbows in the engine compartment. He was somewhere in his fifties and dressed in Levis and a t-shirt. Bob was tapping the side of the carburetor with the butt end of a screwdriver with a deep look of concentration on his face.

"You know you're supposed to be using the other end of that tool. I thought you car types would know something like that."

"Leave me alone, Orly Mann." The man spoke without looking up. "Besides, what do you know, anyway? You just know how to drive 'em and wreck 'em, not how to fix 'em." He spoke with a smile on his face, then he added, "you ready to go?"

"Yeah. Thanks Bobby for letting Hildy and me crash at your place. I'm sorry we got in so late last night."

"Not a problem, Orly. Nancy and I are always happy to see you. I'm glad you feel comfortable here. I expect you need a little break from all the media attention right about now with the chase and what not."

Bob was a contractor in the Napa Valley. He was a very successful builder that made his living building custom homes and wineries for the wealthy that made the Valley their home, or second home, or even their third. Bob's real love, however, was cars. Orly looked around and quietly counted two big block Chevy motors sitting on engine stands and a couple of small blocks in pieces on the workbench. Over in the corner was a Yates Ford motor sitting next to the red Pantera.

"Uh huh, the 'Vette is new. Nice looking. I love that cobalt deep blue color."

"Yeah, we had a good year, and Nancy surprised me. We flew back to Kentucky and picked it up at the factory. She doesn't like to ride with me too much, though. You know how it is. She gets a little nervous if I drop the hammer a bit."

Orly laughed. "I see you got the Pantera running. What's it like?"

"Well, to be honest with you, I'm disappointed. It doesn't handle...well, for beans! It goes like a bat in a straight line, but keeping it pointed that way is a little scary. Then when you toss it into a corner with any speed at all, it's anybody's guess as to what it's going to do. I was going to run it in the Silver Dollar race in Nevada. You know the one where they block off 90 some miles of highway and run time trials against the clock? But I'm just not ready to run that thing. Too spooky right now... I'm going to have to give Bear a call and see what he can tell me. I think we're going to have to make some major modifications to that 1960's suspension."

"Hey, I heard a rumor that you ran that race in a rental car." Orly bent over and looked under the Pantera.

"Yeah, me and my friend Bruce went to watch, and it looked like a lot of fun, so we went down and rented a Cadillac and ran the thing. Finished fourth in class. 'Course the rental people weren't happy when we wore the tires off but we made it right with them. It was fun." Bob rose up from the roadster. "Come on, let's go get some breakfast. What do you want to ride in?"

"Well, not the Pantera, that's for sure. Let's take the roadster. It's a great morning to get some air." It was a testimony to Bob's driving ability that Orly suggested the roadster. Like most race car drivers, Orly was a nervous passenger and was lousy company unless he was driving. But for some reason, he was very comfortable with Bob. Maybe it was because Bob knew when to behave himself and not jeopardize anybody else.

"You sure? It attracts attention you know."

"I don't care Bobby. This is Napa and people are used to seeing...well you know." It was just not part of Orly's nature to call himself a "celebrity" or "famous". But he had no choice. He was a celebrity. He was famous whether he liked it or not, and it affected most aspects of his life. He and Hildy found it bothersome.

It was a testimony to Orly's character that the whole fan thing seemed strange to him even after all these years. He was one of the most popular drivers on the Cup circuit and as a result, everything he did, or didn't do, was newsworthy. He expected the attention at the racetrack and had things set up to deal with it, but now in just the past couple of years, it seemed that he couldn't go anywhere without a media type sticking a camera or microphone in his face. More than once he had a reporter follow him into the men's room at a restaurant or someplace. He tried to tell himself that he didn't mind and it was just part of the 'biz', as Bear called it, but Orly was a private man and didn't like being the center of attention. It was especially difficult now with the Chase being so tight. That was one of the reasons he and Hildy were staying with Bob and Nancy. Their place was off the beaten path, and they had a nice upstairs guest wing in their modest house. Bob and Nancy were pretty good at fielding phone calls and protecting their privacy. They were sweet, and it was a place where Orly and Hildy could just relax. Besides, they were good friends and fun to be with.

Bob was a car guy, but he didn't keep up with all the drama surrounding NASCAR. He could talk racin' and blow tire smoke with the best of them, but he was far more interested in the mechanical side of things. He liked Orly as a person, and the fact that he was a celebrity didn't mean a whole lot. It was refreshing for Orly to spend time with him. He was also a great listener and a good storyteller, and he laughed easily.

Nancy had her own business in downtown Napa. They called it a quilt shop, but it was more of an art center. In fact it was renowned and attracted people from around the country. Nancy had a fantastic eye for design and color and people often came a long way to buy her stuff. She and Hildy shared the same tastes and could talk patterns and fabric for hours. Orly and Bob often complained that they were "chokin' in thread dust" when the ladies got started, but they were largely ignored.

Bob opened the door on the roadster. "Well hop in, unless you want to drive."

"Me! Not me. This thing has way too much power for me. Too scary. I might hurt myself." Orly spoke as he pulled his legs into the roadster.

Bob lit the motor and they idled down the driveway. "What time you supposed to be at the track?"

"Dunno. They just said in the morning."

"The Kid going to meet us there?"

"Yeah, I guess so. Said he would. Then Hildy and Nancy are going to meet us for lunch. Then we'll fly out after dinner this evening for Texas. I think I have an appearance or two tomorrow. Not sure. I can hardly keep track anymore. Did I tell you what happened to Brad, T.K's crew chief yesterday? The Kid is going to be very unhappy when he finds out."

Bob leaned his head toward Orly as they headed down Silverado Trail toward town. "No you didn't. What happened?"

Orly related the story and concluded with the fact that Bear was considering Paolo as T.K's crew chief.

Bob spoke. "Well it seems to me that Paolo is pretty sharp. Bear has schooled him pretty good. He has an aptitude for race cars. But Nancy told me that T.K was dating Alicia. Last I heard she and Paolo were hooked up. Is that all done now? Those kids grew up together and been together practically their whole lives. Seems to me it might be a little problem. You and I both know Paolo."

"Yeah, that's a concern. Bear is trying to think it through. But we are kind of in a fix. We got three and a half weeks of racing left in this year and we have a real shot at this thing. Maybe they can put all that relationship stuff aside 'til it's over."

"Well, maybe they can", Bob said as he wheeled the roadster into the parking lot of the restaurant, "and then from my old man perspective, maybe pigs will fly too. Come on, let's eat. I'm buying."

Breakfast was done. They were interrupted only one time and that was by a fellow that wanted to talk with Bob about giving him a bid on a remodel he was doing. Orly got a few inquisitive looks, but nobody bothered them. A few minutes later after an exhilarating ride down the old Napa highway, they were pulling into the front gate of Infineon Raceway. Bob leaned over to Orly. "Man, this place has sure changed a bunch. Bruton keeps doing more stuff to make it fan-friendly. It's really a nice facility."

"They've changed the track several times as well. I kind of liked the old configuration myself. It was a lot more challenging, although the way they have it now is pretty good."

"Tell me again what you guys are testing?"

"Daytona Prototype. Getting ready for the Rolex 24 hours next February. Riley chassis with a Pontiac motor. Pretty quick, actually. Handles a way bunch different than a stock car. Me and The Kid are co-driving with some Italian F1 guy."

"Does The Kid have any background in a G.T. car?"

"No, not much, but I'm telling you Bob, The Kid is a natural. He can drive just about anything, I think. He's been out here a couple of days already going through whats-his-name driver's school to get some track time. He does well here in Cup cars. Think he got a third or something this year in the Cup race."

Bob digested the information without saying

anything. He idled the roadster to the back of the main grandstands behind the pit lane and glanced over at the transporter sitting in the garage area. The racetrack looked strange with the empty grandstands and nearly deserted garage area.

"Could I ask you a question, Orly?" Bob didn't wait for an answer. "Why are you guys testing at this time of the year, with three races left in the season, and you are working toward a championship? Especially driving something about which you don't know who built it and whether it is safe and all that?" Bob understood the mechanical end of things and knew that no matter how professional a team was, parts could still get mixed up with human error with catastrophic results. He also knew he might have said the wrong thing.

Orly opened the door. "This is a legitimate race team, Bob. These guys are from England, and they've been running this chassis for a while. I think they know what they're doing. Besides, if I didn't, I wouldn't be here. The G.T. guys are working with NASCAR, and trying to get some of us Cup drivers involved to give the series a wider fan base. Besides, it's fun. Come on Bobby, you're starting to sound like Bear."

He grabbed his helmet bag as he stood up and said with a smile "maybe I can talk them into putting another seat in the thing and I'll take you for a ride. It's just a race car, and it is just a test."

- *O* -

Alicia sat on an outside bench in the stern of the ferry as it made the run up the Carquinez Straits toward Mare Island. The San Francisco skyline had long receded into the background and now the Richmond San Rafael Bridge was slipping away as well. She knew if she went up on the bow, she would see the Carquinez bridge approaching, and a little further on, the Bencia bridge that crossed the Straits. But she was happy where she was.

Alicia was sitting next to an older Chinese man with a little boy in his lap. She could tell from the conversation that the boy was his grandson. It was good to hear Mandarin again. She missed hearing her native tongue. She snuggled deeper into her jacket and took a lungful of the cool morning air. *I really miss California,* she thought to herself. *This is home and there really isn't anyplace quite like it. Charlotte is nice, no doubt about that, but it isn't California.*

She also loved riding the ferry. This was a very familiar trip, and it brought back many great memories of excursions to Marine World, USA, an amusement park in Vallejo (back when that's what it was called) and Angel Island with her family and cousins. She was overjoyed when Bear told her that he wanted her to fly to California and meet with the G.T. crew to go over some sponsor details for the Rolex race at Daytona in February.

Alicia worked mostly in the office at the team headquarters in Charlotte doing advance work, setting up accommodations, and making travel arrangements for the team, Monday through Thursday. Then generally she would fly to whatever race track was next on the schedule and co-ordinate with the teams to make sure everybody was okay with lodging, and passes and any other details that might fall through the cracks. With thirty-six races on the schedule, not counting test dates and appearances, it was more than a full time job. But Bear felt that this deal with the G.T. folks was important enough to warrant a hands-on approach, and Alicia was the likely candidate to take care of it. Then when T.K. offered her a spot in his plane and the chance to fly from Talledega to Napa after the race on Sunday, she leapt at the opportunity.

Alicia usually squeezed a day in the city when the Cup cars came to Sonoma for the annual race, but now she had a little extra bonus. She grew up in San Francisco, and the thought of going back if even for just a couple of days was worth the trip. Actually, San Francisco's Chinatown was home. That was her "hood", as Paolo liked to say. She was born and raised there. Many of her extended family, cousins, aunts and uncles, plus tons of friends were still there. She missed the sounds and the smells that were so much a part of San Francisco's Chinatown.

Most of all she missed the atmosphere and the bustling Chinese culture that was her heritage. Chinatown was a unique blend of old China mixed with a west coast lifestyle that covered nearly a hundred and sixty years in the San Francisco area. She loved it and hoped that someday she would be able to move back. But now it was time to get on with the real world. T.K. was testing one of the GT cars with Orly at Infineon, and then he was flying on to Texas tomorrow morning. She could have a sit down with the money people to take care of the sponsor business and then hop another ride to DFW with Orly and Hildy. It made for an easy trip.

T.K. was supposed to pick her up at the Ferry terminal in Vallejo, and give her a ride out to the track, but he would probably be late. He was always late. It was like he didn't think about time too much. He promised to buy her dinner after the session before turning her over to Orly and Hildy. It would be late when she got to DFW, but she could sleep in a little tomorrow. After that, it would be full speed ahead as they got ready for the Texas weekend.

Alicia smiled when she thought of T.K. He was an easy guy to like, and she was genuinely fond of him. He was unique. He was handsome, with blue eyes and a crooked smile. He laughed easy and was fun to be with. It seemed that he always had something going on. She knew that he cared about her and seemed genuinely interested in her. Alicia had often seen him staring at her with a contemplative look when he thought she wasn't looking. She was looking back though, and maybe she had the same look. He could be polite and very funny at the same time. Yet she had seen him agitated and angry, and even go off like a rocket when he thought he was crossed. Orly said that T.K. was one of the most natural, talented drivers he had ever seen, and if he could learn to control his temper would be a phenomenal driver rather than just a talented one. Coming from Orly, that was a pretty good compliment.

She didn't know much about driving, but she did know one thing for sure. T.K. and Paulo didn't like each other very much, and she knew in her heart that she was the reason. Paolo was her friend and had been for most of her life. They grew up together in the same schools and the same church. Even though she was

Chinese and from Chinatown, and he was from out in the avenues in the Sunset district, they had a lot in common. Paolo's Dad was Portuguese and his Mom was Armenian. His culture was radically different from hers. Still, they shared the same values of church and family.Alicia really loved him. He was big and gentle. He could make her laugh when he wanted to. She liked being with him. She always had, and in her mind, she could see them together as husband and wife someday. Paolo was safe, but he had made it abundantly clear that he wasn't ready to get serious with a relationship. "Racing is my life", he said. Well, so be it. Maybe she had waited long enough for him. Maybe T.K. was the guy for her…then again, only God knew.

The ferry eased into the slip and banged the dock as the captain fought the tide. The Chinese gentleman stood the child up and took his hand. He turned to Alicia and said in English, "well that was a pleasant trip, wasn't it?"

Alicia responded in Mandarin. "Yes it was, and such a lovely California day."

As she stepped off the ferry onto the gangplank, she spotted T.K. parked illegally on the sidewalk next to the street. He was straddling a big cherry red custom motorcycle wearing a jacket that said something about Choppers on the back. He was also dangling an extra helmet from his hand. *Oh brother, this is going to be some ride out to the track,* she thought to herself as she waved and smiled at him. He smiled back and motioned for her to hurry.

- *O* -

The two identical race cars sat silently in the pit lane like a couple of aerodynamic, bullet shaped beetles. It was clear at first glance that they were thoroughbred race cars. There was no pretense about being "stock" or anything else. GT cars were closed cockpit endurance race cars. They were slick and stylish, and in Bob's mind, looked like they were doing a hundred miles an hour just sitting still. They were full of intricate curves and scoops, all designed to hold the car on the ground at phenomenal speeds. The lower valence in the front looked like it was touching the ground, and indeed it was barely an inch off the pavement.

The whole design was wedge shaped, ending with a large wing mounted across the engine compartment in the rear. Orly said that they tracked like they were on rails, and it was deceptive how well they cornered. That is as long as you kept them straight. You couldn't slide them like a stock car, and once you got them sideways, you better hang on. They were also equipped with humongous carbon fiber brakes, and could decelerate from 200 miles per down to nothing in the blink of an eye.

Three mechanics were working in the rear engine compartment of one car. They were practically on top of each other and just by general appearance looked a little surly. Bob started to walk over to see what they were doing but thought better of it when one of the mechanics snarled at the other two and threw an expensive torque wrench on the ground and stomped away. Instead Bob walked over to the other car and peered inside the driver's compartment.

It was all business, and reminded him of the cockpit

of a fighter plane except with a lot less gauges. There was a whole panel of switches dominated by two big brake bias knobs in the middle of the dash. By twisting them, the driver could add or take away front or rear brake to balance the car. Considering the speed and the incredible stopping ability of these quick cars, this was a valuable tool. Beside the driver's seat within easy reach were two fire control plungers. When the pins were pulled, all the driver had to do was slap one or both to flood the cockpit or the engine compartment with fire retardant. The carbon fiber seat was form fitted and set at an angle that put the driver's backside nearly on the ground to keep the center of gravity as low as possible. It was also designed with intricate wrap around wings to hold the driver firmly in place. The restraint harness looked substantial to Bob, but it also looked just a tad worn. Both cars looked like they had seen a lot of track time. That troubled him, and he casually opened the gull wing type door to peer inside. He noticed that the gearshift lever was slightly extended so the driver didn't have to move his hand very far off the steering wheel to change gears.

Sequential gearbox, Bob thought to himself, *probably a five speed.* That meant the driver didn't have to use the clutch once he got the car moving. No standard "H" pattern here. Just move the lever back and the box automatically took you up a gear. Move the lever the other way and it went down for deceleration. He reached in and lifted the harness so he could see how it was attached.

"Hey, what are you doing there? Get out of the car!" The voice had a distinct British accent.

"It's all right, he's with me." Orly said from behind

Bob. Unbeknownst to Bob, Orly had already changed into his driver's suit and was sitting in the shade of the grandstand.

"Yeah, well I don't care who he's with. He needs to keep his hands off the car." It was the snarly mechanic voicing his opinion. Then he made a comment to the other mechanics. "Those NASCAR roundy round boys are all show and no go. What a waste of time and money this is."

Before Orly could respond, and as if to emphasize the point, T.K. came blasting up on the chopper with Alicia hanging on to his waist. Bob had a quick image of Cole Trickle from *Days of Thunder* making his initial appearance. He chuckled to himself. Nice timing.

T.K. killed the thumping motor, threw down the kickstand, and allowed Alicia to climb off before he swung his leg and dismounted himself. She pulled the helmet off and shook out her long, black hair.

"Hey guys, how you doing?"

"Doing good, T.K. Grab your stuff and get changed. They're waiting for us. I'll walk with you. We need to talk." Orly's words were clipped and short.

Alicia walked over to Bob. "Whew. I hate motorcycles. Good to see you, Bob."

"You too, Alicia. I don't blame you. Barely looks like enough room for one, let alone two on that thing. By the way, your man there is not going to be too happy when he hears the news."

"He's not my man, Bob, and what news?"

Bob ignored her comment and filled her in on what happened at the shop and the decision Bear had made in regard to T.K.'s team and Paolo.

Alicia didn't respond, just furrowed her brow as she digested the information.

A few minutes later Orly and T.K. came walking back. Neither was talking. Bob could see that T.K. was doing his best to keep his emotions in check.

Ten minutes later, Orly and T.K. were getting strapped in the race cars. Orly was in the front car with the team manager standing beside him, talking into a radio headset. Bob perched himself on the concrete abutment that supported the grandstand and pulled a radio scanner out of his pocket with a couple of small earplugs. The racetrack was still pretty much deserted, and he could see most of it from where he sat. It was a good place to be. He could listen and observe without getting in the way. Alicia had disappeared up into the transporter to discuss business with her counterpart on the G.T. team. Bob adjusted the frequency until he picked up the conversation.

"...I want you to shake it out for a couple of laps and then try a couple of different lines through the esses. We have a new snout configuration pieced together, and I want you to give me a feel for it. We have a bunch of electronics on the cars, so the telemetry will keep us apprised. That way we will be able to monitor pretty much what is going on. T.K., I want you to maintain your distance behind Orly and just keep pace with what he is doing. I want you guys to control yourselves. I will give you the go ahead to spread the jam when we are ready."

"I'm under control. Are you under control, Orly?"

T.K.'s voice resonated in Orly's headset built into his helmet. "Yeah, so far at least. I don't know about spreading the jam though." Neither Orly nor T.K.

appreciated being talked down to.

The team manager was oblivious. "Okay, let's go."

Orly hit the starter button and the car coughed into life. It always amazed Orly that a dead lump of inanimate machinery like a race car could take on life with the push of a button. It was like a heart that suddenly started beating to circulate the lifeblood of oil and coolant and above all, fuel to bring about viability. He eased the car into gear and gently slipped the clutch. Like all race cars, it was bulky and heavy when it was cold. The steering felt stiff as Orly idled down the pit lane. That was to be expected. It was a race car and designed to function at speed, not at forty miles an hour. Orly bounced down the pit lane as the shocks warmed up and headed up the hill toward turn two as he worked through the gears. He gradually fed the beast more fuel as he picked up speed. He glanced in the rear view mirror to see T.K. a few car lengths behind him.

A race car driver by his very nature must be observant. He has to have the ability to see things, analyze them, and then react in a split second. The racetrack was empty. Orly and T.K. were the only two cars using it. There was a crash truck standing by. That was part of the contract in using the track for testing but apart from that, the place was quiet. It had also not been used in a while, and even though the sweeper truck had been around there were still little areas of dirt on the asphalt. The winter rains hadn't moved in yet so the grass was still brown and there was a modicum, of dust blowing around in the light breeze. Orly acknowledged all these things in his subconscious as he gradually began to pick up speed.

The team leader's voice crackled in his ears. "All right, the temps are up, you can turn it loose a little. I would like you to run me three laps at about 85%."

Orly settled his body back in the seat as he came out of the hairpin at turn eleven. "You ready?"

"Check, ten-four." T.K. replied.

Orly banged the gears and flat-footed turn one as he arched up the hill to turn two. The car seemed to squat into the racetrack as it gripped the pavement as he powered up the hill. He chose his line carefully through two, powered through three, and gave himself plenty of room as he exited turn four. They were using the short course which cut out the carousel and the short straight into seven. Instead turn four dumped straight into the sharp right-hander at seven. Orly downshifted and set the car up for the exit and the run down hill through the esses. The car felt good. Orly smiled to himself. This was going to be fun. This race car was incredibly responsive and handled extremely well. Orly ran three laps, then keyed his radio with the button on the steering wheel.

"You there?"

"Check."

"How is it?"

"Good," T.K. replied. "Just a bit of a push through the esses, but when I backed off you, it went away. Think your rear wing was taking a little air off the nose, and it was sliding the front end."

"Ten-four. Hey boss, turn us loose, and we will see what we got here." Orly directed his comment to the team manager.

"Yes, okay. Everything looks good with the telemetry.

Go ahead. give me five laps."

Orly got down to serious business. The way to go fast on a road course is to make it as straight as possible. That means coming closer to inanimate objects. Previously Orly was exiting turn four with two feet to spare, now it was a consistent eight inches. He gradually changed his line so he was flat-footing it down the hill through the esses and floating the car through turn ten before the hard braking for eleven. The telemetry reported that he and T.K. were both doing a hundred and eighty three miles an hour through this section. The car was working, and doing what it was designed to do. T.K. was staying in his tire tracks, although, he was working hard to do so.

"You want to lead for a while?"

"No, I'm back here going to school. I didn't know you were so good. I'm scaring myself trying to keep up."

Bob got off his perch and walked over to the pit wall. The three mechanics were sitting on the wall and the snarly one was smoking a cigarette. Bob sat down next to him.

Orly and T.K. sailed by at full song. "Not bad for a couple of roundy-round boys."

The mechanic looked over. "It's the cars. Anyone can make them go fast. That is what they are designed to do."

"Yeah, sure it is." Bob replied.

"All right boys, bring them in. We'll check tire pressures and fuel load and the usual stuff."

Both cars came idling down the pit road and stopped. Orly and T.K. climbed out and sat on the pit wall next to Bob. The mechanics went to work. T.K.

took a swig of water from a bottle, and Bob noticed that his hand was shaking just a little.

"So Kid, you been in school a couple of days, learning the intricacies of driving this here road course." Bob said to T.K.

"Yeah, but I learned more in the last twenty minutes than the whole two days I was here. You're good, Orly. It took me awhile but I finally figured out what you were doing at the top of the hill. First, I thought you were way off base in the line you were running, but I learned better."

Orly said nothing.

T.K. looked around, then shrugged his shoulders. "Excuse us, Bob, but I need to talk with Orly for a minute."

"Sure, no problem." Bob got up from the wall and walked over to watch the mechanics service the cars.

T. K. looked over at Orly. Orly knew what was coming. "Hey, Orly, it isn't going to work. You know Paolo and I don't get along. It isn't just about Alicia, although he's wrong about that. Me and him are just different or maybe we are too much the same or something. How am I going to work with the guy. Isn't there somebody else that could step in? We got a real chance of winning the championship, and I don't have time to put up with his attitude. You know what I mean."

"This is what you're going to do, T.K. You're going to be a professional, just like he is going to be. He is an excellent mechanic and engineer. He has the experience, and with Bear behind him, He is going to give you the best equipment and call the best race for you. He knows the guys, and they will work for him. This gives you the best chance of winning, considering the circumstances we find ourselves in. We got no other choices. Get used to it and make it work. We got Texas, Phoenix, and then it wraps up at Homestead. "

"Yeah, yeah, well you and Bear are the boss. I've got no choice, but I don't like it much. I hope this doesn't come back to bite me. There is a lot of money at stake." T.K. was clearly irritated.

They were interrupted by the team manager. "All right gentlemen, I think we are ready to run a few more laps."

"Did you hear that, T.K.? We have gone from being boys to gentlemen." Orly's light-hearted attempt at humor fell on deaf ears.

Bob leaned over to the mechanic, who was still wearing his irritation like a bad cologne. "Did you tighten that wheel?"

"Of course I tightened the wheel. Get the ...out of my face."

Bob said nothing, then casually asked one of the other mechanics, "what's bugging that guy anyway?"

The mechanic replied, "Oh, he just found out that he's getting fired. Something to do with some sort of trouble back home in Brighton. Don't know why they told him now."

Bob shook his head then watched as T.K. and Orly climbed back into the cars. This time there was no gentle warm-up. Orly left the pit lane smoking the tires with T.K. doing the same some few car lengths behind.

At the end of the second lap, Bob left the pit lane and climbed up in the grandstand to get a better view of the track. He could sense that Orly was serious and the hammer was coming down. He watched as Orly accelerated out of turn eleven and just, not quite, but nearly, flicked the wall as he came off the corner. T.K. was hanging doggedly two car lengths back. By the fifth lap, all three mechanics were standing on the pit wall, watching in awe as Orly blasted down the hill with T.K. right behind him. This was a master at work with his protégé hanging in his tire tracks. Orly was using every bit of racetrack as the car flattened through the corners. The team manager kept looking at his telemetry, then at a digital stopwatch in his hand. His voice crackled in Bob's ear through the scanner.

"You men are running just a tenth off the track record. Give me three more laps, then bring them in if you would, please." He got nothing back on the radio.

Bob knew what it took to get that much out of a race car. He admired Orly's concentration, and he truly respected T.K.'s ability to stay with him but bit by bit, Orly was pulling away. What once was two car lengths had now become eight or nine. It was obvious that if the session lasted a great deal longer, Orly would come away with a clear advantage. Then suddenly like an unexpected clap of thunder, it happened.

Orly was blasting down the hill in full song with the car looking very much like it was on rails. He crested turn nine flat out with T.K. just a little behind him as he breathed the throttle and set the car for turn ten. Then the rear bodywork literally exploded, throwing pieces high into the air. The car dived sideways, slewing through the dirt as the suspension collapsed on the left rear of the car. It bounced high in the air over the uneven surface but stayed upright until it hit the wall with an audible bang. Bob heard the impact and threw up his hands. "No!" He watched in horror as the car came off the wall completely airborne and pirouetted on its nose, shedding pieces and trailing a lifeblood of carbon fiber, chunks of bodywork and coolant mixed with oil. It did two snap rolls and then landed heavily on what was left of the wheels.

T.K. managed to miss hitting Orly but in the process, spun his car in an acrid cloud of tire smoke as he used up racetrack. He wound up facing backwards in turn eleven with a bird's eye view of Orly, and what was left of his car. His engine had stalled, and the car was eerily quiet. He flipped up his visor and could see that Orly wasn't moving.

He was slumped in the seat with his head down on his chest. Then with a low-pitched "whump", the unthinkable happened as the car burst into flames. Race cars in this day and age are not supposed to burn, but on occasion they do. Carbon fiber, high-octane gasoline, and red hot metal can make for a pretty lethal combination. It is every driver's nightmare.

T.K. keyed his radio and yelled, "Get out, Orly, hurry up man, get out of that thing!" In the meantime, he hit the starter switch, jammed his car in gear and burned rubber up the track toward Orly. He slid to a stop, popped his belts and threw the door open. He didn't bother to disconnect his radio or his cooling hose. He just jerked them loose as he made a fast exit and sprinted to Orly's car.

The fire was already inside the cockpit as he pulled what was left of the door away from the body. He flipped his visor down as he reached across Orly to hit the plunger for the fire bottle. Somebody had forgotten to pull the safety pin, and it wouldn't depress. He didn't waste time with it. He could hear the crash truck coming as he pulled Orly's belts away from his body and started dragging him out of the car. Suddenly Orly came alive and with T.K.'s help scrambled out of the car. Both drivers stumbled away from the car and watched as the fire crew put out the fire. T.K. helped Orly get his helmet off and surveyed the damage. Orly's fire suit was charred in several places and his helmet had a couple of burned spots. T.K. could see that he was visibly shaken. "You okay?"

"I think my thighs are burned a little."

Just then the medical personnel came running up, and T. K. led Orly over to the waiting ambulance.

Bob punched numbers into his cell phone as he walked around the destroyed car. This was not good. This was a lot more than just a wrecked race car. This could be the whole season all wrapped up in a smoldering heap with a hurt and incapacitated driver. He held the phone to his ear as he watched the ambulance race up the hill toward the helicopter pad.

In the thirty some odd years he had known Nancy, he had never seen her rattled. She had a calmness about her that was "matter of fact". It was a good trait. Even when he rolled a bulldozer down the hill in a spectacular fashion at a job site and got tossed out on his head, she didn't overreact and go hysterical or anything. Later, after they determined that he was okay with just minor bruises and a concussion, she did tell him she thought he was an idiot for trying to do something impossible.

He was counting on her calmness, especially now. Of course he doubted whether Hildy would panic or fall apart. She had been around racing most of her life. It wasn't like she didn't know the risks in her husband's profession.

Nancy finally answered the phone and Bob wasted no time cutting to the chase. He didn't even say hello.

"Tell Hildy he's going to be okay. He's conscious and everything. He was stunned for a couple of minutes. They've choppered him to the burn center in San Rafael. I don't think he is hurt bad at all. Legs got toasted a little. Just blistered, no third degree. Heck of a crash though. Some jerk left something loose. That's what I think, anyway. You guys get going, and I'll meet you there. You know where it is, Nance. It's right below Kaiser off 101. I'll bring Alicia. She'll have all his paperwork. I got to call Bear."

Chapter Two

*"A real cowboy don't have to tell anybody who he is.
The boots, the hat, and most of all,
the heart define his character."*

R. W. Coburn, Rodeo Stock Broker

Paolo was upset but doing his best to hide his irritation. This whole thing was ridiculous. He was a car chief in the midst of a run for the championship, and he needed to be back at the shop making sure everything was done the way it was supposed to be done on his race car. For crying out loud, he didn't have the time nor the energy to be playing games, especially now. He'd been forced to leave the shop early this morning to catch a flight to Texas, which meant that most likely there were several things undone on the car. Things that he would have to get done as soon as the car was unloaded at the racetrack, but that wouldn't be until Friday morning. Then the car would have to go through tech inspection before it could get on the track, and that really could be a hassle.

Besides that, he had never been to a rodeo in his life, and the only time he was ever on a horse was when he was five years old at the circus for a picture. That was only half the story. He actually had no interest in any of this cowboy stuff.

Now here he was, standing behind the rodeo chutes, checking out some of the most expensive bucking bulls in the country as they waited patiently for the opportunity to stomp on another cowboy. The bulls looked massive, and what was that word that Alicia used? Malevolent, yeah that was it. They looked malevolent. Paolo wasn't exactly sure what that meant, but it had something to do with evil, and that is exactly how these big animals looked… They were a lot bigger than he imagined they would be. Somehow the thought of throwing a leg over one of those broad backs seemed like more than pure foolishness. It looked downright suicidal.

Paolo kept to the middle of the aisle as he wandered from pen to pen. He stopped in front of an enclosure and studied the animal behind the fence. There was a nameplate on the front of the fence that read "Sweety Pie". Paolo laughed out loud and shook his head. Somebody had a strange sense of humor.

Paolo watched as the big animal nosed about in the hay for another mouthful of feed. This guy was huge with thick heavy muscles across his shoulders and a pair of sawed off horns that looked like table legs sticking out of its head. It filled its jaws, then raised its head, looking Paolo square in the eye as if sizing him up as it chewed. Satisfied that Paolo wasn't a threat, at least for the moment, it pawed at the hay pile with a hoof about the size of a piston from a top fuel dragster and put his head down for another mouthful. Paolo was impressed.

"Hey dude, I think he likes you," Doug said as

he walked up next to Paolo. They both regarded the immense creature in the pen with their arms folded. "Man, they smell don't they? I never expected them to smell like they do. In fact this whole place stinks. Is this what a barnyard smells like?"

Paolo ignored Doug's comment. "What are we doing here anyway, Doug? I never felt so out of place in my life. We don't know beans about horses and bulls and rodeo and stuff. This is not our gig, dude. We are car people. We know about stock cars and racing. This whole thing is sketch if you ask me. Besides that, I feel like I'm dressed up for a Halloween party or something."

Paolo tried to put his hands in his pockets but snorted in irritation. His jeans were too tight. He was dressed western style with a pearl button shirt, jeans, boots, a big belt buckle and a black resistol cowboy hat that felt just a little too small. In fact, everything felt a little too small. At six foot two and two hundred and forty pounds, he was a big guy. He grew up a city boy in San Francisco, California, in the midst of the generation where loose was in. Comfort was prime. Tight clothes made him grouchy. This outfit really did feel more like a costume than real clothes.

"You know why we are here, Pally. Let me 'splain', as Bear would say. Bear, as you know, is also known as Henry Erickson, the team manager and half owner at Orly Mann Racing and as a result, is our illustrious boss." Doug mimicked Bear's North Carolina accent and mannerisms as he spoke.

"To go racin', which we do, costs money, which it does. Lots and lots of cash. Moola, so to speak. Sponsors supply most of the money, and in exchange, we display advertising for their products. Besides that, they pay our salaries. We have a new western wear company coming on board the Orly Mann team as an associate sponsor and they decided that you and me would be good material for a photo shoot, wearing their products 'cause maybe they are thinking of using us in an advert campaign next year. That is why we are here at this PBR in the Will Rogers Coliseum, in Dallas, Texas. PBR, being the Professional Bull Riders event. That is also why that dude over there is following us around with a camera taking a picture every time we scratch or pick our nose wearing these wonderful western outfits. And that is why that bull rider over there talking to that other bunch of cowboys, which this company also sponsors, is going to join the Orly Mann Team on Sunday at the world famous Texas Motor Speedway so some photographer can follow him around and document when he spits or scratches."

Paolo, despite his irritation, laughed. "Not bad, Doug. You do sound just like Bear. But you left out the part about us winning lots of prize money if we do well in the race, which is also a substantial part of our income."

The bull tossed its head, snorted and blew a stream of mucus out of its nose as if to emphasize Paolo's point.

"Sweet." Doug said sarcastically.

"Oh that ain't nothing, son. Wait 'till you get rubbed real good in what comes out the other end." A Texas tinged voice twanged from behind them.

Paolo and Doug turned to be greeted by a stocky middle-aged man dressed pretty much the way they were, except he looked natural and perfectly at ease.

He stuck out his hand.

"Hello, boys. The name is R.W. Coburn and I have been asked to squire you around this event, which is a polite way of saying to keep you out of trouble." Coburn motioned to Paolo and Doug. "Come on, follow me. Things are just about to get underway. Either one of you boys ever been rodeoing?" He didn't wait for an answer. "Yup, I didn't think so. You both look as nervous as a cat with a long tail in a room full of rocking chairs."

Paolo and Doug exchanged a look.

Doug leaned over to Paolo and said in a low voice "Do you know who that is?"

"Not a clue."

"That guy is a rodeo stock broker. He owns most of these bulls, which are worth more than a good Daytona car. They really baby these big suckers and treat them like real prima donnas."

"Yeah, well, they just look like a lot of beef steak to me."

Two minutes later, they found themselves sitting on the top of the fence that surrounded the bull chutes with the rest of the railbirds. It gave them a clear view of the activity and also a view of the capacity crowd that filled the amphitheatre waiting impatiently for the event to get underway.

"Now you boys stay loose. I'm assuming that you aren't crippled or slowed down. You got to stay sharp as a tack 'cause anything can happen when one of these big fellas gets riled up. If they head for the fence and come at us, throw your leg over and vamoose."

In the meantime, the photographer had switched lenses and was set up with an angle that let him focus on Paolo and Doug, and cover the action coming out of the chute at the same time.

Coburn climbed up on the fence between Doug and Paolo and began talking.

"See those fellows sort of dressed like clowns? Now bulls are mean, and once they get you on the ground, they have a tendency to want to stomp you into mush. That is why the cowboys wear those flak jackets. Kind of distributes the weight, I guess. Those three clowns are some of the best in the business. It's their job to keep the bull off the cowboy 'til he has a chance to get out of the way. They have to be pretty good athletes, and believe me, every cowboy treats them with respect." Coburn stopped talking for a minute to unwrap a cigar. Once he got it going, he went on.

"See those chutes there? Once the cowboy pays his entry fee, he draws for a bull. Both the bulls and the cowboys get scored and the total is a compilation of both scores. Once they get the bull in the bucking chute, they put the bucking strap around the bull's flanks. It don't hurt them none, but it makes them a little testy. Then with help from the chute crew, the cowboy puts his rigging around the bull and wraps his hand so he can hang on. Every cowboy has his own tailor made glove and he wraps it special. It's got to be wrapped in a way that he can hold tight and yet at the same time when he lets go, it has to come loose. He's got to stay on for eight seconds to get a score."

"Eight seconds doesn't sound like very long." Said Doug.

"Yeah, well, I suppose it depends on which side of the bull you're on. If you're trying to stay on him it can seem like an eternity." Coburn blew out a puff of acrid smoke. "You'll see."

And see they did. The first bull was prodded down the chute and stood patiently while the crew did their work. He was a wily veteran named Cold Steel. Paolo watched intently as the rigging was pulled tight. The bull hardly moved, but Paolo could see the muscles ripple beneath his skin.

The cowboy carefully wrapped his right hand with the strap pounding his fingers with his left as he did so. Satisfied, he pulled his hat down, then nodded to the gate man. The gate man did his job and the bull literally exploded out of the chute. He twisted his massive body then arched his back as he crow hopped across the arena floor. The cowboy stayed with him through three jumps and then with an acrobatic twist, the bull unseated him and launched him through the air to land on his face in the dirt. The clowns immediately jumped to his aid. Two of them distracted the bull while the third made sure he was up and okay.

Paolo leaned back on the fence and looked at Doug over Coburn's back. He smiled and Doug nodded back. They exchanged a look that only good friends really understood. This was a macho game, and they immediately understood that it took skill and a whole lot of courage to do it right. A lot like stock car racing. Maybe this gig wasn't so bad after all.

They watched as the bulls were fed into the chutes and the cowboys did their thing. Paolo lost count, but he knew that so far there had only been three complete eight second rides. Doug reached around Coburn and poked Paolo, then motioned with his thumb at the chute. Sure enough, here came Sweety Pie. He looked docile for the moment, but Paolo could see that his head was up, and he was very much aware of what was going on around him.

Sweety Pie was prodded into the bucking chute and stood quietly. Then with a crack that could be heard over the noise of the crowd, one hind foot shot out and kicked the boards in the chute. It was such a quick motion that it took Paolo by surprise. It also opened his eyes to the realization that this big animal was fast and experienced as well.

"Looks to me like he's getting ready for the green flag." Paolo yelled over the noise of the crowd to Doug, who nodded vigorously.

Sweety Pie pawed the dirt as they put the bucking strap around his flanks. Then they fished the rigging around his huge chest and pulled it tight.

"Watch him. See him blow up his chest so they can't get it tight. This bull has been here many times before. They'll put the rigging on him, then he will blow up while they pull it tight. As soon as they stop he lets the air out and the rigging gets slack. Cowboy ain't got a chance of staying on." Coburn yelled in Paolo's ear.

The cowboy and the chute crew did their best to get the rigging pulled snug. Finally, the cowboy gently eased down onto the broad back of the bull. Paolo could see the concentration in his face and maybe just a hint of fear. *I'd be wetting my pants just about now,* he thought to himself.

The cowboy pounded his gloved fist with his left hand as he wrapped his fingers tight around the strap. He pulled his hat down as tight as it would go then raised his head and nodded to the gate man.

Sweety Pie came out of the chute in one gigantic twisting leap with all four legs off the ground. It was a spectacular move. Sixteen hundred pounds at least two feet off the ground in contorted concentrated motion designed to put the cowboy in the next county.

The cowboy was game and rode it out with his left arm flailing the air while he did his best to stay centered over his right hand. Then the bull kicked both back legs straight out and landed on his front legs with his head down. The motion put the cowboy down over his neck, and as he did, the bull snapped his head back, catching the cowboy on the forehead with the side of one of those sawed off horns.

The man went limp and his hat went flying as he flipped off the side of the bull. Unfortunately his hand was still in the rigging and when he rolled he twisted his wrist making it even tighter. The bull crow-hopped around the arena dragging the unconscious cowboy by his right arm. The clowns did their best to get him untangled, but it was no match.

One clown risked his life as he tried to reach over and untangle the rigging. He caught a horn himself for his effort and was tossed into the fence to lay stunned in the dirt.

Coburn threw down his cigar and yelled, "This ain't good, boys!" He hopped off the fence into the arena and set off at a run. In the process, he inadvertently grabbed Paolo's leg and dragged him down off the fence as well. The next thing Paolo knew, he was caught up in a rush of six or seven cowboys that had run to the rescue of the unconscious cowboy.

They threw themselves into the side of the bull, trying to hold him while undoing the rigging. Five seconds later, some of them were flying around the arena like bowling pins. Paolo managed to slam the bull with his shoulder and grab hold of the rigging. Two or three other cowboys grabbed Paolo and were doing their best to get a piece of the bull as well. He didn't have time to think. He was just reacting as he was bounced around the dirt. Later that night, while lying in bed, he would reflect on the latent power of the animal. It made about as much sense as throwing his arms around a Cup motor while it was turning nine grand on the dyno.

Coburn, despite his age and portliness, managed to get a hold of the rigging with one hand. In between the bull's jumps, he was waving the other hand and yelling, "Somebody give me a knife. Ain't nobody got a knife? Give me a pocket knife!"

Finally it was Doug that had the foresight to put an opened pocketknife in his hand. Coburn sawed at the rigging strap until it finally parted and the cowboy came loose. Everybody fell away from Sweety Pie. He made a couple of victory laps tossing his head in celebration, then headed for the gate. The party was over.

Doug looked down at Paolo on his knees in the dirt and grinned. "You okay, Dude?"

"I think so," Paolo said as he got to his feet. "Man, I don't think I want to do that again. How about you?"

"Yeah. Hey...Dude, what is that green stuff on your shirt there? And look, there is a big gob on your pants! I hope it isn't what I think it is..."

Paolo looked at his hands and down the front of his pants. Yes, it was true. He had indeed been rubbed all over with what came out of the other end.

Coburn walked over. "Good job, boys. You fellas got sand, I'll say that. Thanks for jumping in there. That cowboy might've lost his life or worse if we hadn't helped out." He looked carefully at Paolo. "Look at you. You got bull pucky all over you. You look like a real cowboy now!"

All at once they realized that the crowd was giving them a standing ovation. Coburn waved and bowed taking his hat off in the process, then he motioned to Doug and Paolo as the applause grew louder.

"You boys are real cowboys. Yessir."

In the meantime, the photographer kept clicking away.

- O -

Dr. Roger Miller sat at his desk and wondered if he had done the right thing. He folded his hands and stared out the window of his small office at the Texas Motor Speedway complex. Whether he did the right thing or not didn't matter any more. He'd done it and hopefully it would work out in a way that made everybody happy and brought glory to the Lord. He opened the file folder in front of him and picked up the letter.

He had read the thing so many times, he practically knew it by heart. It was written in pencil in a labored scrawl on lined binder paper. Obviously it was from a kid, but Miller could see that it was done with carefully delineated margins and perfect spelling and punctuation. It looked as if each letter in each word was laboriously printed to fit exactly between the lines.

Dear Dr. Miller, it began. *My name is Silas Biggs and my friend Jeffery said just before he died that you were the one I should write to.* The opening line got Dr. Miller's attention. At first, he thought it might be a hoax of some sort, but after he read the thing, he knew that it wasn't. It was a sincere letter from an adolescent young man with a genuine request.

Dr. Miller stared at the paper. Even though he knew what it said, he found himself reading the letter once again in its entirety for probably the twentieth time. In the past couple of weeks he had learned a lot about Silas Biggs. The kid was a gamer and that was a fact. Silas had written to him specifically with a request. He wanted to attend the Cup race this weekend. That in itself was not a big problem. Texas Motor Speedway often gave away numbers of tickets to underprivileged and handicapped children and did everything possible to make them welcome. Make A Wish and some of the other charity programs worked very closely with NASCAR and many times brought kids to the events. NASCAR worked hard to accommodate them, and a number of drivers were involved in the programs and gave of their time and resources to meet and greet them.

But Silas' request didn't fall in that category. He not only wanted to attend the race but was asking to spend the weekend specifically with the Orly Mann Team. He was wanting to spend every moment with the team and watch them do everything that they would do for the whole weekend. That would mean that he would stay in the motor home compound at the track.

Silas also said that he felt like he had some things to talk over with the team. He wanted to talk to Orly

Mann privately, *just me and him* his letter said. He also wanted to talk with Bear. He called him *Mr. Henry Erickson*. Then he said he had some words for Paolo Pellegrini. Paolo had been with the team for a number of years now and was listed as the car chief for Orly Mann's car. He went on to state that he was probably the most knowledgeable Orly Mann Racing fan there was, although he didn't use that language. He pointed out the fact that he had been a fan nearly his whole life, and considering that he was thirteen, that was a long time. But it was the last bit of the letter that was the most compelling and somewhat shocking.

It read, *Even though I am in a wheel chair, sometimes, my doctor, Dr. Eilersen, says he thinks I would have no problems for the weekend as long as I got my rest and took my meds. Dr. Miller, I am going to die pretty soon. They think I don't know but I do. I am only telling you that because you are a pastor and you understand. If you could help me it would be wonderful. I haven't asked God for very much because I don't want to bother Him too much but I am praying he would let me do this. I have put my telephone number, my email address and you could request to be my friend on my FaceBook page. All you have to do is go and register and you can read about me. I even have a picture on there.*

Dr. Miller was a Godly man. He was a Baptist pastor and did his utmost to live his faith in a way that was pleasing to God. He knew that in God's providence, letters like this didn't just happen. There was a reason for these smudged pages in front of him. As a result, he had to follow through with this kid's request. The first thing he would have to do was verify if it was all genuine. He dutifully made the request on FaceBook and checked out the kid's profile.

It was a typical young boy's page with the usual juvenile stuff. He learned that Silas lived with his Mom and was home schooled most of the time. He was a devoted Orly Mann Racing Team fan with several NASCAR and Orly Mann links. His personal picture showed a fresh faced kid with a great smile but only from the neck up. There was no mention of his disease although he did have a link to a site that outlined the cause and treatment of juvenile arthritis.

He did a little further research and found Dr. Eilersen's name in a town close to the address on Silas' letter. He called and left a message on Eilersen's voice-mail asking him to return the call. Eilersen did an hour later and Miller explained the letter.

"Well, with the privacy laws and so forth, I really can't tell you whether Silas is a patient or not. If his family gives permission, then perhaps I can. In the meantime Dr. Miller, I suggest you get on the Net and look up Juvenile Idiopathic Arthritis or JIA for short. Sometimes it is called JRA. There are basically three manifestations of the disease. If I were you, I would educate myself about the effects of the disease for those who have suffered long term. Most notably check out Systemic JIA with many of its related side effects. JIA is somehow related to an immune system malfunction and as a result has multiple symptoms. We don't completely understand how the disease works. We just know that it can cause major problems not only with the joints but major organs as well. There are occasional high fevers and inflammation of the soft tissue. It also sometimes manifests itself with a condition called uveitis, which is an inflammation of the eye. We do know that all these symptoms combined makes life extremely difficult, and for some, the long term prognosis is not good."

Miller understood that even though Dr. Eilersen could say nothing about Silas specifically, he had given him a lot of pertinent information. He thanked him and told him that maybe they would talk again.

The next decision he had to make was to determine if it was even feasible to do what the kid was asking. Maybe he should talk to the boy first but then again, maybe he should talk first to the people that could make it happen. He elected to talk to the people before he talked with the boy. The one thing that Dr. Roger Miller knew and understood was that because of who he was and who he represented, he was a man of influence. He had been around racing for a long time. His home base was Texas Motor Speedway and in fact, his office was located in the main building. He worked hard to build the reputation of the NFRM with speedways across the nation. People in high places knew that he didn't make requests very often and as a result when he did, they listened. It was a huge mantle of responsibility.

He knew he would have to go upstairs and talk things over with Eddie G., the CEO of Texas Motor Speedway. Eddie was a good man and he treated Dr. Miller with genuine respect. As well as being good, Eddie was wise and he knew how to make things happen. His reaction was to say that as long as Dr. Miller was convinced that this was a good thing, he would back him all the way.

Eddie even went the second mile, telling Dr. Miller that the race track would not only make space in the motor coach lot where the drivers and crews stayed, but would supply a motor coach for the weekend. They would also see to it that the boy and whoever accompanied him would have all the appropriate passes to get them wherever they wanted to go.

It was a very generous offer, but then Eddie G. was always generous with TxArm, which was the Texas connection to the NFRM. He appreciated the numbers of volunteers that staffed the information booths and took care of a multitude of tasks around the track that made things easier for the race fans. Things like making sure the workers got their lunches and running the golf carts that transported the handicapped from the camp grounds to the grandstands and back. Most people didn't realize that for a brief few days Texas Motor Speedway became the fourth largest city in Texas, and it took a lot to make it run smoothly. TxArm was a big part of that process.

Miller was encouraged by Eddie G.'s response, so he went on to the next step, which was to talk with Bear and Orly. When he called the shop, Bear was busy and up to his eyeballs in difficulties, and really didn't have time to talk. That was the life of a crewchief, especially one who owned half the team. But he took Dr. Miller's call anyway and after listening for a few minutes, essentially told him to do what he thought best. He did understand that they were in the midst of a tight points race with two cars, but he would trust Miller's judgment. He would talk with Orly when he had a chance. In the meantime, he was to just let him know what he needed.

So that was that. Now it was time to talk to the kid

and more importantly, his parents. It took two days to make the connection. The kid lived about four hours west from the track, so that meant practically a whole day out of his own schedule. After a brief phone call and a short conversation with Silas' Mom, he made an appointment for a Monday afternoon. He discovered that the boy and his Mom lived in a modest ground floor unit in a middle class apartment complex just outside of town. When he knocked on the door, an attractive blonde haired woman that looked far too young to have a thirteen-year-old son opened it.

"Are you Ms. Biggs?"

"Yes, and you must be Dr. Miller. Call me Sarah. Please come in. Silas has been waiting for you all morning."

"Oh I'm sorry, am I late?"

"No, no. I just meant that he's very excited about you coming. Patience is not one of his virtues. Actually, he's thrilled. I really do appreciate you making the trip. I hope it wasn't a major bother. I had no idea that Silas had written you. When I found out, I wasn't too pleased. But he does have a way of getting what he wants."

The place was clean and well kept. As he entered the living room Silas, who gave him a large smile, met him. He was standing with the help of aluminum crutches, but that didn't keep him from extending his hand.

"Hello, Dr. Miller. Thank you for coming to see us."

As Miller made himself comfortable in the living room, he made two quick observations.

First, the boy was very articulate and not only communicated well, but was also extremely charming. He hogged the initial conversation in his desire to make

Dr. Miller welcome. He had a great smile and flashed it often. He was absolutely delighted to meet him, and did his best to bring his Mom up to speed in what Dr. Miller did, telling her what an important man he was, and how he knew all these famous people, and he even did the prayer before the race started.

"You know Mom, the invocation." His freshness was genuine and his enthusiasm was contagious. Were it not for the misshapen knees and spindly legs and the crippled joints of his hands and wrists, it would be easy to ignore the fact that he was ill. He was just a fresh, vibrant, thirteen year old kid full of life and energy.

The second thing Miller observed was that the boy was engaged in a war. He was fighting an awesome physical battle with a very debilitating, crippling disease. His body was frail and he was very thin. He spent most of the time sitting, but on occasion would get up and painfully make his way around the house on his crutches gesturing as he spoke.

"Sometimes I have to use my wheelchair, but I try not to use it too much. I don't want people to think I'm crippled or something. My Mom home schools me most of the time and I have lots of friends. I don't ever miss a NASCAR race, Dr. Miller. I'm a big fan. I've been watching the Orly Mann Team practically my whole life. I visit their website almost every day and oh yeah, I visit the NFRM site as well. I keep track of you pretty good, that's why I wrote you."

Miller listened intently as the boy spoke. He learned a great deal in a short amount of time. The young man was matter of fact when he spoke about his disease.

"It's just something I have to deal with. I don't know

why God chose me to have it, but you know, Dr. Miller, things happen. I just have to live with it. Most of the time, Mom and me do okay, though sometimes I do have to go to the hospital. My Doctor, Dr. Eilersen, is a good guy and he takes pretty good care of us. Huh, Mom."

Sarah Biggs said nothing from across the room and simply nodded her head in agreement.

"I don't think it will get in the way, Dr. Miller, if I get to go to the track. I will be just fine."

Sarah interrupted Silas, "Dr. Miller, can I get you a cup of coffee? I made a fresh pot."

"Yes, that would be great, Ms. Biggs."

Sarah left the room and Miller turned to Silas.

"Silas, you said something in your letter that disturbed me. You mentioned that you were dying. That nobody thought you knew, but you know. Is that true?"

Silas looked at the floor. "Yes. I overheard a conversation between my Mom and Dr. Eilersen one time, and I also heard the nurses talking when they thought I was asleep at the hospital. I'm thirteen, Dr. Miller, and I know how to use the web to find out what I want to know. I know exactly what type of disease I have and I know that most kids don't live past their early teens." Silas spoke with his head down, not making eye contact.

"Are you sure you're right? Have you talked this over with your Mom?"

Silas looked up and fixed his eyes on Miller's.

"It isn't that easy, Dr. Miller. If I try to talk with her, she gets all teary and starts to cry and then I don't know what to do."

At that point, Sarah walked back into the room

carrying a tray.

"My, you guys look serious. Silas, have you shown Dr. Miller your car collection?"

"Before you do that, Silas, I need to ask your Mom a couple of quick questions. Would you mind excusing us for a minute?"

"No, I don't mind. Come on back to my room when you're done, and I will show you some neat stuff I have collected," Silas said as he hobbled out of the room.

"Ms. Biggs, I mean Sarah, is there a Mr. Biggs and do you want to include him in the trip?"

"The answer to your question is both yes and no. I met Silas' Dad while we were in high school. We fell in love, or at least what we thought was love. I got pregnant. We never got married. That is why Silas has my last name and not his. His Dad is from a broken home like I was and neither one of us knew anything. He tried, but he was just a kid. So was I. He finally left, and we agreed that I would raise Silas. He lives up in Oklahoma somewhere. I don't think he has seen Silas since he was three years old. He sends us money, but not on a regular basis. Silas doesn't know him at all." She spoke in flat matter of fact tones.

"I make our living doing accounting work, which means I can work from home and keep track of Silas at the same time. It's just the two of us. I'm a CPA."

Miller had planned to only spend an hour or so with the kid and his Mom, but before he knew it, three hours had gone by and he had to be on his way back. He told Silas he would do what he could to answer his request. At this point he could make no promises, and Silas had to understand that the Orly Mann Team was in a major battle for the championship and neither he nor Silas could do anything to jeopardize that run. This was serious business. Silas said he understood completely.

Silas' Mom walked him out to the car. "Dr. Miller, I want you to understand something. Silas is not a typical thirteen-year-old. He's been fighting this disease for almost all of his life. In some ways, he is very mature because of what he has had to deal with. He has spent a great deal of time in the hospital, and his understanding of the whole medical aspect of his illness is phenomenal. On the other hand, he hasn't been able to spend much time in school, so socially he isn't typical either. Practically all of his friends are on the Net." She paused before continuing.

"I appreciate all you're doing, but you also need to know that Silas has good days and bad days. When he has a bad day, he suffers a great deal, and sometimes it can be very difficult. I just am not sure he should do this. I am his Mom and I just don't want him to hurt anymore. I don't understand why God allows him to suffer so much and I don't want him to overdo and hurt himself. Having said that, I also know that this is the most exciting thing that has ever happened to him, and it is the fulfillment of his dream." She paused again a moment.

"I guess what I am saying is that if you can make this happen, I would be so very grateful." Her eyes misted up and she quickly wiped a tear off her cheek. "I'm sorry."

"We will do what we can Mrs. Biggs. I will let you know in a couple of days. Would you mind if I talked with Dr. Eilersen about Silas?"

"No, not at all. He is a wonderful doctor and has been a great friend to Silas. I will contact him and tell him to share with you anything he thinks you might need to know. You know, Dr. Miller, like I told you I didn't even know he had written to you until you called. He is a remarkable boy."

"I can see that he is, Ms. Biggs. I will do what I can."

The next day he talked at length with Dr. Eilersen, who did indeed agree that Silas could more than likely handle the stress of the weekend. He felt that it was a worthwhile risk and would be a tremendous source of encouragement for Silas. He would make sure that all the proper meds were in order and gave Dr. Miller his personal cell number in case he was needed.

Then Miller asked Dr. Eilersen if he was aware that Silas thought he was dying. He went on to share what Silas had shared with him, both in the letter and at the house.

"I wasn't aware of that, no. Silas is extremely smart. He keeps me on my toes. He would make a good doctor. Is he terminal? Yes, I would say that he is. It is not the disease itself, it is the collateral damage it causes to certain of the internal organs. How long does he have? I don't know. I am not God. He could live another ten or fifteen years or he might develop pneumonia and die next week. I am concerned about his attitude. I will talk with him about it first chance I get. I will do my best not to violate your confidence."

Miller had no doubts. This was the right thing to do. He put the wheels in motion, and it was done.

Some of TxArm's folks would pick Silas and his Mom up Thursday afternoon at their apartment. He knew a fellow with a limousine service that owed him a favor. He was willing to pick up Silas and his Mom and bring them to the track, then take them home on Monday morning. It would be a nice touch. A little frosting on the cake.

Lord I hope we are doing the right thing and it all works out, Dr. Miller prayed for the hundredth time.

Chapter Three

*"The good Lord doesn't tell you what His plan is,
so all you can do is get up in the morning
and see what happens next."*
Richard Petty

Paolo sat on the edge of the bed in his underwear in the DFW Marriott while he talked to Bear. "So when do you think the Hauler will be here?"

Doug was gingerly shoving Paolo's manure laden clothes into a plastic bag muttering to himself.

"Making the whole room stink." Then he stopped what he was doing and put his whole focus on Paolo and his conversation when he said

"How bad is he hurt?" Paolo grimaced at Doug as he listened.

"Man, that's no good. What a dumb thing. Somebody must have screwed up big time. Can he drive this weekend?" Paolo was silent as he listened to Bear's answer. The pause went on for a long time while Doug waited impatiently. Finally Paolo spoke. "Yeah, I know, Bear. Stop leaning on me." Paolo shook his head, scowling. He was speaking in short clipped tones, which was a signal to Doug that he was getting irritated.

"Okay, we'll be waiting. I know he likes a different setup than Orly. Yeah, I know exactly what Brad has in that car. You know I do, Bear. Yes, I'll give him a call as soon as I can. Yeah, I can do this. You know I can, Bear. We've got a race to win. I'll give him everything I can. The guys on the Blue Saber side are a smart bunch. You know that, you hired them. I can work with them. I do already a lot of the time." Paolo waited while Bear spoke. Then he began to talk again.

"Now listen, just because I don't like him doesn't mean I can't do the job. It will be fine. I'll see you in the garage. Hey Bear, lighten up. Yeah, okay. Bear, listen. Email me any of Brad's notes that you think might help and what time do you think the Hauler will get here? Is Brad going to be able to talk tomorrow in case I have questions? Yeah, I know that Dobson is his car chief and I have his number. I'll call him as soon as I can." Paolo's mind was racing.

"Who are you going to get to handle the jack for the Thunderfoot Ballet?" That was Paolo's usual job on race day. "Yeah, he's good. Okay, Bear. No problem. We can do it. Yeah, stay in touch and I will see you at the track." Paolo clicked off the phone.

"What's up, Dude?"

Paolo looked up at Doug with a hard look on his face. "I'm not sure where to start. For starters, Orly got hurt today in a testing accident at Infineon. He was driving a GT Daytona prototype, and destroyed it, and got banged up."

"How bad? Can he drive? Who are we going to get for backup? Let's see, we used. . . ."

"Slow down, Doug. Yeah, they think he can drive. Seems some Wrench left something loose or something on the car, and then they didn't pull the pin on the fire bottle or something, so it got pretty hot in the cockpit. Orly was stunned by the impact, I guess. I don't know. Bear didn't know all the details. Anyway, he lost it going into or coming out of ten, and crashed real heavy into the fence. The car flipped but landed on its wheels, but then caught fire. It burned him a bit on his leg and hands. I guess T.K. pulled him out. It must have been pretty sick. It will be interesting to hear T.K.'s version."

"Burned! Holy crap! Painful, I bet. He can drive though?" Doug said with a question mark. "You sure?"

"Yeah. He is Orly. You know him. It's not like he hasn't been hurt before..."

"What's the other news?"

"Well, you're looking at the new crew chief for the Blue Saber car."

"Dude...really? What's up with Brad?"

"He tripped at the shop and broke an ankle. They had to do surgery and put some pins in. He's laid up for a while. For sure the rest of the season. Looks like I'm the guy to finish up the championship run."

"What! Everything happening at once. Man, poor Brad. That guy was about the only guy in the shop that could understand T.K. They got along pretty good." Doug sat down on the bed next to Paolo and put his hands in his pockets.

"You up for that?" Doug was the kind of guy who took things as they came. He shared that trait with Bear. Whatever the situation, he was convinced that there was a way to deal with it. He also knew Paolo and his capabilities.

Doug grew up in the North Carolina NASCAR world. His father had been a crew chief and mechanic and was one of the very first people Bear and Orly hired. He was retired now. Doug didn't necessarily share his father's mechanical abilities, but he was a most valuable tool to the team in his administrative capabilities. He was one of those unique guys that could watch a race with 43 cars and tell you virtually every position of every car, and who had stopped for fuel only, and which cars took four or two tires, and how many laps had been run, and who was gaining and who was losing. Bear relied heavily on Doug's ability to see the big picture.

Doug was also very tech savvy. Everyone in racing nowadays was computer literate. It was just a sophisticated part of the game. Most teams employed people that did nothing but their I.T. stuff. But Doug took things in a different direction. He was an observer, and as Bear called him, "an assimilator of information."

It seemed like Doug knew everybody and everything that was happening in every NASCAR series. He also knew that "stuff happens" and virtually anything could and often did go wrong in the racing "biz", as Bear called it. He also knew generally there was a solution if one just dug hard enough.

"Yeah, I'm up for it. I can do it. The hardest part will be staying on the same page with T.K. He likes his car a lot different than Orly. I'll have to get used to that. But I can do it. It's what I have been shooting for. It's what I want to do. Besides that, I can rely on Bear and his knowledge. I still work for the Orly Mann Racing Team. At least, I hope so."

"Of course you can do it, Paolo. Kind of an odd way of getting the position. Kind of like coming off the bench when the star quarterback goes down, but stuff happens. Not usually everything at once, though." Doug paused, thought for a minute then said "hey Dude, what about Alicia?"

"Doug, don't go there, man. This isn't about her. Let's go get something to eat." But Paolo knew in his mind that she did play a part. A big part. He wondered to himself *yeah, what about Alicia?*

About that time the phone in the room rang. Both men jumped a little. Doug reached over and picked it up. "Yeah. I dunno, I'll ask him." He put his hand over the mouthpiece and said to Paolo "It's some reporter dude from ESPN. He wants to know if he can interview you. I guess we're all over the tube. They have video of you mixing it up with the bull and he wants to get your take on Orly's injury and Brad and being the new crew chief and all. What should I tell him?"

"Tell him sure, if he's buying. I'm starving. Tell him we'll meet in the restaurant downstairs in a few minutes."

- *O* -

Hildy sat back in the seat in the private jet and tried to close her eyes. She couldn't. Every time she tried to relax she snapped awake and her mind took off. They were flying at thirty something thousand feet sometime in the middle of the night, and most likely were over Arizona, or New Mexico, or maybe even Nevada. She wasn't sure, and she didn't particularly care.

It seemed lately that they spent way too much time in this airplane. She wasn't complaining. It was quick and comfortable, but at the same time it was cramped and stuffy. Besides that, it was an absolute necessity, considering Orly's schedule.

She studied Orly in the seat beside her. He was sleeping in his shorts with his legs extended and a sheet draped across his left thigh. He looked uncomfortable and occasionally his lips twitched in pain. Were he an ordinary human being, he would be heavily medicated and probably would be sleeping stretched out. Truthfully, he most likely would still be in a hospital bed.

But he wasn't. He was a race car driver with three races left in the season sitting on a strong chance to win the championship, and he wasn't going to risk failing a random NASCAR drug test.

Drug testing could be a chancy business these days, so he was making do with over the counter ibuprofen painkillers. Under the circumstances, he probably could have gotten permission from NASCAR to take something a little stronger, but he absolutely refused to even contact them. He wanted to do nothing that would cause anyone to ask any type of questions. As a result, he was hurting, and from the looks of him, he was hurting pretty bad.

Hildy looked at his hands curled in his lap. They were strong hands, she knew that for a fact. She held them often. She also knew that he had calluses across his palms from gripping the steering wheels in countless different race cars. Right now his hands looked soft and vulnerable...and hurt. He had blisters on the back of them from the fire. She loved this guy. She wanted to reach out and take those hands and pull him close and hold him but she didn't want to hurt him any more.

Hildy resisted the impulse and instead studied Orly's face. He was a handsome guy. At least, she thought so. He wasn't movie star perfect, but he was rugged looking and usually sported a half-crooked, almost sardonic grin. Right now he just looked tired and worn out. He furrowed his brow and shook his head and groaned softly. She could tell he was dreaming and it wouldn't be long before he snapped awake. She had seen him like this many times before.

Orly jokingly told her one time that he didn't dream often except when he was stressed or in pain. He never told her what he dreamed, but she knew. He thought he kept it hidden, but because she loved him and understood him so well, she saw it. It was like a pocket of sissy emotional hurt that was buried deep inside him.

Most of the time, it was encapsulated by scar tissue, but somehow physical pain or injury or extreme stress seemed to open the wound all over again and the stuff would come boiling to the surface. When it did, it brought with it more pain. It was just something he lived with. She knew that there was nothing she could do to heal it except hold him close in the dark.

When they first got married, she used to think that she could "fix" it, but she had learned that it was his thing and she couldn't. She leaned back further and slipped her fingers gently around the back of his arm, stroking him softly. She willed herself to relax and closed her eyes and let her mind drift.

She had loved this guy most of her life. Hildy first

met him when she was a young girl. Her father was Harry Hornbrook, the founder of the Speed King Oil Additive Company. He was an innovative man and decided the best way to market his products was to sponsor a race team. Initially, he didn't have much budget to work with, but he found a couple of very young men who had teamed together and were scorching the dirt car circuit.

Her father often told her that Henry Erickson, better known as Bear, was the best race car engineer/ crew chief that he ever met. He understood the nuances of setup and was incredibly adept at wringing the most out of any race car while Orly Mann had the uncanny ability of communicating to Bear what the car needed to go faster than the other guys. Orly was smooth and easy on equipment. He knew when to press and when to lay back. Together those two guys were phenomenal.

As the fortunes of the Orly Mann Racing Team rose, so did the Speed King Company. A number of years back, Orly and Bear decided to make the switch to NASCAR and Cup racing. Speed King went with them. The rest, as they say, is history. Orly won two championships and was now in the hunt for a third.

Growing up, Hildy always thought she might marry Orly Mann, but it wasn't meant to be. At least, not then. Oh yeah they dated and were sort of serious, but they spent more time arguing and butting heads than anything else. Finally they both realized that they were too much alike. They were both driven and both felt like they had something to prove to the world. They called it quits. It was the hardest thing Hildy ever did and in her heart she knew she never got over it. She went on to school, then got her law degree, and opened a small independent practice in San Diego, working mostly with the Hispanic population. She didn't make a lot of money and did a lot of pro-bono work, but she was satisfied. She had several relationships, but nothing serious.

In the meantime, Orly moved on. He met a girl and married her. Hildy didn't know her and never met her. She went to the wedding, but didn't stay for the reception. It was a hard day.

Then not quite two years later, Orly's world came apart. His wife and brand new baby daughter were broadsided in a suburban intersection just a few blocks from the house and killed outright. A drunk driver, who was driving at a high rate of speed, running from the police, hit them. It was one of those inexplicable tragedies that only the Lord understands. At first Orly was completely immobilized, but he came out of that and tried to drown his sorrow on the racetrack.

There was a period of time when he would drive anything anywhere and did everything he could to fill up every spare moment. He drove with a vindictiveness that scared those that cared for him and loved him. Bear bore the brunt of Orly's rage and there were those who questioned why he hung around. Bear loved him as friend and a brother, and he knew that Orly needed him.

During that time Orly was in several bad crashes but always managed to come away with minimal injury. He developed a reputation as an "iron man", which wasn't far from the truth. He did his best to make himself impervious to pain whether it was emotional or physical.

83

Were it not for Bear and Pastor John of Raceway Ministries, Orly would have self-destructed. Perhaps it was a weakness in his character that made him take responsibility for everyone and everything. Somehow he felt that if he had only done something different, the accident would not have happened, that it was his fault. Of course he was wrong, but Hildy knew that even today, he still struggled.

Then Hildy's own world came apart. Her Mom died, and then her Dad was diagnosed with terminal cancer. There was a group that thought they might swoop in and snatch up the Speed King Company in Harry's weakness, but he coerced Hildy into coming in and running the organization after he passed. She didn't want to do it, but she did, and wonder of wonders, she was very good at it. It was during this time that she and Orly got together.

They were both older and wiser and they both realized that they did indeed love each other, that they were truly, no matter how cliché it sounded, soul mates. They were better together than when they were apart. That was a fact.

But now she had a decision to make and it wasn't an easy one.

Thank the Lord for Nancy. She was a wise lady and Hildy needed advice. That is why she was delighted to spend the day with her while Orly tested. Nancy was a little older and understood pain and suffering. She also understood men, particularly competitive ones. Hildy was pregnant. She just found out a few days ago and she wasn't very far along. The question was whether to tell Orly now or wait until after the end of the season in three weeks. The truth was she was a little scared. Considering Orly's past, she wasn't sure what kind of reaction she might get from him, and the last thing she wanted to do was distract him from the business at hand.

Nancy didn't waste words. It took two to make a baby, and a baby was a love gift from the Lord, and far more important than any kind of championship or anything else in this world.

"Get your priorities straight, girl," she said to Hildy. Hildy had to laugh when she said that. Nancy was right. She was prepared to tell him this evening when they went out to dinner with Bob and Nancy, but then Orly got hurt, and instead they spent the time at the hospital. Now finally they were on their way to Texas, but Orly was asleep and hurting. It would have to wait.

Orly snapped awake with his eyes wide open. Hildy put her head on his shoulder as she held his arm. "It's okay, Orly Mann. I'm right here."

- O -

Silas Biggs emptied his backpack out on his bed for the third time. He was so excited he could hardly breathe. They were picking him and his Mom up late Thursday afternoon in a real limousine. A big black one, they said, and it would take him right to the Motor Coach lot at the racetrack.

He would have his own motor coach, and it would be parked right next to Orly Mann's coach. It had a TV and a bathroom and everything. They would be sleeping right next to where Orly Mann slept. He could meet all the drivers and famous people he wanted to. He would even be able to go into the garage area. They said they had a special golf cart for them that would take him anywhere he wanted to go.

Dr. Miller said he could even go to the Chapel Service before the race and maybe they could allow him to go to the driver's meeting as well. He carefully took inventory to make sure he hadn't forgotten anything and gently placed each item back in the pack. Binoculars that his Mom gave him for his birthday. They were good ones that were easy to adjust. Swiss army knife. The big one with all the attachments, just in case. Extra batteries and two memory sticks for his camera. Mini tape recorder, which fit in his pocket. A piece of string and a small roll of racer's tape, just in case and a little bungee cord. His Bible, of course. Two pencils and two pens and two sharpies for autographs. His autograph book and a small notebook to take notes in.

Then there was the #37 Speed King Chevrolet with the special Speed King paint job that was carefully kept in the box. His Mom got that for him, too. She had to order it special on the internet. He was hoping to get Orly Mann to sign it, if he could. He methodically put everything back in the backpack and hefted it. It wasn't too heavy. He could manage, it he thought.

Silas turned around and sat down on the edge of his bed. The pain wasn't too bad tonight. It was manageable. Sometimes it wasn't and he had to take more medicine. He hated when that happened because it made him so groggy and out of it. Sometimes it was a hard choice. Hurt or be groggy and feel dull and stupid. He put his awkward misshapen hands on his knobby knees and bowed his head. He could feel the fever lurking in the background. Sometimes it came leaping out of the bushes and ambushed him like a big striped tiger. He would suddenly feel all hot and incredibly sweaty and there would be lots of "achy-breakyness", as his Mom called it.

Other times it just started like a little nagging voice that got louder and louder that made his ears ring and hurt his head until he thought he couldn't stand it anymore. It was hard when the fever broke and the chills came and he shivered uncontrollably. Sometimes it felt like he had fallen in a frozen lake and he just couldn't get warm enough. His Mom kept a stack of blankets next to the microwave just in case, so she could warm them before she piled them on.

Silas prayed. "God please let me not get sick this weekend. Please Lord. I will do anything you want me to do, Lord, but please don't let the fever come now. Please Lord."

- O -

T.K. hummed the old Lynard Skynard song *They Call me the Breeze*. He couldn't quite remember the words but they went something like *they call me the breeze 'cause I'm always blowing down the road*. Yeah, that was what he was doing. Blowing down the road.

He was relaxed into the rhythm of the big motorcycle and kept his speed just slightly over the speed limit. It was a wonderful night for riding. Clear and crisp with little traffic. His leathers kept the wind out and the heat of the big motor warmed him as it effortlessly propelled him through the darkness.

T.K. was on the old river road between Antioch and Sacramento running along the levee. Soon he would cut off toward Lodi through the cornfields. A few zigs and zags and then another back road or two that would take him into Kettleman City where his Mom lived. He would arrive after midnight, but that was plenty okay. She would still be up waiting for him.

It would be a short visit. With his schedule the way it was, he didn't have much time to hang around. It was okay, she understood. She was good that way. They would probably stay up all night talking, which is what they usually did. He couldn't stay long even if he wanted to. He was supposed to meet his plane at Bakersfield tomorrow afternoon and fly on to Texas. Bear had called a team meeting tomorrow night, and he obviously had to be there for that.

T.K. not only loved his Mom, but he had great respect for her. In his own mind, he owed her and he had made a vow to himself that no matter what, he would take decent care of her. After all, she had sacrificed to make sure he and his sister had a decent place to live growing up, particularly in the difficult times after "Slick Willie".His Dad died when he was five and his sister was three. His Dad was a hard worker that always did his best to provide for his young family. He died unexpectedly, but he had the foresight to make sure he had enough life insurance to keep things together. That plus he had a little inheritance from his own parents that he had invested wisely. They did okay. They weren't rich but they had enough to live fairly comfortably.

Then when he was fourteen his Mom fell in love

with a guy named William Williams. She married him and they moved to Phoenix. It wasn't T.K. that named him "Slick Willie", it was what he was called behind his back by everyone who worked for him. He was a crook, plain and simple. He went through his Mom's money in about three years and then dumped her and the family like a bag of worthless trash. Willie threw them out of the house that he bought with T.K.'s Mom's money.

They ended up moving back to the Bakersfield area into a rundown trailer park, and his Mom went to work as a waitress. It was all they could afford but they managed. All three of them felt the effects of what Slick Willie did to them. He came across as such a nice guy, but in truth he had no conscience at all.

T.K. went to work part time while he finished school doing various jobs. He was working for a grocery store when a great man named Walt Porter offered him a job. Walt had a body shop and also spent a lot of time building race car chassis. He was a wealth of knowledge and T.K. was a sponge. He started out sweeping floors but it wasn't long before Walt had him welding and fabricating.

One thing led to another and through a set of interesting circumstances, T.K. got his break in racing on a couple of local dirt tracks. T.K. was a 'natural'. He had a great feel for the car and a whole bucket load of talent. He was also fearless and a touch arrogant, but it was all good. The rest, as they say, is history. T.K. progressed to sprint cars and the late model circuit. He ultimately moved into the NASCAR West Series and from there made the jump into Cup racing. He started out driving for a low budget team run by a great guy. But it was obvious that they weren't going to be able to compete with the multi-car teams with the big wallets.

In the meantime old Slick Willie never left them alone. It was kind of like he recognized T.K.'s talent and he wanted a piece of the pie. Slick was hooked up with a guy named Thornton Vertner who wedged himself into the ownership of the Blue Saber Team. Supposedly Slick Willie brokered a deal that put T.K. into the seat although T.K. never saw any contract. He took major credit for getting T.K. the "ride" and he felt that T.K. owed him agent's fees, which was a bit of a joke because Vertner was notoriously slow at paying his people.

The bottom line was that he sued T.K., not once, but several times. Then when Vertner went down for his crooked financial shenanigans, Slick Willie caught some of the spin-off and nearly did a little time himself. Later on he did do time when some anomalies showed up at his dealership in Phoenix, and as far as T.K. knew, he was still in the pokey.

At least he hoped he still was in jail. Slick Willie was one of those guys who never gave up, and he had made T.K.'s life miserable for a period of time. He knew T.K. was now making big money and he wanted what he felt was his share. At one point, he had become so obnoxious that T.K. was granted a restraining order that was supposed to keep Slick Willie at a distance. At any rate he was out of the picture...at least for now.

T.K. glanced down at the speedo on the bike and realized that he was booking way too fast on a two-lane country road in the middle of the night. The last thing he needed to do was run over some unfortunate critter and crash the bike. He backed off of the throttle and smiled to himself. Funny how just thinking about Slick Willie got him fired up. The guy was a jerk. A narcissistic self-centered egomaniac, plain and simple.

His Mom lived in a nice house now, out in the country with her dogs and cats, a few chickens, plus the odd horse or two. T.K. bought the house for her and got her out of that run down trailer park as soon as he started making decent money on the racing circuit. He actually bought her the house before he spent any money on himself.

His Mom worked hard to hold it together to make sure he and his sister got what they needed growing up. She had confessed to both of them that she was very sorry that she allowed William, as she called him, into their lives. She was lonely and he was so charming and so full of fun, and she thought it would all work out.

It was okay. Things had worked out. His sister was happily married with three kids already and lived fairly close to Mom. The kids loved spending time at "Grandma's house" with all of her animals, and they adored Uncle T.K.

T.K. let his mind wander as he rumbled through the night. Whew! What a day. Orly came really close to getting seriously hurt or burned. If he was testing by himself, it would have taken help a lot longer to get to him.

It was fortunate that T.K. was just behind when the car broke. Well, he wasn't 'just' behind him. T.K. was having a hard time staying with Orly when he put the hammer down.

Orly was an incredibly skilled road racer and it took every bit of talent that T.K. possessed to try to hang with him. Orly didn't even look like he was breathing hard, he was so smooth. A couple of times he was certain that it was going to be him in the dirt and he wanted to yell "uncle" and whine like a little girl. Then when Orly's car broke and the bodywork flew off, he was faced with an instantaneous decision. He knew Orly was going into the fence and more than likely would come ricocheting back across the track.

He could throw his own car into a spin and try to miss him or he could just try to drive through the corner and get by before Orly came back across the track. Of course, if he miscalculated he would t-bone Orly and probably hurt them both. He didn't hesitate and did his best to flatfoot through the corner.

The problem was there was fluid of some kind dumped on the track when Orly's car came apart. He managed to clear Orly, but lost the car in the process and spun down the short chute between turns ten and eleven. He was fortunate that he didn't hit anything, but by the time he got the thing stopped and could see through the tire smoke, he realized that Orly was on fire.

The acrid black smoke and the ugly yellow flames were creeping out of the engine compartment, and it looked like it wouldn't be long before the thing was going to be fully engulfed. Once again he didn't hesitate. He was closest and dressed in fireproof material, so he was the logical one to get Orly out of there. He drove up as close as he dared, threw the door open, popped the harness and pulled his communication cables loose.

He sprinted to the wreck and pulled what was left of the door out of the way. He reached across Orly to hit the fire bottle. He realized then that some name-less idiot had left the safety pin in. Orly should have checked that himself. He didn't take time to mess with it. It was only a race car, He didn't give a fig if the thing burned to the ground. Instead he got Orly's belts undone and started dragging him out of the car. There was a lot of smoke, and flames were coming out of the dash panel. He jerked Orly's radio wire loose without bothering to unplug it.

All of a sudden Orly came to and started scram-bling himself. T.K. grabbed Orly around the waist and literally pulled him out of the flames. He led him a good distance away from the car and helped him sit on the ground while they waited for the emergency crew. T.K. helped Orly get his helmet off, and it was then he realized that Orly's gloves and the left thigh part of his driver's suit were darkly singed. He also realized that at that moment Orly looked older and more worn out than he had ever seen him.

T.K. remembered asking Orly if he was okay. Orly's voice came out in a hoarse croak, "I think I am burned some. It is starting to hurt. Help me get these gloves off."

He told Orly to hang on a minute, and let them cut them off so he didn't hurt his hands any more than they were. Orly had nodded in agreement. Shortly after that, things went to pieces in a hand basket as they say.

The team boss came screeching up in a van with the other mechanics. He never even looked at Orly but went straight to the car. The fire crew snuffed the flames in short order with a healthy dose of foam and fire retardant. The boss stomped around the wreck twice then came goose-stepping back to Orly and T.K. "You bloody idiots. You have completely wiped out the car. That's what I get for putting you NASCAR chumps in the seat. The paramedics were cutting Orly's gloves off and he paid no attention to the pompous verbiage, but T.K. had enough.

He couldn't remember exactly what he said but it had something to do with carelessness and shoddy workmanship but not necessarily in those terms. It was also after he grabbed the guy by the front of his shirt and almost literally lifted him off the ground. He did recall Bob pulling him off saying something over his shoulder to the guy about being lucky not to have his "nose broke".

Ah well, it was fun while it lasted, as they say. He had other business.

T.K. now had a new crew chief. He knew that some people would think that he was going to be really upset about that. Particularly with Paolo doing the job. He was ticked at the beginning, but he had a chance to think it through and reason it out. Paolo was good. He knew his stuff. As a result he wasn't upset at all. Paolo was the logical choice. He didn't have the emotional energy to invest in it. It was what it was. Paolo would do the job and together they would make it work. There was no other choice. It would have to work. He wanted this championship so bad he could taste it. Three races to go and he needed to make up some points.

When Orly talked with him he mentioned Alicia and asked him if that was going to be a problem. Little did Orly know that as far as T.K. was concerned, she didn't factor into the equation. Oh yeah she was beautiful and intriguing and a lot of fun to be with, but he was dead serious about racing and nothing else. Besides, when it came time to settle down he could have his pick. In the meantime, *I have the need for speed.*

T.K. checked his mirrors. Nobody on the road. He took a fresh set on the handgrips and cracked the throttle on the bike. *They call me the breeze...*

Chapter Four

"I read once where some guy said that if you work hard for eight hours and do a good job you might get promoted and make more money then you could work hard for twelve hours. That is kind of how this sport is. More responsibility...more hours."

Paolo Pellgrini on being promoted to Crew Chief

Thursday morning found Paolo buried inside his laptop with his head down and mind racing. He was linked into the shop computer and was going over some of Brad's notes on the Blue Saber car. He was humming to himself as he sorted through the data. He knew that T.K. liked a much looser setup than Orly, but he didn't know exactly what they had been running in the way of springs and track bar.

Paolo had been on the phone for an hour with Randy Eaton, the car chief for the car. Randy's responsibility was pretty much the same as Paolo's had been with Orly. Bear made most of the decisions and his responsibility was to see them carried out. *That had been an interesting conversation*, thought Paolo to himself.

Now he was the one making the calls. Randy said

one of the first things Bear did was call all the crew together and inform them that he, Paolo, was the boss. He was the final guy on all decisions. Randy was more than agreeable on the phone and reassured Paolo that all the crew guys were okay with Bear's decision. Randy also assured him that whatever Paolo wanted done he would see to it that it got done. That was his job. They had a championship to win, and the whole crew was geared to that goal. They had confidence in him and would work their tails off for him. It was an encouraging discussion, but it also defined the enormous responsibility that Paolo faced.

Now he was working through some algebraic equations, figuring fuel mileage, axle ratios and barometric pressures combined with the aero package they were running. *Then, let's see...throw in the banking at Texas and the carb setup,* he thought to himself. It was a bit ironic because math was one of his weakest subjects in school, but through the years he had developed a lot of skill in that area.

Amazing how circumstances could motivate. He was almost there on his engineering degree, but doing it part time was slowing him down some. Bear said he was a natural. Of course working with Bear was an education in itself.

Paolo pushed his chair back and took a couple of deep breaths. He was trying to think of everything and all it was doing right now was making him anxious. He was *chomping at the bit,* as Coburn the rodeo guy would say, whatever the heck that meant. He guessed it had something to do with horses, but in truth he wanted to get started.

The Haulers would be in the area this afternoon, but they wouldn't be allowed into the track until 7:00 this evening. Tomorrow night was the truck race, and Saturday was the Nationwide race, so things were going to be pretty hectic. Of course the truck guys would take off right after their race, and the Nationwide guys would all be gone after their race as well. He couldn't remember if T.K. was entered in either one of those races. He drove for other teams in those series and occasionally drove all three events if the demographics worked out. Never mind all that. It didn't concern him. He was only worried about one race and that one was Sunday afternoon.

Let's see, he thought. Even if the Haulers were parked at the track tonight, they couldn't unload until the garage opened at 7:00 AM tomorrow morning. Bear had promised to make sure that he brought everything in terms of notes and computer stuff when he came in this afternoon. Then he informed him that Alicia would be his "go-to" person. That meant that she would take care of all the details in regard to the paperwork and whatnot. She would also be on the pit box as the official scorer. That would be excellent as well.

Brad had his own way of doing things and Bear cautioned him not to change too much, especially this late in the season. But Bear also understood that there would be certain things that Paolo would want to do his way and Alicia was to help with that. He was also going to give him Doug or at the very least split him between both teams. That would be good.

Paolo got up and paced around the room. As soon as they got the car off the truck, he wanted to give it a meticulous going over. Then they had to get the car through the "room of doom", which was the tech inspection and get the car certified before it could go on the track. Get their competition sticker stuck in the window, then they were good to go.

Of course, the car was already certified at the NASCAR headquarters back in Charlotte. The way the rules were, once the car was fabricated in the shop, it was sent over there to be carefully looked at by the officials and then registered. It saved a lot of time at the track. It wasn't like they didn't know what they were doing. They had been doing this all season long so everybody on both teams knew the drill.

Paolo sat down at his laptop and punched in the schedule for Texas Motor Speedway. The first practice wasn't until noon on Friday, tomorrow, and lasted an hour and a half. That could be a pretty frantic time.

It all depended on what the car was doing and what changes T.K. wanted. They would start with a race setup and then make the subtle changes for a qualifying setup. Texas could be funny this time of the year. It might be gray and cold or then again it might be ninety degrees and the track could be hot and slick. Fortunately they had two practices on Saturday to fine tune the race setup, but he better dial in enough adjustment for whatever the conditions might be. Bear was the greatest weather prognosticator he had ever seen, so he could rely on that.

Qualifying was Friday afternoon at 3:30. When they went out depended on how they practiced and what practice speed they posted. The faster they went in practice, the later they qualified. Be nice to be in the last ten cars or so. Qualifying generally lasted only an hour or so. It would be nice to qualify well so they could pick a decent pit box. It was going to be a busy time. Orly was a fairly consistent qualifier. He was usually in the top ten or twelve somewhere. He only had one pole this year, but he generally started the race toward the front. T.K. on the other hand, was wildly inconsistent. One week he would be on the front row and the next week be back in twentieth or worse. It would be anybody's guess as to how they might take the green flag. It was certainly a lot easier to start the race toward the front as opposed to being back in the pack. Bad stuff could happen, especially on low air pressure and a bunch of unknowns. No sense in worrying about that, Paolo thought to himself. Cross that bridge, and all that, when you get to it.

Then Paolo sat back and grabbed his head with both hands as he was overwhelmed with a thought. Devin! Devin could be big trouble. Devin was T.K.'s cousin, which didn't count for much, but he was also T.K.'s spotter. T.K. wouldn't run a NASCAR race without him. T. K. swore by him. He trusted him and listened to him before he would listen to anyone else.

The guy is funky, thought Paolo to himself. Brad managed to deal with him okay, but then Brad was a pretty calm guy. There had to be good communication between a crew chief and a spotter. It was essential.

The NASCAR rule was that a car could not be on the racetrack at any time without a spotter. Spotters must be in radio communication with the driver at all times. Generally the spotters were grouped together and perched high atop the highest point of the track.

At Texas, they observed from the top of the suites on the front straight. As a result they had an overview that allowed them to see the race car all around the track. Because of the Hahn's device, the wrap around seats and the basic configuration of the car, it was the spotter's job to keep the driver apprized of who and what was going on around him. But if he knew what he was talking about, he could work well with the driver and crew chief to make the necessary adjustments on the car to make it faster.

Devin had a high-pitched, squeaky voice and sometimes when he got excited, he talked so fast that nobody but T.K. could understand him. Several times Bear had made the suggestion to T.K. that maybe, just maybe he might do better with a different guy calling the shots. T.K. wouldn't hear of it. Finally Bear gave up.

T.K. was doing pretty good up to this point and Bear's attitude was, "if it ain't broke, don't try to fix it." Devin was a short, heavyset guy with spiked hair who wore a diamond in his nose. That upset a lot of people in the NASCAR world, but Paolo could care less. The big issue was that Devin was opinionated and could on occasion be argumentative. He also didn't like Paolo very much. Paolo wasn't sure why and didn't waste much time trying to understand the issues, but now he would have to work with the guy. That was the last thing Paolo needed as he tried to keep this team together.

Paolo's reverie was interrupted when Doug came crashing into the room.

"Hey Dude, you won't believe what happened! I just talked with Bear. The Blue Saber hauler caught fire and burned to the ground at a truck stop in Tulsa, Oklahoma. Total loss." He started to go on, then exploded with laughter and held himself as he looked at Paolo's stricken face.

"You jerk! That isn't funny. They don't even go through Tulsa. But the way things have been going, it really is within the realm of possibility. You had me scared for a minute."

"Yeah! You should have seen your face." Doug continued to chuckle. Then he changed the subject. "I did talk with Bear. He is going to be here this afternoon. He's coming in early and wants to meet with you. He has called a meeting for tonight with everybody from both teams. Wants to go over some stuff with the whole bunch of us. Give us the old pep talk I bet."

"Yeah I know. I talked with him too. I also talked with Randy and I guess Bear informed everybody that I am the boss now, which means that you are fired. Did he say when T.K. was going to be here?"

"You can't fire me. I don't work for you! No, he didn't say when T.K. was coming in, but you know as well as me, that guy is on his own schedule. He will be here I'm sure, but I don't know when."

"I hate to tell you this, Bub, but you do work for me now. You have been demoted."

"Oh man, listen to this guy. Been a crew chief for all of twenty minutes and already it has gone to his head." Doug paused. "Seriously. Bear wants me to work with you? That's cool."

"Hey Doug, do you know when Alicia is getting here?"

"No, not exactly. I know she flew in with Orly

this morning. Give her a call. She is probably around somewhere."

- *O* -

Alicia was indeed "around." She was in her room, which was just down the hall from Doug and Paolo. She was tired and was contemplating taking a nap. It had been what seemed like an endless flight from California to Texas. The company plane was fast but the seats weren't all that comfortable for sleeping. More than once she had seen Paolo and Doug stretch out on the floor between the seats to sleep, but she wasn't going to do that.

The whole thing with Orly getting hurt and everything seemed like a nightmare. When they got Orly to the hospital, the doctor started making noises like they were going to keep him. Orly wouldn't hear of it. She supposed that the doctor could have been insistent. He told Orly that he needed to be under observation not so much for the burns, but because he blacked out. Orly worked a little charm on him, and finally, the doctor let him go, which meant that they could all go.

As soon as they got out of the hospital, Hildy asked her to call Carol, Orly's publicist, and cancel his appearances for today. She also told her to tell Carol to put out a press release stating that Orly was okay and that he planned on racing at Texas.

Carol was shocked at the news that Orly was hurt and muttered something about "race car drivers" and their constant need to "push the envelope". Alicia had been around long enough to share her sentiment, but she kept her mouth shut.

When they finally got on the company plane, Alicia could see that Orly really was in pain. She marveled at Hildy's ability to deal with it all. Alicia simply kept her mouth shut and stayed in the background. As soon as they landed, Hildy and Orly took off for the track. Their motor home was already there and they were going to try to sneak in the back and hide out to rest.

She was just about to crawl under the covers when her cell rang. It was Paolo.

"Hey, where are you?"

"You could at least say hello, Paolo. I just got in and I am in the hotel."

"Yeah I'm sorry. I got a lot on my mind. Hey, you want to get some lunch? I need to go over a few things with you."

"No, I'm tired. I think I'm going to get a nap."

"I'm serious Alicia. I need to talk with you and go over some stuff. Brad got hurt at the shop, broke his ankle and I am now the crew chief for the Blue Saber team. Bear has made you my secretary and 'go-to' person."

Alicia tried to keep the surprise out of her voice. "Well, congratulations, I guess. Give me an hour or so and I will meet you in the lobby."

"Okay. Hey, how bad is Orly hurt really?"

"I don't know for sure. I couldn't see, but I was told the backs of his hands are blistered a little, but not too much. The worst burn is on his left leg, just above his knee on his thigh. Apparently some of the ...what do you call it...the composite, yes that's it, melted and dripped onto his leg. From the looks of him on the plane, it hurt pretty bad."

"Ugh. Sick! Well for Bear's sake, I hope he can drive. Five hundred miles at Texas is going to be tough." Paolo paused. "Hey girl, let's be friends. I need your help. I feel like I am in a little over my head. I am seriously asking for your input."

Alicia's heart melted. In all the years she had known Paolo, even when they were kids in San Francisco, she could never say no to him. He had never abused that privilege and she doubted whether he knew that about her, but when he got that tone in his voice she was gone. "Okay Pally. I know this is a big step, but you can do it. I'll see you in the lobby in an hour."

- O -

Dr. Miller stood with his arms folded and contemplated the TxArm compound. He was pleased with what he saw. In fact, he couldn't be happier. Robert, one of the co-leaders of the ministry, stood beside him.

"What do you think, Robert? Is it going to be a record weekend?

Robert was an unpaid volunteer, but he had years of experience. He was also a good friend of Dr. Miller.

"I don't know, but the weather couldn't be any better. It is only Thursday and we got a pretty good group already. We got three races this weekend with the trucks and the Nationwide cars. We have a real tight points race for the championship in Cup so we have all the pieces. Could be a record weekend. I know one thing, the campground is sure filling up fast."

The TxArm compound sits like an island in the

middle of a vast sea of RV's and tents. It's easily recognizable because of the huge opened-sided circus tent that dominates the center of the grounds. Round tables are set up with folding chairs, which give a sense of intimacy in the large space. It's the place of the never empty coffee pot and warm greeting. It's staffed twenty-four hours a day throughout the week, and someone is always around to lend an ear or a helping hand or answer a question. There is most always popcorn, donuts or some form of goodie on the tables between the stacks of literature and pictures. Free for the taking. No fuss, no pressure. Good Texas hospitality. The goal was to offer genuine friendship and an attitude that said "how can we help you?"

The staff was all volunteers with a deep heart for ministry and saw their obligation to the Lord Jesus as Christians in adopting his role as a servant. They worked hard for no pay, often sleeping in a tent for the week and cooking over a camp stove with nothing but porta-potties for convenience. They seldom got to watch a race, and spent most of their time sorting out the problems of the people who do.

"Do you really think we are the fourth largest city in Texas twice a year?" Robert asked.

"I don't know about that, even though I have heard it said over and over. But I do know that we have a lot of folks out here for the races." Dr. Miller replied. "Look at that rig over there. Isn't that one of those Prevost motor coaches? Those things don't come cheap."

"That's more my budget." Robert said while gesturing with his thumb toward a converted 1956 school bus that had been spray painted with a camouflage motif.

"Yeah, somebody told me that those guys drive that thing all the way from Fort Smith, Arkansas every year. I think they have more Dale Earnhardt flags flying than anybody. Die hard fans."

It was true that hundreds and hundreds make the trek to the Speedway in RV's that range from the absolutely state of the art luxurious to the converted junkyard specials.

No matter what they come in, everybody has to stop by the TxArm location at least once during the course of their stay. It might be to sign up for the horseshoe tournament and check out a concert on the flatbed trailer that serves for a stage. It might be to examine the different types of race cars that occasionally make an appearance on the grass next to the tent. Maybe it is to hear the testimony of a NASCAR crew chief or driver. Whatever it is, one thing is certain. There is always something going on.

"Have you heard from Dwight?" Dr. Miller asked. The high point of the weekend for the kids was the pinewood derby run on Saturday afternoon after the Nationwide race. Kids of all shapes, sizes, and colors were encouraged to come in and choose a pinewood racer, and then paint it in the colors of their favorite drivers.

Once the cars were painted, they'd go into the "impound" area where they were put on display and held for the competition. Dwight Sisk was from Alabama, and he coordinated what was called the Timothy Program, which incorporated the pinewood derby. Come Saturday afternoon, the tent would be full of whooping and hollering as everyone came together to support their favorites. It generally was a hotly contested program, and the winner got a nice trophy. But the TxArm people made sure every kid was recognized and went away a winner.

"Yes, we're picking him up tomorrow afternoon. He keeps tweaking the track to make the competition tighter and tighter. We already have a number of cars sitting on the table, and it is still early. I think we're in for just a great weekend."

At that moment, three men dressed in TxArm shirts walked up to Dr. Miller and Robert. It was obvious that they had been talking among themselves and had come to some sort of agreement. Their names were Harold, Ricky and Sam, and they were good guys. It seemed Harold was elected spokesman so he spoke first.

"He's back. Ricky just saw him coming in the gate. He is headed to the same old campsite...right there," he said as he pointed to one of the sites close to the compound.

Dr. Miller felt his stomach knot up and he almost groaned out loud.

"You're kidding, right? You guys are putting us on. Maybe it's somebody else and you just thought you saw him," said Robert in his soft Texas accent. He looked at Miller. *I thought he was in jail and we wouldn't have to worry about him this year.*

"No Robert, it's him. I checked, too. Same motor home, Phoenix license plate, got his dealership stuff splashed all over it, the whole enchilada. Ricky is right." It was Big Sam who spoke this time. He was known as Big Sam because he was not only big in size but had a heart to match.

"Yeah it's him." Ricky said. "We think we all ought to pay him a visit first thing and tell him that he isn't welcome, and maybe he ought to turn that rig around and head it back to Arizona. We would be glad to help him. We might even take up a collection and buy him a tank of gas. At the very least, we need to tell him to stay away from the compound here."

The other two men nodded in agreement. He paused. "But I guess we can't do that, can we?"

"No, we can't do that, although I wouldn't be adverse to several of us paying him a visit and telling him we don't want a repeat of last year." Robert said this with a shake of his head. "Of course it won't do any good."

Dr. Miller listened quietly. *Well Lord, what purpose do you have in this?* he thought to himself. Last year William Williams nearly brought the TxArm ministry to a stop with his antics. It was amazing how things just 'happened' when he was around.Somehow the coffee pot got knocked over and ruined all the literature on the handout table. The main cable got kicked out in the midst of the Saturday night concert. Stuff disappeared and other stuff was damaged beyond repair.

TxArm used a fleet of golf carts to shuttle disabled individuals back and forth from the campground to the grandstands. One morning they discovered that over half of them had flat tires. If it wasn't one thing, it was six others…and Miller knew exactly why.

William Williams wanted something from Dr. Miller, and he wasn't about to give it to him. As a result Williams was making Miller pay, and he was doing it by trying to disrupt the TxArm ministry. More than likely, Williams would be paying him a visit as soon as he got settled. *I can hardly wait*, thought Dr. Miller to himself.

"Well men, there isn't anything we can do about it but leave it to the Lord. Let's start right now. Why don't we put our heads together and a couple of you lead out in prayer. Obviously the Lord has a purpose in bringing him here. We will just have to deal with it. Hey, you know he might be different this year."

These were solid Christian men and they did not doubt God's ability to change people, nor the power of prayer. Their own lives were a testimony to that, but not one of them shared Dr. Miller's optimism.

Bear started the meeting with prayer, as was his custom. Both traveling teams were combined, so there were about forty people sitting in a small conference room at the hotel. With over a hundred employees at the shop, not everyone made the trip. These guys were the mechanics and tech people that worked "hands on" at the track and took care of the hundreds of details that were necessary to run two cars in the race. Everybody had at least one specific job and generally could fill in where needed.

The "over-the-wall" guys, the actual pit crew people wouldn't show up 'til early Sunday morning. They would come in on a charter flight with a group of crew-members from other teams that flew out of Charlotte in the wee hours. They generally were not mechanics and were hired for their athleticism, and their ability to move fast changing tires and fueling the car. They traveled on the same plane, but fiercely competed with each other at the track. Most of them had regular day jobs.

The first thing Bear did was to give everyone an update on Orly.

"Orly got burned some. He is sorry that he isn't here but he felt he just needed to rest before the weekend got cooking. I'm sorry. Poor choice of words." There were a few groans in the background.

"His hands are tender, but we think we can make some adjustments with his gloves that will help out. The doctor is going to take care of the burn on his leg. They will pad it, so it shouldn't bother him too much. We will have to help him in and out. It hurts to bend his leg. He's planning on driving the car just like normal but we'll have a relief standing by just in case." It was short and sweet, but everybody in the room knew that if there was a relief driver standing by, there was a lot left unsaid.

The second thing he did was give them all an update on Brad.

"As you know, Brad took a tumble and broke his ankle and hit his face. His face is swollen some. I've talked with Rosie. She says he looks like he has been ten rounds with a heavyweight. He came through surgery just fine, and thank you for your prayers, but he's done for the year. What there is left of it, anyway. Most, if not all of you, know that Orly and I talked it over and we have made Paolo the crew chief for the #36 car and you Saber guys."

There was a round of applause with a couple of whistles at this announcement. "At this stage of the season, we felt it better to promote from within rather than bring somebody in from the outside. Just want you to know that Paolo, myself and T.K. had a meeting this afternoon and we are all on the same page."

Yeah right, thought Paolo to himself. T.K. was his usual flippant self and essentially dumped the success or failure of the team directly into Paolo's lap. Bear tried to tone him down but he was pretty cocky. Paolo did his best to keep his mouth shut and listen, which wasn't easy. A couple of times he felt like coming across the table. The guy was so obnoxious!

Well he would just have to make the best of it. No choice. As long as he drove his guts out and did his part, Paolo would make do with the rest of it. Suddenly his attention snapped back to the meeting.

Bear was holding up a copy of the Dallas newspaper with a large photo on the front page.

"Now I know many of you on this team have different hobbies and avocations, but I think we are all surprised to learn that Paolo has aspirations of being a rodeo clown. A friend in the newspaper biz slipped this to me. It will be on the newsstands tomorrow morning. It shows our illustrious hero exercising his talents to save a poor unfortunate cowboy who got trapped on the back of one of those four-legged monsters they call bucking bulls. IIf you look real close, you can see that our resident cowboy has got his head under the hood, so to speak, and is tuning this critter's exhaust system." Indeed, it was a great picture that took up half the front page. It showed Paolo with his head buried in the side of the bull with his boots off the ground and his hands wrapped around the bucking strap. The headline read "NASCAR Crew Chief puts Wedge into Sweety Pie".

"I have been informed by the PBR folks that if things don't work out for you, Paolo, in the world of

Stock Car racing, you're more than welcome to try your hand with them."

The room erupted into laughter as Paolo slunk down into his seat with a stupid grin on his face. T.K. seemed to be laughing the most. Alicia gave him a sympathetic look.

"Now before we break up I want to inform you of something else. We all know how important this weekend is in the Chase, but there is still one thing far more important... and that is people. Dr. Miller, whom most of you know, asked us if we would do something special this weekend...well, I am going to let him explain to you all."

Dr. Miller came forward. "I know this is a busy time for you. I'll be brief. Awhile back I received a letter from a thirteen-year-old young man who has a terrible debilitating illness. The illness is a form of juvenile arthritis. It is bad stuff and attacks the joints, but it also affects the internal organs. This kid lives with constant pain, but at the same time he is a typical thirteen-year-old. His name is Silas Biggs. He is a great kid. His wish was to join the Orly Mann Team for the weekend. I have to tell you that he is your biggest fan. He knows all your names and your pertinent stats. Pretty impressive. I have been to his house, or actually his apartment, where he lives with his mother. Just the two of them. I was just struck at how we might make a difference in this boy's life. For us, racing is what we do and most of us take it for granted. Like I said, his life isn't easy. Maybe we could give him an experience that he could look back on. You folks know what I mean. So I talked with Bear and he agreed to it. Then I talked with Eddie G. and the racetrack has made a motor home available to the boy and his mom inside the driver's compound. NASCAR has agreed to give him limited access to the garage. We will do our best to keep him out of your way, but if you could reach out to him through the course of the weekend, it would really be a wonderful thing for him. Thanks, folks."

"Thank you, Dr. Miller. You people are good people, so let's do our best to make this weekend memorable for the kid. Maybe we could even win. Who knows? Please close us out in prayer, Dr. Miller. Remember, the garage opens at 7:00 AM sharp and so it begins. Get some rest and be on time."

Paolo was gathering his stuff up to leave when Devin walked up to him.

"Hey man, I just want to tell you, I'm not happy having to work with you, but I'm going to cut you a little slack anyway. Me and T.K. talked it over, and we figure it is best if we all work together…you know what I mean." He turned to leave but Paolo reached out and spun him around.

"Hey Devin, let me lay it out for you, Dude. I'm really not happy having to put up with your attitude, but you need to remember something. Whether you like working with me or not, I am the boss, and if you give me any more grief or crap or hassle I will can your butt so fast, it will make your nose bleed. You do your job, and I will do mine." Paolo stood with his hands on his hips. "You get the picture? Oh yeah, and be sure and tell T.K. exactly what I said."

Chapter Five

"Five minutes with Silas Biggs you forget all about any disability he might have. His fresh and inquisitive personality helps you see things from a new perspective. It is great fun."

Kay Benton, TxArm volunteer, on meeting Silas for the first time.

Friday is an incredibly busy day at the Speedway. NASCAR has its hands full juggling the schedule for all three major NASCAR events. The garage area was quiet at the moment, but in ten minutes, it would be a veritable sea of noisy chaos and sometimes frenzied activity. The truck series qualified yesterday and wouldn't be back on the track until race time tonight. But in the meantime, they took up valuable space. The Nationwide boys were already off-loaded and in their garage stalls at the east end of the garage area. They would be practicing first this morning in preparation for their race on Saturday. They would qualify after the cup cars this afternoon. In the meantime, the Cup Haulers all sat in a quiet row waiting to be unloaded. They were parked in the order of the point standings with their rear cargo doors facing the garage stalls.

It gave Paolo a thrill of excitement to see the Orly Mann yellow and orange Hauler parked second and the deep cobalt blue of the Blue Saber Team parked fourth. He looked down at his watch as he bounced on the balls of his feet. Three minutes to go.

"Do you think that's true?" Bear said to Paolo as they stood in the crowd of crewmen waiting for the NASCAR official to unlock the gate to the garage area. Bear was looking up at the sign that hung over the entrance. It read, *Through These Gates Pass The Greatest Drivers and Mechanics In The World.*

"Heck yeah it's true! We are the best and what's more we're going to go on and get us another championship." Paolo was fairly quivering with excitement as he stood impatiently waiting for the gate to open. He was working hard to maintain an outward calmness, but Bear wasn't fooled.

Bear gave Paolo a critical look, then leaned over and spoke into Paolo's ear so no one else could hear.

"Just take your time, Paolo. Think before you decide anything. You got this thing. You are not the car chief, you are the crew chief. Let your guys do what they are trained to do. Your driver has a tendency to get wound up. Just remember the tighter he gets, the calmer you get. When he starts yelling on the radio, you just get calmer. Works every time. By the way, that dark blue suits you. It matches your eyes." Bear was referring to the fact that Paolo was now wearing a Blue Saber uniform instead of the familiar orange and yellow of the Orly Mann Team.

"Thanks Bear, but my eyes are brown. Yeah, it feels

a little strange, but that is the least of my worries. Yeah, that's my plan in dealing with T.K." Paolo's response was genuine. He was smart enough to listen to what Bear had to say. "Speaking of drivers, how is yours doing?"

"I met with him last night after our meeting. He's still hurting quite a bit, but I think he will be okay."

Bear's words didn't match the expression on his face. Paolo could see that. Something was going on, but right now Paolo couldn't take time to worry about it. He had his own business to take care of. Just then, the gate swung open as the weekend officially began for the Cup teams. Paolo gave Bear a wave, then headed off to the Blue Saber hauler.

Bear was indeed worried. He was a fretful man by nature, which made him detail orientated, or maybe it was the other way around. He always tried to think of everything and usually wound up focusing on what could go wrong instead of the positive. Orly, on the other hand, was one of the most positive guys around. In his quiet way he had the ability to see the silver lining in even the most difficult situations. Except for last night. When Bear visited Orly's motor home, Hildy answered the door looking tired and very frustrated. Orly looked worn out himself, and it was obvious that Bear had interrupted some sort of heated discussion. Bear was tempted to excuse himself and head on down the road, but Orly insisted that he come in.

It didn't take Bear long to realize that the issue was not Orly's burns. Those would heal and were mostly a minor physical distraction at the moment. However, him getting hurt did have an obvious impact.

Race car driving was dangerous, and it wasn't like

Orly hadn't been hurt before or couldn't get hurt again. There was always the serious possibility that something major could happen. That was a given.

No, Bear suspected it was something that had been lurking on the horizon for the better part of this year. Something called "retirement". Orly had been hinting that Hildy would like him to quit. Bear's response was non-committal. He simply told Orly that it was his decision and Bear really had no say in it. When the time came, and it would, ultimately, it was purely Orly's call. Maybe this was it.

In the meantime, he counseled Orly that they had three races left in this season. Everybody was used up. It had been a long grind, but now wasn't the time to contemplate quitting. Now was the time to reach down into the barrel and gather as much resource as possible and go for it.

If Orly did decide to retire, it would be very sweet to go out with a championship in their pocket. Bear wasn't sure Orly heard him. Hildy hardly said two words the whole time he was there. In the meantime, they needed to get this show on the road and get after it.

Bear came out of his reverie as he joined the crush of crewmen heading through the gate. His progress was suddenly halted when the security guard put his hand on his chest and stopped him.

"Sorry, buddy, but you can't come in here without a pass." Bear stood with his mouth open for a second then realized that he wasn't wearing his ID credential that had his picture on it. NASCAR issued every crewman and people connected with racing that had a need to be in the garage area an identity card. The credentials didn't come cheap. They weren't free for the race teams. They cost somewhere around two grand a year per crewman. It was NASCAR's method of keeping control over the garage area and dictating who could get in and who couldn't. Otherwise the area would get so crowded, it would be difficult to do the necessary work on the cars.

Bear gestured at his yellow and orange uniform with his name written over the left pocket.

"I am half owner in the Orly Mann Team and I am the crew chief as well. Everybody knows me!"

"Yeah, and I am the king of Siam and nobody knows me. No one gets in this area without a pass. Now step out of the way, you're blocking traffic."

Bear could feel his blood pressure rising. This was no way to start the weekend. Suddenly someone grabbed his arm and put something in his hand.

"Dang, Bear. You must be getting old. You left this on the sink in the restroom." T.K. said as he handed Bear his credential and headed toward the Blue Saber Hauler.

Bear nodded. "Thanks. Yeah, maybe I am."

- O -

Silas was looking through the side window of the motor coach trying to figure out if that was Orly Mann's coach on this side or maybe it was the one on the other side. He couldn't tell.

"Hey Mom, do you think Orly Mann likes black better than brown?"

"Silas, I have no idea. Why don't you come over here and eat breakfast? You need to get some nourishment inside you." Sarah Biggs looked around the inside of the motor coach. There was a word to describe this thing, she thought to herself. She rummaged around in her mind, then smiled as she said the word out loud. That was it. This thing was opulent.

It was absolutely beautiful, with paneling in various muted tones accented by the gorgeous fabric of the blinds that covered the windows and the dividers. It was plush. She was impressed by the craftsmanship and quality that surrounded them. They were being treated like royalty.

She expected Silas to be excited and saw herself as staying in the background as he had his "experience", but the TxArm people were making sure that she was not left out of the process. They made that evident from the beginning.

The plan was to pick them up at the apartment after she got off work and drive them to the track. The idea was for Silas to get settled in and get a good night's sleep before the weekend. Then he could wake up fresh on Friday morning ready to go. She knew that probably wasn't going to happen because he was so excited, and it didn't. When the limo pulled up in front of the apartment complex, Silas was bouncing around on his crutches with a lopsided grin on his face. Kay Benton from the TxArm group was in the limo and informed Sarah that she was there to help her anyway she could. She told her that the TxArm people were all excited for her and Silas and just wanted their weekend to be very special. If there was anything, anything at all that they could do to help, she wasn't to hesitate to ask. That brought tears to Sarah's eyes.

Then watching Silas looking so proud as he sprawled out on the huge back seat made it even better. She had to laugh when Silas looked at her, gave a wink and said, "Pretty cool, huh, Mom."

"Yes, pretty cool, Silas. You look very important. My, what a handsome young man you are. Are you somebody rich and famous?"

"Aww, Mom."

The limo ride was smooth and fast as they sailed through the Texas evening. As they got closer, Kay pointed out a large complex that lit up the night in the far distance. "There it is," she said.

The racetrack looked like a huge jeweled crown rising up out of the prairie. It was a lot bigger than she imagined that it would be. And my goodness, there were people all over the place. It was a beehive of activity, even at this late hour. The campgrounds were filling up with lines of RV's and pickups and all kinds of vehicles driving through the gates.

Kay was so kind to her and Silas. Sarah recalled that she must have said at least five times that it was their privilege to be a part of this weekend for her and Silas. Then they were there, or here, she thought. The limo bypassed all the traffic as the security guards waved them through. They entered the infield and then drove right into the motor coach compound as the guards opened the gate. It stopped in front of a motor coach in the middle of a line of coaches. Kay opened the door with a remote as the driver brought in their luggage.

Sarah was breathless and didn't know what to say when she stepped inside. "Wow" was all she could utter. She was doubly impressed when the driver of the limo showed Silas how to operate the steps so he didn't have to climb up into the coach. He simply stood on the bottom step and pushed a button. It lifted him up like an escalator and deposited him in the front living quarters.

"Pretty cool, Silas, don't you think? They put that in special just for you," Kay said as she winked at Sarah.

Kay walked her through and showed her how everything worked.

"Yes, it has two bedrooms and two bathrooms as well. Don't worry about running out of hot water. Take a bath, use the Jacuzzi, whatever. I don't know exactly how much it has, but they tell me it is plenty. Everything is here to be used, so don't be afraid to avail yourself of whatever you find. Eddie G. made sure his people stocked it full of food, and there are all kinds of toiletries in the bathrooms and anything else you might need. Washer and dryer as well. Now let me show you this." Kay showed her a little speaker on the wall with a switch.

"If you need help or anything at all, there is someone on the other end 24 hours a day. It goes right to the TxArm office and there are always two or three people in there. When you get ready in the morning just give us a whistle and the golf cart will be right over. Now Sarah, if you need anything, any kind of help, anything, call us. We want you to relax and enjoy the weekend. We want to be a blessing to you." Then she gave Sarah a quick hug and she was out the door.

That was it. They were settled in. It didn't take Silas long to figure out how the big screen TV worked along with every other gadget he came across. Finally Sarah got him settled down and they were both off to bed.

"Did you sleep good Mom?"

"Like a rock. That bed is big enough to play tennis on. Now eat your breakfast."

Silas was just starting to eat his breakfast when there was a beep on the intercom. Sarah looked puzzled.

"What does that mean, I wonder?"

Silas laughed. "It means there is someone at the door Mom. Here watch." He reached over and pressed a switch. "Hello from inside the Enterprise. Who is it?"

"Is this the world famous Silas Biggs?"

"No he is out signing autographs, but I know where he is and I can get him for you."

"Great, then you must be Captain Kirk. Would you tell him he has a couple of visitors?"

"Okay. We will beam you up." Silas pressed a button on the remote and the door to the coach opened.

Orly Mann came up the steps followed by Hildy.

"Good morning you all. I hope we didn't disturb you. My name is Orly Mann and this is my wife Hildy. We just wanted to stop by and welcome you."

Sarah found her voice. "Come in, come in. Please sit down. I apologize for my son. He can get a little too playful sometimes. May I offer you a cup of coffee?"

Orly looked at his watch. "Sure, we have time." He and Hildy sat down opposite Silas who sat speechless with his chin on his chest and his mouth open. Orly reached across the table and offered his hand.

Silas could see that the back of it was bandaged. He offered his own misshapen hand with its enlarged knuckles and crooked fingers. Orly took it gently.

"Good to meet you, Silas. Hildy and I have heard

a lot about you. Dr. Miller thinks you're a pretty good guy."

"You really are Orly Mann, aren't you?" Silas said smiling. "Mom, it's Orly Mann. Look!"

"Silas, where are your manners? It isn't polite to talk about someone when they are right in front of you."

Hildy spoke. "Yes it's him Silas. He is a real person. I can attest to that."

Orly didn't consider himself gifted with "people skills". Oh, he knew how to deal with the media and make public appearances and whatnot. He didn't mind speaking in front of groups and could be entertaining, but when it came to one on one, it was different. Being famous had its drawbacks. Seemed like most people had an agenda and were more interested in getting something from him rather than just knowing him. That added to the fact that they knew all about you, and you knew nothing about them. As a result he had few close friends. But Orly truly liked kids. Not only that, but he had the ability to get inside their world. He didn't come across as an adult that needed to assert himself and above all, he didn't pass judgment. Instead he listened and took what they said at face value and showed genuine interest.

It wasn't long before Silas relaxed, and he was telling Orly all about his collection of stock car stuff. Orly listened attentively and made the appropriate comments with raised eyebrows and the occasional whistle. Silas asked questions, like any inquisitive thirteen-year-old.

Orly answered them simply, with terms and definitions that Silas could understand. Orly asked about school and church and friends. They shared stories and experiences with one another. Silas even told Orly his favorite thirteen-year-old kid joke and Orly laughed appreciatively. Then Silas excused himself for a minute and came hobbling back with his backpack. He reached inside and brought out the die cast #37 Speed King Chevrolet still in the box and produced a sharpie to go with it.

"Would you sign this for me, Orly?"

Orly carefully took the treasure and turned it over in his hands. "Boy, they do a nice job with these don't they? You bet I'll sign it. Where do you think is best?"

Later Orly asked him about his disease and Silas was trusting enough to give him honest answers. "Does it hurt much?"

"Yeah, sometimes, but I'm used to it. The fevers are hard. I have to take a steroid for the inflammation and sometimes that has bad side effects. Other times, it messes up my thinking, but it's okay. I know kids that are dealing with a lot worse stuff. I try not to complain."

Sarah interjected "He seldom complains, Mr. Mann, except maybe when I make him go to bed."

Hildy didn't try to interact in the conversation. She kept her mouth shut and listened. She always knew that Orly related well with kids, but now she was seeing him in action. It made her heart even softer as she reflected on how much she loved him. He was a unique guy.

Orly checked his watch. "We have got to go. Hildy and I have to meet with some people. Now remember what I said. Dr. Miller will be by in a little while with your passes. You know we get real busy during practice. You can watch but don't ask any questions until the session is over. Okay? When the garage goes hot, then you have to leave or stay on the Hauler. You know why. The drivers are concentrating on getting their adjustments made as quick as possible and getting back out on the track. It gets real busy with all the cars coming and going."

"Yes sir, Mr. Mann. I got it." Silas said as he watched Orly painfully stand up. Then he leaned over and whispered so his Mom couldn't hear.

"Mr. Mann, I need to ask you something in private. Could just you and me talk sometime?"

"You bet. I'll find you later when I get a chance. Maybe after qualifying."

After Hildy and Orly left, Sarah said, "Hot? What does that mean Silas?"

"Oh that is when the cars are going back and forth from the garage to the track and then they come back so the crew guys can make adjustments. You know, Mom. They don't want anybody rolling around in a wheel chair when the cars are coming and going."

"Oh, of course. That makes sense."

Once they were outside Hildy said to Orly, "Why do you suppose he wants to talk with you?"

"I have no idea, but it's the least I can do. He doesn't have the easiest life. Did you see his hands? Here I am complaining about a few minor burns. At least my stuff will heal. Miller told me his condition is only going to get worse. They can slow it down some but that is about all. Treat his pain, I guess. Remind me later Hildy that I promised him. I might get busy and forget."

"You won't forget."

- *O* -

126

Paolo was not prepared for the reception he received in the garage area. He expected to field questions about being the new crew chief, but he was surprised when several people walked up to him with a copy of the newspaper with his picture on the front and asked him to autograph it. One of the crew guys from another team came charging over and asked him quickly to autograph a cowboy hat. A TV reporter and two radio guys were waiting for him at the Hauler. He tried to deal with them as quickly as he could without being rude, but it seemed the only thing they wanted to talk about was the bull riding fiasco.

The final straw was when Jeff "what's his name" from the network sports show pulled him into an interview and challenged him to compete with him in a bull riding competition. Paolo respectfully declined while Doug and the crew grinned out of camera range. Finally he made it clear that he had a job to do and got disentangled from them. In the meantime, the crew had gone to work and had the car off-loaded into the garage. The toolboxes were in place with all the other assorted paraphernalia they needed to get the car ready and fine-tune the adjustments.

The garage area at any NASCAR event is a busy place. The cars are parked close together with just enough room to work on them. NASCAR does this on purpose. It keeps the competition on a level playing field. Everybody knows what everybody else is doing. The cars are in plain sight and at any given time, anybody, including officials or other team members can walk by and take a look. However, there are certain unspoken rules and invisible lines that shouldn't be crossed. Nobody touches or crawls underneath another team's car without permission. Nobody touches another team's stuff.

That kind of "cheek by jowl" parking makes for a sometimes chaotic work environment, especially when two or three cars are idling at the same time with their eight hundred horsepower open exhausts. But it is a system that has been in place a long time, and it works well.

Paolo spent a few minutes in the Hauler gathering his thoughts and picking up his setup sheets, then headed across to the garage. He started to roll up his sleeves and get busy, but then checked himself. Randy the car chief already had the guys organized, which was his job.

They knew what to do and were quickly running down the check-off list. It was a big transition for Paolo. It was so much easier to stay focused on the task at hand with your head down and refer any questions or decisions to the crew chief. Now he was the crew chief, which meant that he was the one answering the questions and making the decisions. It also meant that he had to keep his head up and be aware of the big picture. He couldn't get bogged down in the details... but at the same time, he had to make sure the details were carried out.

"Randy, you seen T.K. yet?"

"Yeah, he went over to the Nationwide garage. They're putting his seat in the car or something and wanted to make sure they had it right. He said he would be back in a few minutes, and he wanted to check with you before he went over there for their practice sessions."

T.K., like a lot of other Cup drivers, competed in the Nationwide series when the schedule allowed. The Nationwide cars were a little slower and handled quite different than the Cup cars, but a good driver could learn a lot that would transfer for Sunday's race. They generally ran their race the day before the Cup race. It used to be they were considered a support race, but the series had become so competitive they were almost a "stand alone" event.

T.K. was under contract with an independent team and had done pretty good this year. He was out of the running for the championship, but he was always a threat to pick off the occasional win. Orly and Bear had no problem with him running the series as long as there were no sponsor conflicts. Orly used to run it himself when it was called the Busch Series and had an early championship under his belt.

Sure enough, as if on cue, T.K. came walking up to Paolo. He put his head close, so they could talk in the midst of the noise. They were about the same height, but Paolo was much heavier and thicker through the shoulders and chest.

"Hey Cowboy, we good to go?" T.K. asked with his hands in the pockets of his driving suit.

Paolo ignored the "cowboy" comment.

"Yeah, we will be. If you don't mind, I am going to monitor a little of your Nationwide practice sessions. I'd like to get a handle on what the track is doing. The truck guys say the top groove is pretty bumpy. If it is, we might want to start with a little different setup than what we got now. We might want to tighten you up a bit."

"Yeah, cool. I'll mention it. If you're listening, I'll give you a heads up."

"Is Devin spotting for you over there?"

"Yeah. He's good and we communicate pretty well together. He has been with me all year as you know. He can just stay up there for the Cup practice session." T.K. motioned toward the front grandstands behind the start/finish line.

"Okay. Our first session is at noon so we'll see you as soon as you finish over there."

Silas was trying to see everything at once as Dr. Miller pushed him through the garage area. Race cars were all over the place and crewmen were working on them, in them and under them as everybody got ready for the first practice session. His pit pass was on a lanyard around his neck, and he clutched it in one hand like it might get away. Occasionally, he would let it briefly go as he snapped a picture with his camera. His autograph book was on his lap and he had his sharpie in his pocket. Dr. Miller was well known in the Texas garage. Several people stopped what they were doing when he walked by pushing Silas' chair and took the opportunity to greet him. He was careful to introduce them to Silas, and they greeted him warmly.

"Wow, Dr. Miller! Everybody seems so nice."

"Yeah, well racers are good people. Hey Silas, you aren't afraid of heights, are you?"

Silas thought a minute. "I dunno. I don't think I have ever been up high."

Five minutes later they were stopped behind the Orly Mann Hauler. "Here is what we are going to do.

We are going to go up on top of the Hauler and watch the practice session from there. It is the safest place for you and besides that, NASCAR won't allow a wheel chair in the garage when it goes hot."

"Yeah, Orly told me. Uh, Dr. Miller how am I going to get up there? I don't think I can climb that ladder. I could try, though."

"No problem, Silas. Just watch."

A couple of minutes later, Silas watched with wide eyes as a crewman pushed a couple of buttons and dropped the hydraulic car lift/tailgate to the ground. Dr. Miller rolled the wheel chair onto it and then it lifted them into the air in majestic fashion. A quick push up a short ramp and Silas found himself high in the air on the observation platform bolted to the roof of the Hauler. His view was perfect. He could see almost the whole racetrack. Paolo was standing in the corner with one foot on the bottom bar of the railing and his arms resting on his knee. Bear was standing beside him. They both had radio headsets on as they watched the Nationwide cars practice.

Silas painfully worked himself out of the chair and grabbed his crutches. He hobbled over to stand next to Paolo. Paolo looked down at him and kicked his headset back so his ears were exposed.

"Hey kid. How ya doing?"

"I'm good. Are you Paolo Pells...Pella ginni."

"Pelegreeeni, Pelegrini kid. Yup, that's me. But you can call me Pally. That's what my friends call me. Just don't call me 'cowboy'."

"Yeah I saw the picture in the paper. That was pretty impressive. That bull looked pretty mad. Were you scared? Is that Mr. Erickson next to us?"

"The answer to all those questions is yes sir, right on. The bull was mad, I was scared and that is the world famous Mr. Erickson, better known as Bear."

Bear was listening to the conversation with a smile on his face. He reached over and put his hand out. "Nice to meet you Silas. I'm glad you made it."

In the meantime Dr. Miller had procured a couple of radio headsets and plugged them into the console on the platform. He offered one to Silas who slipped it over his baseball cap so it covered his ears.

"I'm loose in. It feels like I am sliding a lot. The front end doesn't want to stay nailed. I am not anywhere close to getting down into the track."

"Roger that. Give us one more, then bring it in and we will fix it."

Dr. Miller looked down at Silas and mouthed the word "T.K."

Silas nodded as he watched Bear and Paolo turn in a circle as they followed T.K. around the track. T.K. ducked low going into turn three and let the car slide using the whole track. Bear yelled, "Look out" as T.K. came off four sideways. The car broke loose and T.K. spun then slid down the track trailing tire smoke. Fortunately, there was no one around him at the time.

"Weeeha! Ride 'em cowboy. I told you I was loose. Make that wicked loose." T.K. said as he straightened the car out and limped it to the pits. "Gonna need some tires, boys."

"Seen enough?" Paolo said to Bear as he took his headset off.

"Yeah. It was what I expected. You're going to have

to rein in some of that boyish exuberance, at least for a while, anyway." Bear turned to face Silas. "Hey boy, hop back in that chair and we will take you downstairs to the lounge in the Hauler. Get you out of the wind for a bit. Maybe introduce you to some people, and you can get a couple of autographs."

Silas dutifully worked his way back to the wheel chair and settled in. Bear turned to Dr. Miller and spoke in a low tone so Silas couldn't hear. "He looks pretty tired, Roger. We don't want to use him up. "

"Yeah, I know, Henry. He wants to watch the truck race tonight and Eddie G. has made a suite available this evening. He said the whole Orly Mann Team is welcome to come up and watch. Sarah, Silas' Mom, told me that he really needs to rest this afternoon. I'll take him back to the motor coach just before the garage goes hot."

Chapter Six

"*It is just all about opportunities,*
knocking doors down and see who answers."
Denny Hamlin, NASCAR Driver.

Bear stood in the infield and surveyed the front stretch of the Texas Motor Speedway. It was one thing to stand on top of the Hauler and watch the Nationwide cars go by, but it was quite another to stand flatfooted and look at the racing surface close up. Texas is fast. It took a good handling car and a big gob of courage to get around this place quick. Bear knew that for a fact. Like Darrell Waltrip was fond of saying, "When you come to Texas, you better put your work clothes on." The track is 1.5 mile in length with 24 degree banking in the turns. Some call the mile and a half tracks, like Vegas, Charlotte and Atlanta "cookie cutters" because they think they are all the same. Not so.

Each track has its own personality that is shaped by nuances in surface and weather. They might look the same, but coming off turn four at Texas and Vegas was a whole lot different. There is a lot of subtlety to racing a cup car. The variables are infinite in terms of adjustments. Just when you think you have the track figured out, something will change and the car will start "pushing", or suddenly get "loose", or won't turn in the middle of the corner.

When you are searching for that little, tiny bit of extra speed, a minor adjustment can be big. The cars change as the tires wear and the track surface "rubbers" up. A fluctuation in the weather and track temperature can make a mountain of difference in how the car grips the track. For instance, California Speedway in Southern California was right on the edge of the desert, and no matter what the weather, the wind was always blowing. As a result, there always seemed to be a fine dusting of sand on the track, which made the cars loose. It takes experience to figure those things out. Bear and Orly had been here in Texas many times, and they knew how this track worked.

Bear knew that if you stood flatfooted in the infield between turns three and four, you have to look up to see the cars flash by. Twenty-four degrees of banking doesn't seem like much, but in actuality, it is a lot. The track is plenty wide enough for drivers to pass one another and that made for good racing, and Orly liked that.

Through the course of the race several "lines" or grooves may develop, and it took a skilled driver to find the fastest line. In the latter stages of the race, when the competition is the fiercest, it is not unusual for drivers to run near or faster than their qualifying speeds. This was partly due to the crew chiefs making the right calls and getting the adjustments figured out just right, and the drivers finding that little bit of extra "intestinal fortitude" which most people called guts.

Some thought the track was just a big oval. It wasn't. The front straight has a dogleg with the start/finish line at the apex. The qualifying record here is 196.235mph, which was set in 2006. Orly has come close but never matched that. Bear knew also that the times have dropped a tick since then as the surface of the track has weathered and aged, but in the language of race car drivers, it is still.

Bear surveyed the track surface in front of him. It looked about the same, but the vagaries of the Texas weather took their toll. Sometimes the place was full of grip, and other times it got pretty greasy and plenty loose. Especially at 190 mph. One of the things that make this place extremely tricky is the transition from the banking in the turns to the nearly level surface of the straights. The drivers say it is most noticeable coming off turn four onto the front dogleg. If the car is right and the suspension and tires cooperate, and the driver has the courage, it is possible to "flatfoot" around the place.Bear would take Orly's word for it.

Practice schedules vary at different tracks. Here at Texas the first session for the Cup cars was at noon. The Nationwide cars had already been out for two sessions of their own, and put some rubber down on the track. It was important to "rubber up" the track a little. It made a big difference in how the cars gripped the surface. The first practice session on any race weekend is always full of uncertainty. No matter how much preparation is put into the car and no matter "what worked last time", there still are a number of variables that can affect how the car performs. The track surface may change. It might be a brand new chassis, or perhaps the motor has been tweaked. There might be a little extra rubber on the track or maybe not enough.

A team never knows exactly what they have until you run what you brung, thought Bear to himself. Most teams only ran a few laps then brought the car back in for adjustments. Then back out to run a few more laps to see what you had. Some teams would spend a lot of time running a qualifying setup in the later part of the session to get an indication of what they might have. Bear and Orly didn't waste a lot of time doing that.

Qualifying was at three thirty or thereabouts. It was generally televised with a lot of hoopla for the pole winner. Once qualifying was over, the teams could concentrate on the race set-up. But the next session was not until Saturday morning and then only for 45 minutes. The 'happy hour' or final hour of practice followed shortly thereafter. The cars were then 'put to bed' and wouldn't be back on the track until Sunday where they were parked on the pit lane in preparation for the race.

How a team approaches practice depends a lot on personality. Orly and Bear had been together for a long time. They started working together "back in the day" when they were running sprint cars on the dirt bullrings in the Midwest. *We were both a lot younger back then*, thought Bear to himself. Bear was working for a guy that had more money than brains and he coupled that with the ability to blow up motors and tear up chassis faster than Bear could build them.

In the meantime, Orly was driving outdated equipment and doing his best to simply survive on his winnings. Bear finally got fed up one night at a small track in Kansas and quit. Orly followed him out of the track and offered him a partnership on the spot. They pooled their resources and the rest is, as they say, history. There had been some hard years but the chemistry was good. They learned a lot through those lean times, but now they understood each other and could communicate almost without speaking. Bear had a solid feel for Orly's driving style, his preferences and what he wanted the car to do. Those lean years taught them that the money wasn't paid until the last lap was completed and the race was over. In other words, *practice don't pay*.

As a result, their approach was methodical. Seldom would Orly's name appear at the top of the speed charts for any given session. It didn't mean he couldn't go fast. It just meant that he wasn't going to tip his hand and show the field what he had until it counted.

T.K. on the other hand, was just the opposite. He attacked practice like a school yard bully looking for a fight. T.K. was aggressive. Somebody once accused him of driving "angry", which was close to the truth. He was hard on equipment and didn't believe much in "saving his stuff". His theory was to push it hard as you can. Tweak it a little and then push it hard again. If it broke, then it better get fixed, and it was smarter to find it out now than later in the middle of the race.

He saw a race car as a disposable commodity. It was designed to be used and used up completely. From the first lap until the last, he was doing his best to wring every last drop of speed out of the car that he could get. He liked to lead, he would lead every lap if he could. That was just one of the reasons that Bear said T.K. was the only guy "who could go three wide through a corner all by hisself."

He preferred a much looser setup than Orly. Bear was reluctant to lean too much on T.K. to change his style. Race car drivers were a unique bunch and they all had their opinions and idiosyncrasies. So far T.K. had been successful, otherwise they wouldn't be sitting fourth in the points right now. This wasn't the time to force changes. Bear had confidence that Paolo knew the difference between Orly's and T.K.'s style. It was just something he had to adapt to and hopefully he would.

Bear slipped his headset on as he watched two crewmen help Orly get in the race car. The usual way was to slip the right leg into the car, grab the roof with both hands and slide into the seat. Orly had done it thousands of times. But the burn wound on his thigh made it nearly impossible to bend his left leg at the proper angle.

As a result two men cradled his back while he fit his legs through the window and eased into the seat. A photographer was trying to get shots of Orly as they slipped him in the car but somehow somebody always seemed to be standing in the way. Miraculously, as soon as Orly was in the car the photographer could get all the shots he wanted.

Orly worked his custom fit earplugs in, put his helmet on and plugged in his radio.

"You good to go?" Bear asked over his headset.

"Yeah. I'm okay. Hands feel a little bulky but I will get used to them. I think we are fine. Simpson did a good job fitting the gloves over the bandages."

"Well at least you won't have to worry about this car catching on fire. We won't allow it. How's the clutch?" Bear was referring to Orly's ability to depress the clutch pedal.

"Good. The leg is a little stiff, but it will loosen up."

"All right then, let's go to work and see what we got."

Orly flipped up the switches that energized the fuel pump and ignition box with his left hand. He lifted up the big red switch marked "start" and the motor cranked over a couple of times before it rumbled into life. Orly cleared the throttle then let it idle down to a throaty grumble. The sound reverberated off the walls of the crowded garage. It was a familiar ritual for Orly. This was his office. This was home. It was a place where he felt comfortable. The Daytona GT prototype car was fun to drive, and even after the accident, he would have no compunction about getting back into one, but a Cup car was where he lived. Right now the world with all its complications and difficulties was out there while he was in here. He had one job, one focus and that was to make this car the best it could be.

Bear snapped up the window net over the driver's side window and patted the top of the car. The crew pushed him backwards out of the garage as he cut the wheel. He eased the car into gear and headed out of the garage area toward the Sunco fuel station. He cut the switches as his crew carefully monitored how much fuel was put into the car.It was something every competitor did but Bear was extra careful. More than one race had been won on fuel mileage, and he wanted to be dead certain about what kind of mileage they were getting. Three to three and a half miles per gallon was good. Four was exceptional. It all depended on how rich the carb was set and where the power curves were and how much finesse the driver had.

The crew pushed Orly away from the pumps, and he

restarted the engine as he rolled down the slight incline.

"Turn the coolers on."

Orly clicked the mic switch twice as he reached over and flipped the rear end and brake cooler switches. By clicking the mic button twice he was giving Bear a "roger" or affirmative answer.

"You there, Jimmy?" Jimmy, Orly's spotter was perched in the spotter's roost on top of the suites above the main grandstands. He was leaning on the guardrail, along with several other spotters, enjoying the sunshine. They all had a commanding view of the whole track. He was also one of the Hauler drivers for the team and had been for what seemed like forever. His familiar voice had been with Orly almost as long as Bear. Jimmy was good. He never got rattled and was nearly unflappable. Even in the midst of dire circumstances, his voice never changed. When the big crash happened last week at Talladega, it was Jimmy's calm voice that guided Orly through the cloud of tire smoke and raining debris. Orly trusted him. It was hard for a driver to see behind him with the Hahn's device and assorted cables attached to his helmet. The "wrap-around" seat supports also limited his peripheral vision. All in all he had to have Jimmy's "eyes" to keep him out of trouble.

Jimmy knew that Orly seldom liked to chit-chat on the radio. Orly needed to stay focused, so he told him what he needed to know and nothing more or nothing less. At the same time, he communicated with Bear to give him insight on what the car was doing. Jimmy was a pro. Several teams had tried to hire him away from the Orly Mann team, but his loyalties rested with Bear and Orly. He was also renowned for his soft Texas accent.

He was from Texas originally and made his permanent home out on a ranch near Lubbock where he and his family raised horses.

"Yesiree, I am here this fine Texas morning and so glad to be back in civilization in the wonderful lone star state."

Orly clicked the mic twice as he eased out into the pit lane and waited his turn to get on the track. He pulled into the line of cars and killed the motor.

Today was different than usual for some reason. Orly had a lot on his mind, and even though he was focused, there was a part of him that was thinking about other things. He and Hildy were not doing well. There seemed to be a grating friction between them. The accident at Infineon only made things worse. A whole lot worse.

He was a race car driver. What did she expect? Stuff happened. He had been in worse crashes, although that wasn't entirely true. Yeah, he had crashed harder and broke stuff, but never, in his whole career, was he burned. When he drove sprint cars, he was on his head on a regular basis but he never caught on fire. Quite frankly, he would trade a broken bone for a burn anytime. Burns were very painful, and Orly was in a lot more pain than he let on. Right now he needed her support. He didn't need her criticism.

It seemed like she was preoccupied. Like maybe she had something going on that she wasn't talking about. Three more races and then this season was in the bag. Then they could take a little time off over the holidays and maybe he could get to the source of her irritation. Of course if he won the championship, he would be busy making appearances and things.

With thirty-six races in the season, there really wasn't much time off. He and Bear were already making plans for next year. With the economy the way it was, sponsorships were hard to come by. But he and Bear were blessed. They were one of the few teams that already had everything in place and were good to go for next season. Hildy knew he was a driver when she married him. It was what he did. Besides that, it gave them a very nice living. Of course they didn't have a lot of time to enjoy it because they were on the road practically all the time. Women were hard to figure sometimes.

But then there was another side to it. He was tired. Bone tired. Maybe it was time to quit. No, quit wasn't the right word. Maybe it was time to find something else to do. Something that wasn't so all consuming.

"Hey! Let's go." Orly's thoughts were interrupted by the voice in his ear. He jumped as he came out of his reverie and started the engine as the NASCAR official pounded on the roof. He ground the car into gear and eased out onto the track watching the gauges as he gently accelerated.

Three laps later, he was putting the car through its paces. He pushed the "talk" button on the steering wheel.

"The track is fast Bear. I can tell you that. It is also a little rougher than it was in the spring. There seems to be a nice set of bumps coming off four that upsets the car as I make the transition from the banking to the straight. I can already tell it is going to be trouble. Seems to want to suck the car into the wall. Let me run a few more laps, but I think I am a little tight right now. I am going to try a couple of different lines. We might want to loosen this thing up a little, but not too much. I'll let you know. Probably do it with air pressure adjustments."

"Roger that."

- *O* -

Silas was back in the motor coach. He was laying on the big bed basking in the glow of the morning. He was holding his precious autograph book with both hands and kept flipping the pages. He also had a set of radio earphones on his head. He was monitoring Orly and T.K.'s conversation on the radio while watching the Speed Channel coverage of the practice session on the huge screen in the bedroom. The time up on the Hauler and in the garage was great but it wore him out. He felt very important standing next to Paolo and Bear. They even had an Orly Mann Racing Team jacket for him and it fit really good.

They treated him just like a regular person. Which he was, of course. Just because he had physical problems didn't make him any less than anybody else. He was just a regular kid. He voiced that opinion out loud to himself...but he didn't really believe it inside. He knew he was different. He didn't have much stamina and was very weak most of the time. Even though his mind was willing to go, sometimes his body just wouldn't cooperate.

Dr. Miller was cool with pushing him around in his chair and he did get some great autographs and meet some cool people. Richard Petty and Darrell Waltrip even signed his book for him. Morgan Shepherd signed it and even put in a bible verse. Wow! But the best thing was when Bear said he could sit in Orly's race car. It looked so shiny, sitting in the garage with its yellow and orange paint job. It said Speed King on the side and the hood. A big number 37 was on the door in black paint with purple shadows. It looked cool. Then Bear asked him if he wanted to sit in the car? He was so excited he could hardly speak. He just nodded his head.

Bear said, "Yeah, I thought you might."

"I don't know how to get in."

"Here stand up and we will do it this way." He worked his way to his feet and Paolo picked him up like a sack of sugar with his arms around his shoulders and under his knees. He gently guided his legs through the window and eased him into the seat. Then they even put the steering wheel back on. He felt like a real race car driver sitting there.

Silas looked all around. It was a little more cramped than he thought it would be. The interior was painted gray and everything was so clean. It looked very business like. It smelled, even. Sort of like metal and oil and maybe rubber, he wasn't sure. He could see that the gauges were turned a little in the dash. When he asked Bear why, he said it was because when Orly was going fast, if everything was okay, then all the gauges would be pointing the same way. He wouldn't have to take time to read each one. He held onto the steering wheel with both hands. It was big and pretty thick around with a pad in the middle. Bear reached in and pulled the belts down so they went over his chest. They practically covered him up. He said to him, "There, we will put a helmet on your noggin and then you will be safe and good to go."

Silas smiled. "When I get old enough I'm going to drive for you, Bear."

"Of course you will. We'll give you a try."

Silas jumped when the crew of the car next to the Speed King Chevrolet started the engine to check for oil leaks. The loud noise startled him. He looked up at Paolo with big eyes. Paolo gave him a thumbs up and mouthed the words. "It's okay." Silas peered through the windshield and imagined himself roaring down the racetrack.

"Hey Mom, I got to sit in Orly Mann's car. It's the very one he's going to race in on Sunday. It was so cool."

"I know you did, Silas. I have a whole bunch of pictures to prove it. We'll look at them later and you can choose which one you want to frame for your room." Sarah leaned over him and quietly touched his ear with the thermometer. I want you to rest Silas. We are going to be out tonight and you need to be up for it."

"Aw, Mom, I don't want to rest. I want to go and watch Orly and T.K. qualify."

"Now Silas, we talked about this. You can watch it on TV and listen to them on the radio. Come on now, we agreed." She turned her back to him and checked the thermometer. So far, so good, although he did look a little pale.

Silas' attention was brought back to the radio.

"Now I'm too loose, Cowboy. Maybe we ought to take that packer off the front shock. I'm loose going in and the front end is all over the place. I'm having to chase it up to the wall. I don't feel in the track. Feels more like I am skating on top of it."

"Roger that. Bring it in, T.K. We got about fifteen minutes left." Paolo responded.

The Speed Channel cameras were focused directly on T.K. as he exited turn four. The speculation was that he just over cooked it coming off the corner. Maybe it was the bumps that sucked him into the wall. He never publicly said what happened. He came sliding off the corner with the throttle wide open searching for grip. Unfortunately, he ran out of racetrack and talent at the same time and banged the turn four Safer barrier hard. He came off the wall with a flat right rear tire, and despite the inner liner, it shredded into pieces tearing bodywork off the car. He then did a snap spin and collected another car that was doing his best to stay out of his way. That impact practically tore the front end off.

Silas sat up. "Oh Mom, T.K. just crashed!" he yelled.

- O -

Paolo was standing in the pit lane with a clear view of turn four when T.K. lost it. He watched him hit the wall then collect the other car. It was instantly obvious to his trained eye that they wouldn't be able to fix this one in the garage.

Devin's high-pitched voice rang in his ears, "It's toast. Front clip is gone along with the right rear corner." *Tell me something I don't know*, Paolo thought to himself. There were parts all over the track. It would have to go back to the shop for a front clip and probably a rear one as well. He made a mental note that he would have to apologize to the other crew chief when he had time. It didn't look like his car was in any better shape. Well, that is what you get when your driver doesn't exercise the good sense that God gave a fence post, as Jimmy would say. He spun on his heel and set off on a run for the garage before the cars had completely stopped.

The Blue Saber crew was waiting in the garage stall for T.K. to bring the car back so they could make some final adjustments before qualifying. They were standing around in various relaxed positions. Each man was wearing a headset so he could hear what T.K. was saying and what Paolo wanted done to the car in the midst of the noise of the garage.

"All right guys, let's get the backup off the Hauler. We got some work to do before qualifying." Nobody asked questions. It wasn't the first time T.K. had wiped out a car in practice. They sprinted toward the Hauler to fish out the secondary car.

Paolo groaned as he ran. There was no time left in the session. By the time NASCAR got the mess cleaned up, the session would be over. T.K. would have to qualify the backup without any track time to see where it stood. This should be interesting. Not many race car drivers liked having to flatfoot a car that hadn't been shaken down. In the meantime, they would have to bust their hump to get the thing ready.

The backup car was similar to the primary car but it wasn't identical. They had been tuning on the primary all morning. Now if he could just dial those same adjustments into the backup they might be okay. He would have to talk to Bear about a couple of things. Bear always supervised every car when it was on the surface plate back at the shop just before they got loaded into the Haulers. He would have to get the notes on this car out of the Hauler.

At least they had a couple of hours before qualifying started. It meant non-stop work for the team. But that was what they got paid for.

Qualifying was important. It meant a great deal in terms of track position during the race but it was also important in regard to pit stall selection. Pit stalls were picked by the order of qualifying. The guy on the pole got first choice, second next and so on. They needed a championship run this weekend, and the last thing Paolo wanted to do was start the race in the back of the pack with a lousy pit stall location. His mind was in overdrive as he sprinted into the garage. Bear was already there talking with Randy. He and Orly had finished practice early and parked their car, and Bear was monitoring T.K.'s radio. As soon as T.K. Crashed, Bear walked down to take charge. Paolo would have none of that. He was the crew chief, and he was in charge. He interrupted the conversation.

"Randy, let's get the thing ready for tech and get the sticker. Make sure it weighs right and the spoiler is set good. I want to check the height first thing. Then we will go over the checklist to make sure we haven't forgotten anything."

Randy looked from Bear to Paolo with a question on his face. One look at Paolo told him he was dead serious.

"Got it." And he was moving.

"We can handle this, Bear. I want to check a couple of things with you on the setup but we got it. Come on and let me do my job."

Bear never said a word. He just folded his arms and got out of the way.

Speaking of getting in the way, the media people knew better than to bother the Blue Saber team as they prepared the car. More than one reporter had been impolitely elbowed out of the way by a crew guy trying to work against the clock. But drivers on the other hand were fair game. They generally stood around while the crew fixed what they had broke. T.K. already had been interviewed twice by the television and radio professionals.

He also had to endure an angry confrontation with the driver he wrecked as he made references to T.K.'s aggressive driving style and his bonehead errors in judgment. T.K. was noncommittal and kept his mouth shut, much to the disappointment of a network cameraman and several photographers. He took no umbrage at the man's comments. He knew the guy was probably right anyway, but he wasn't going to say so. More than once, he was on the other end of the argument. In the meantime, while he was reaping the fruit of his transgressions, his team was building him another ride.

Nor did T.K. apologize to Paolo. They both knew the situation and there was no sense in talking about it.

"I'm going to try to get it as close as I can for you but I'm not certain just exactly what it's going to do."

"No problem. I'll just work with it. You guys build good stuff so it should be ok. I'll try to keep it off the wall this time. Where are we in the order?" T.K. was referring to the order in which they qualified. The order was determined by practice speeds.

"Alicia says we go out 27th and Orly is 21st."

"Cool."

Chapter Seven

*"Driving a race car is a very intense experience.
I mean it can make you see stars. Believe me
I have seen my share."*

T.K. Kittridge, NASCAR Driver.

One by one the cars were quietly pushed out of the garage area to take their place on the pit lane. They had been polished and primped, tuned and adjusted. What could be done to make them go fast for one quick lap had been done. It was up to the drivers now.

Orly was patiently leaning against the crowd side of the Speed King Chevrolet. He turned and looked over his shoulder. The grandstands were starting to fill up and he could hear the noise of the crowd. The Texas fans were a knowledgeable bunch and knew what was at stake. Orly looked over and saw several people pointing him out to others. He turned and waved. He was trying not to put too much weight on his burned leg and look natural at the same time. The thing was paining him some and he was trying to put off getting back in the car as long as possible.

Orly didn't like qualifying much anymore. He had his share of poles throughout his career, but now they just didn't seem to matter as much. Starting toward the front was essential. No doubt about that, but pounding your chest and going for broke and running the risk of wrecking the car didn't make much sense at this stage of the championship chase. Of course he would give it his best shot and take what the car gave him, but there just wasn't anything to be gained in bouncing it off the wall. He was going to chill today. Yeah, that made sense.

He mentally gave himself a poke in the stomach. He knew better. He also knew that as soon as he started the engine and left the pit lane, his competitive juices would be flowing. He would be screwing his foot to the floorboard and be hunched over the wheel working to wring every last drop of speed out of this machine whether it was willing to give it to him or not.

Orly could see one of the network media crews as they worked their way down the line of cars interviewing the twelve chase drivers. They would be in his face in a few minutes asking the same questions they asked every week. This week might be different with his injured leg and his burned hands. He would have to deal with the details of the accident all over again and explain that he really had no idea what broke, and yes it was scary, and yes it was part of the business, and it happened, and yes he was grateful for T.K. helping him out of the car, and no he probably wouldn't drive for that particular team in the Rolex race at Daytona in February, and yeah, of course, he would be fine for Sunday's race, and yes indeed he thought he had a shot at the pole, and of course he thought he could win the championship…

blah, blah, blah. *Same old stuff, but that's the price one pays for fame and fortune,* he thought to himself. Orly did think he could win the championship. He wanted it bad, but then so did the other eleven guys. *T.K. probably wanted it more than anybody,* thought Orly. If he ever got his emotions under control, he would be an absolutely fantastic driver. He had more natural talent than anybody that Orly had ever raced against.

He bent down and peered inside the driver's compartment with a critical eye. Got to be a way to make it more user friendly. Bear and the crew had done everything he asked, but it was still painful sitting in the car.

Running a cup car for five hundred miles was physically demanding. At least Texas had some straightaway, which gave him a chance to rest, but the g-force in the corners was fierce. He hoped he could hang in there. If he didn't, Sunday's race was going to really be an endurance test of his ability to withstand pain.

Fortunately he was able to negotiate with the medical center doctors and they had removed some of the bandages on the back of his hands, making them less bulky. Still, by the end of the race tomorrow, they would most certainly be throbbing pretty good. Oh well, it was what it was. Pain was something that just was. No sense in worrying about it. Orly smiled to himself. That is exactly what Silas told him.

Orly watched as Bear, T.K. and Paolo walked up to join him.

"You guys good to go?" Orly said to T.K. as he leaned against the car. It was obvious to the other three that he wasn't putting much weight on his bad leg. It was also clear that he was in considerable pain, but no one asked him how he was feeling. It didn't matter how he was feeling. He had a job to do, and whether he was in pain or not made no difference. Nobody understood that better than the other men standing with him.

T.K. Smiled.

"Yeah, as far as I know we are. We'll light it up and see what it does." T.K. brought both hands up in a palm out expression of "I dunno".

"The Cowboy here tells me everything is okay so I guess I'll take his word for it."

Bear wasn't talking, just observing as he glanced sideways at Paolo out of the corner of his eye to see how he took to being called "Cowboy". Paolo's face stayed expressionless and the only indication he gave that he heard the comment was a slight grunt under his breath. Then he put both hands in his pockets and spoke.

"Like I told you, partner." He drew the word out cowboy style. "Just put the hammer down and see if it sticks. I think it will, but you're the 'pro from Dover'. You're the ace wheel man. Give it your best shot, or as they say in the cowboy world, grab aholt and let er' buck."

Bear could see where this was going and quickly jumped into the conversation. The wear and tear on the teams with the pressure of the chase was starting to take its toll. Everybody was on edge. Maybe after they got both cars qualified things would settle down a little bit. He changed the subject.

"Never mind that, you guys. T.K. come up and join us in the tower tonight and watch the truck race. Mr. Eddie G. has made arrangements for us to use one of the suites. Silas and his Mom are going to be with us."

T.K. was still reacting to Paolo's comments. "Oh

yeah, that's that crippled kid, isn't it?"

"Better not let him hear you say he is crippled," Orly said with a disarming smile. "He is just as liable to jump up and bite your ear or something. Silas doesn't consider himself a cripple, and he doesn't like it much when other people label him like that."

T.K. was about to reply when the media team walked up with their assorted paraphernalia.

"Well, I see we have the four kingpins from the Orly Mann Racing Team all together for once. Would you folks mind giving us a few sound bytes for the broadcast today?" The producer spoke with an ingratiating smile, but everybody knew that there was no option but to give him what he wanted.

Twenty minutes later the qualifying session was in full swing. The times were about what Bear expected. He was hoping that they might come away with a top five, which, considering their practice times was well within the realm of possibility. Bear glanced up at the scoring pylon at the end of the pit lane that listed the times. Yup, the chase cars were right up there. Looked like pretty much everyone so far had brought their "A" game. This race this weekend was going to boil down to experienced veteran teams against experienced veteran teams.

When it came time for Orly to get in his car, he managed it without help. It wasn't easy. It was downright excruciating, but he managed. Bear helped him get hooked up with his radio and belts. He spoke into Orly's ear as Orly adjusted himself in his seat.

"Just take what it gives you. If we have to start a little further back, it will be okay. We will just tweak it some and make it better. You know I didn't take too much of the race trim out of it but we did adjust it a little. The usual stuff. Everybody is saying that the track has a lot of grip this afternoon, but feel it out. You know what you are doing." Bear was nervous. He was always nervous when Orly qualified. Funny how that worked. He trusted Orly during the race in any type of situation, but when it came to qualifying, he almost felt like it was up to him, and he somehow had to ride along with Orly to "get 'er done", as they say.

Bear started to snap the window net up when Hildy brushed past him and leaned in the window. She kissed the end of her fingers and touched Orly's cheek. "Go fast." is all she said, then she stepped back.

Orly was left alone with his thoughts as Bear and Hildy headed back in the garage area. They would watch Orly qualify from the roof of the transporter.

Orly sat in the car collecting his thoughts. He couldn't see much out the side of his car but he could see just a little bit of the pit stalls on the other side of the wall. Nobody had their boxes setup for qualifying because everyone was still working in the garage. Besides they hadn't been assigned yet. As a result, it made a good vantage point for people to stand and gawk at the various drivers and other assorted celebrities. He watched the people standing behind the wall that were watching him as the crew pushed him forward another spot. Five more cars, and then it would be his turn. Suddenly he spotted a familiar face in the crowd. Damn! Orly seldom (if ever) swore but this was an exception. He keyed the radio.

"Do you know who is here?"

"Yeah I saw him too. Forget about it. We will deal with him later. You need to stay focused right now." Bear's voice was calm and even.

Orly clicked the mic button twice.

- ***O*** -

Paolo was standing beside the Blue Saber car with a sense of ownership and pride in accomplishment. The car was ready. He and the crew had done their part, and the only thing missing was the driver. In the meantime, T.K. was in no hurry to get mounted. To Paolo, it seemed like he had talked with half the people milling around the pit lane and been interviewed by every media group at the track, including the weather network. He really enjoyed all the attention, and Paolo wasn't used to that. Bear and Orly treated their fame as a necessary evil and endured the interrupted privacy it brought. T.K., on the other hand, went out of his way to be seen and rub shoulders with every celebrity he could. He pretty much basked in the notoriety.

Unlike Bear, Paolo had elected to watch qualifying from the pit lane. Once T.K. was on the track, there wasn't anything he could do, but at least he could watch the lap on the JumboTron big screen that faced the grandstands. Besides, he would still be in radio contact if it quit running or something. By watching the whole lap, it would give him some indication of what the car was doing. He and his Blue Saber crew had busted their humps getting this thing ready. He was pretty sure he had it dialed in, but you never knew until it was on the track. He helped push the car forward another spot.

T.K. was walking beside the car and Paolo was tempted to tell him to get in the "frickin' seat", but he held his tongue.

T.K. was looking at the crowd on the other side of the pit wall when he suddenly stiffened. He balled his hands into fists and hunched his shoulders. Paolo looked over quickly himself to see what had drawn his attention. Then he saw the man. Was it him? It couldn't be. He was supposed to be in jail. He couldn't be here now. This was exactly what they didn't need. Paolo quickly put his headset on and keyed the mic button.

"Bear. He is here. I thought he was uh, you know."

"Yeah, I know he is here. Whatever you do, don't let him get close to T.K."

"Yeah, right." Paolo shifted his focus. "T.K., we need you to get in the car"

T.K. stared at him with an unfocused look on his face then he turned and methodically climbed into the car. Paolo positioned himself beside the drivers' window, blocking T.K's view. He leaned in the window and helped him straighten his belts and plug his radio in. When he had the Hahn's device lined up right, he helped T.K. pull the belts tight then he snapped the steering wheel into place as T.K. put on his gloves. Paolo keyed his radio.

"Hey man, don't worry about it. You got to put him out of your mind. Let's get this car qualified then we will deal with it. You can't think about anything else right now. Got it?" Then he locked the window net into place, sealing T.K. into the cocoon of the cockpit.

T.K. looked at him through the window net and gave him a thumbs up. "Got it." It was a lie.

Paolo turned around to see Alicia walking up behind him. "Paolo, Bear sent me over. He didn't want to use the radio but he said to be sure you told T.K. that the restraining order was still in effect. The guy is not supposed to come within a 100 feet of T.K., and he is by no means to talk to him."

"Yeah, right." Paolo unsnapped the net and said, "You lean in an tell him that."

Alicia leaned in as T.K. flipped his visor up and looked into her eyes. Alicia repeated the message. T.K. nodded his head then spoke from the confines of his helmet. "Did you know that you have the most beautiful eyes?" His voice was muffled, but she understood. She playfully flipped the visor down.

"Did he understand?" Paolo said as he snapped the net back into place.

"Oh yeah, he understood. He will be all right."

Maybe, then maybe not, Paolo thought to himself.

T.K. put both hands on the steering wheel and closed his eyes to try to clear his mind. He could feel the crew push him up as another car began a qualifying run. His brain wouldn't obey. It was like he stepped off a precipice and dropped into a black boiling pool of bitterness and anger. He could see the man in his mind's eye, standing in the pit lane just staring at him with that cocky grin on his face. All the past history came screaming to the surface. The abuse of his Mom, the lies, the deceit, and the embarrassment...it was just too much, and here the guy was hanging around again. *Maybe I should give him what he wants*, thought T.K. *No that's wrong. If I do, the guy will just demand more.*

- O -

Slowly, the line crept forward. Some guys were fast and some were very fast. The pole position bounced around as the qualifiers fought the clock. From his position atop the Hauler, Bear studied each car carefully. He keyed the mic with the radio set so he could speak to both T.K. and Paolo. "I am hearing that there is a lot of 'grip' in the track. Looks like the really fast guys are using the low groove."

As Bear ended his comment, Orly reached over and flipped the ignition switches, then hit the toggle for the starter. It was his turn. The pit Marshal waved him out, and Orly eased into the gas. He took the car through the gears, slowly building speed as he rode up the banking in turn one.

He settled himself back in the custom seat and pulled his shoulder belts tight. He slipped his toe under the restraining strap on the gas pedal and gently stood on the pedal. The eight hundred horsepower in the Chevy engine came alive as he rolled off the second turn, building speed. Orly watched the tach out of the corner of his eye as he sailed down the back chute.

The car seemed to hunker down and hook to the track surface. Orly could feel every vibration, every little ripple in the pavement as he put his entire focus on his entrance into the third turn. He went low, allowing the car to climb the banking, feeling the g force as he exited the apex of the corner. The car went light as he flashed across the bump coming off turn four. Then he was through the dogleg as the starter waved the green flag. The official clock was ticking.

Orly kept his foot on the floor, fighting the impulse to lift, if ever so slightly, as he laid the car into turn one. He could feel the car start to push, but he was careful not to overcorrect with wheel input. Every adjustment of the steering wheel scraped off just a tiny bit of speed, but when qualifying speeds were measured to the thousandth of a second, it could make a difference. He kept it clean and smooth as he rocketed off turn two and roared down the back chute once again. He felt rather than heard Bear's voice in his ear. "Nice, lookin', very good".

Now came the critical part. He was faster than before. He chose his line carefully and laid the car into the groove like a new mama laying her sweet baby down for a nap. He was flat out. One mistake, one miscalculation, could move him from a decent spot on the grid to eating dust at the back of the pack. His apex was perfect. The car drifted up the banking and he came off four with at least six inches between the car and the wall. He whistled past start finish, picked up the flag and boom he was done.

"Nice run, Orly. You are on the outside of the front row. You missed the pole by two hundredths of a second. I really don't think anybody left to qualify is going to go any faster. Maybe T.K., but I doubt it. Nice job."

Orly took a deep breath and clicked the mic, "I may have left some on the table, but not much. Hey Bear, come down and help me get out of this thing. I think we might have to adjust the seat a little more."

- O -

The NASCAR pit official pointed at T.K. and then motioned over his shoulder. T.K. dumped the clutch and left tire rubber on the pit lane as he accelerated on to the track. He ran the motor to the rev limiter on each shift as he slammed the lever through the gears.

Paolo's voice echoed in his ears, "Hey Buddy, remember we've got to run that motor in the race."

T.K. didn't bother to acknowledge.

Paolo's voice rang out again. "T.K., the car is fresh. Be careful, man. Feel it out." Again T.K. didn't bother to acknowledge.

T.K. came off the back chute and pointed the car into turn three. He knew immediately that he had his hands full. The car was loose on entry, which was about the worst handling characteristic a driver had to face. As he set up for the corner, he could feel the car drift sideways. It felt like it was skating on top of the track as opposed to settling in the groove. He fought the wheel and finally got the thing pointed down the racetrack exiting turn four. *Man, this thing is twitchy*, he thought. The Starter waved the green flag as T.K. flashed by. T.K. set the car for turn one and took a deep breath. "I hope this thing sticks," he said out loud.

Whether T.K. misjudged the corner or the car was just too loose was anybody's guess. It did remain a hot topic of conversation for the rest of the weekend, and the input was about 50% each way. It didn't matter.

As T.K. laid the car into the corner, the front end stuck…but the back end didn't. T.K. did his best to correct, and the car made a sudden move up the banking to head directly for the wall. There was no saving it. T.K. smashed the wall not quite but nearly head on. Later

NASCAR would say it was one of the hardest impacts they ever recorded.

When the car hit, T.K. shot forward in his seat, but the Hahn's device, and his belts and all the rest of the safety equipment did their job. The impact still knocked the wind out of him, but he had the presence of mind to take his hands off the wheel and grab his shoulder straps just before hitting. It saved him from a broken wrist or sprained thumbs.

The car ricocheted off the wall, tripped over the mangled front end and commenced a series of barrel rolls ten feet in the air, shedding parts in the process. It landed on its roof then rebounded into the air again, rolling over and over. Finally it stopped upright on what was left of the body, only to burst into brief flame as the ruptured oil tank and lines caught fire.

T.K. was conscious through it all and absolutely furious. He was literally cursing out loud as the car tumbled through the air. As soon as the car stopped he ripped his belts off his shoulders and punched out his window net. He unsnapped the bent steering wheel and pitched it out of the car onto the racetrack. He was halfway out of the car before the crash crew could reach him. They arrived just in time to help him stand upright.

"You okay?" the first guy said to him as he started to take T.K.'s arm.

T.K. was ripping off his gloves as he snarled "I'm fine. Don't touch me," as he jerked away from the man and his attempt to help him.

"Go easy man, you just had one heck of a ride. You better take a minute and make sure you got all your parts working."

As T.K.'s head cleared he looked up into the crowd in the turn one grandstands. The racetrack was eerily quiet. Virtually everyone was standing silently watching him. He threw his gloves into the wreck of the car and turned, put his forearm across his stomach and ceremoniously bowed to the crowd. The place went nuts as the gesture was broadcast all around the track on the giant TV screens. Practically everyone in the place was cheering and whistling. This time he allowed them to help him as he was ushered into the waiting ambulance for the mandatory trip to the care center.

Paolo wasn't cheering or whistling. He stood with his arms folded watching the infinite replays on the big screen. Doug was standing beside him saying nothing. A crew chief from another team walked up and stood beside them. "Did something break or did he overcook it? Don't look like anything broke."

Paolo shook his head. "I haven't a clue, but we aren't going to fix that one, that's for sure."

"Well, I got to admit that in all my years of racing, I don't think I ever saw a crash more spectacular than that one. Son of a gun, he hit hard. Musta been ten feet off the ground doing barrel rolls. Pretty amazing that he walked away. 'Bout the only thing you're going to save out of that mess is the gearshift knob. I think even the radiator cap is bent." At the end of the replay, he patted Paolo on the back, "Well, so much for number two," and walked away.

"Two write offs in one day. There goes a chunk of change," Doug said indignantly. "This is sick, Paolo. What is wrong with that guy?"

Paolo didn't reply. Just nodded his head in affirmation. He keyed his radio, "Well, now what?"

"I'm not sure yet. We'll have to talk with NASCAR." Bear replied.

- *O* -

Five minutes later Bear was on the phone to the head of fabrication at Orly Mann Racing, Mike Manning.

"Hey Mike. Had that baby yet?"

"'Lo Bear. Nope, not yet. Any day now. Mama is ready and so am I. Yeah, I am on my way to the shop. I was watching qualifying and I figured you would be calling. You want to use chassis 177? That one has been good to us. Has two wins. Been certified and with a couple minor tweaks, it will be a done deal. Besides, it is all decaled up with the shrink-wrap, so it is good to go. Take us a couple of hours to detail it out."

Like all Cup Teams, the Speed King Team had ten to fifteen rolling chassis in various states of preparation. It used to be that the logos and sponsor signs were painted on the cars. With modern technology everything was applied with a very thin plastic film, then shrunk to fit. Almost but not quite like using decals.

"Yes, that is the one I had in mind. Get her going then use the small transporter and get it on the road. Going to take him twelve to fifteen hours to get here. Our first, last practice ends at eleven tomorrow morning. We still have to stuff a motor in it, so that don't leave us much time."

"Okay Bear, you got it. Tell that kid he owes us for this. Tell the Hauler guys to just drop that wreck off at the junkyard on the way back. I don't think I'll be able to use much off it. Whew, what a crash. I am just glad he's all right."

"Yeah, me too. Keep me posted so I can coordinate with my guys here."

- *O* -

It was late in the afternoon. Qualifying was done and the racetrack itself was quiet, but it seemed that every fan on the Speedway grounds was on the move. Dr. Miller liked it this way. He was sitting in his golf cart in a line of traffic waiting to make a left turn into the infield. Suddenly a burly man with a handlebar mustache and a cowboy hat stepped into the cart and sat down beside him.

"Hey Most Holy Dr. Reverend, how you doing? Some crash, hey? That kid really knows how to tear things up. I sure wished I had the rights to the film of that thing. They're going to be showing that for years to come. A guy could make big money off that."

"Doing fine, William. Yes, T.K. was very blessed to walk away. That was a tough one. I must say I am surprised to see you. I thought you were on a little vacation at the government's expense."

"Yeah, well things being what they are with the economy and crime rate and all, they decided to turn us good boys loose a little early. Have you reconsidered my offer?"

It was William Williams sitting next to him. T.K.'s notorious stepfather. He wanted one thing and he was willing to do just about anything to get it. He wanted a share, a big share of T.K.'s earnings.

He knew that Miller had ties to the Orly Mann team. He wanted Miller to use his leverage to force the team to capitulate and put pressure on T.K. Somehow, he felt that Miller had the ability to do this. That assumption was wrong on two counts. First, nobody told Bear and Orly what to do. They made their own decisions. Second, Miller was not about to get involved in anybody's personal business. It wasn't his job.

When he politely explained all this to Williams, it fell on deaf ears. That was when Williams upped the ante and strange things began to happen around the TxArm compound. They could never prove that William Williams was responsible, but he always seemed to be in proximity.

Dr. Miller pulled the golf cart to the side of the road and killed the motor. "Look William, my answer is the same as it was last time. No. If you want to sit down with T.K. and talk, I would be glad to mediate. I would be willing to act as a go-between. You know that there is a restraining order forbidding you to get within a hundred feet of him. Apart from that, I don't want anything to do with this. They have thrown your lawsuit, I guess I should say lawsuits, out of court. That is the end of it. You need to let it go. I will be praying to that end. Now, I need you to get out of my cart. I have things to do."

Williams made no move to get out. He smoothed his mustache. "Look Miller, how about if I donate 10%, no make that 20%, of what I collect from the kid to your organization. How about that? Would you be willing to help me then? Sure you would. You would be a fool not to." Williams clapped Miller on the back. "Come on, man, help me out here. Together we can collect what the kid rightfully owes me, and you will reap the benefits." This last comment was made with the best used car salesman smile that Harold could muster.

"No. The answer is no, William. No further discussion needed."

Dr. Miller could see the anger in William's eyes, although he was still smiling. Well I guess I will just have to try another approach. Wonder what would happen if the Orly Mann Team began to experience some, how shall we say, anomalies."

Dr. Miller could feel his adrenaline start to come up. "William, you are right on the edge of blackmail or extortion. I have a mind to turn you in to the authorities!"

"What, me? I don't have any idea what you are talking about." Williams said this with a completely innocent look. It was the look he reserved for the customer when they discovered that the interest rate quoted by the dealership didn't match that of the finance company.

Dr. Miller took a deep breath. "William, let me tell you something. When you mess with TxArm, you are messing with the Lord's ministry. We bathe this outreach in prayer and I don't think you want to get in the way of that. I know you don't care, but I want to remind you there are bigger things at stake here. If you mess with the Orly Mann Team, you better 'gird up your loins', so to speak, for a fight. They are a tough bunch and they stick together. Now, I don't want to see you anywhere around the TxArm compound or I will call security. Get out of my cart before I throw you out."

"My, my, a clergyman resorting to violence. What is the world coming to." This was said as Williams slid out of the seat.

Dr. Miller started the cart and muttered, "forgive me, Lord but I would like nothing better than to mash that guy's nose" as he drove away.

Chapter Eight

"Some folks are as slick as an adobe creek bank in a rain storm. If you believe everything they say you generally wind up in the creek."

R. W. Coburn

T.K. was sore.

They were talking about keeping him in the Infield Care Center for observation, and maybe even sending him on to the hospital, but he managed to talk them into letting him go. The doc was amazed that he didn't suffer any major injuries. Even so, he could feel his body tightening up. His neck was very sore, and he had a tender spot on his ribs where the seat bar punched him. His right knee was also a little swollen. He wasn't sure what caused that.

Doing all those flips in mid-air took him back to his sprint car days. He had images in his mind of staring down at the black asphalt of the track then up to the blue of the sky. Asphalt...sky...asphalt...sky. Made him dizzy thinking about it.

He hadn't had much time to think about the crash, but the one thing he did know was that initial impact into the wall was big time. It was just like getting punched in the sternum. It just knocked all the air out of him.

He was almost reminded of when Slick Willie used to get angry and haul off and hit him in the stomach when he was a kid. It just kind of collapsed his lungs and paralyzed his diaphragm for a few seconds. Of course he always punched him when his mother wasn't around. Speaking of that jerk, maybe it was time to take him in a back alley and beat the stuffing out of him for once. No if he did that, he would just sue him and then he would get what he wanted, which was money.

He was also surprised to see Bear and Orly waiting for him just outside the Care Center. Of course there were hordes of reporters and media types waiting for him. He made a brief statement, and then Carol, the PR rep for the teams, took over. Bear took his arm and guided him to a golf cart. Orly was driving and headed them toward the motor home lot. After they pulled into the lot, Orly stopped in front of his coach and shut the thing off.

"You okay, really? That was a heck of a crash."

"Yeah, I think I'm okay. Just sore already. Look, I am sorry, guys. I probably should have backed off and brought the thing in and let them fix whatever was wrong. It really did feel like something wasn't quite right."

Bear took over and reminded him this was the eleventh cup car that T.K. had totaled this year, and it was costing the team a big bunch of money. T. K. nodded his head. He couldn't blame Bear. He knew that a few of those wrecks were avoidable, but some weren't.

Everybody expected attrition, but he was pushing it. He just nodded his head again and agreed with everything Bear said, waiting for him to finish. When he couldn't stand it any more, he cleared his throat and interrupted.

"Look, I know you guys are ticked, but I want you to remember something. I'm in the Chase. In fact, I'm sitting fourth, and I have every possibility of winning the championship for the Orly Mann Team. So back off me a little, and let's finish this season, and I will try to do better…and all that." With that said, he got out of the cart and limped to his motor home.

As soon as he got into the motor home, he headed straight to the custom built bathroom. He ran the taps and eased into the Jacuzzi tub and let the hot water do its work. That felt good, but now he was really starting to stiffen up and hurt. *I will be okay. A couple of aspirin and I will be just fine*, he thought to himself as he soaked in the water.

By the time he got out of the tub, his cell phone message box was full. Seemed like every media organization in the world, including the Hispanic Television Network, wanted to interview him. He ignored them all. They would catch up with him, eventually. Somehow they always did.

T.K. microwaved some mac and cheese and sat down to eat. While he was eating, his cell phone rang yet again. At first he ignored it then looked down to check the number. It was Alicia.

"Hey Beautiful, whatcha doing?"

"You're a tough guy to get a hold of. Are you okay? No teeth loose or anything? They told us to keep an eye on you to see if you did anything funny. We told them that was normal for you."

"Thanks a bunch. Yeah, I know I'm hiding. That big boyfriend of yours is probably looking for a piece of me right about now. Wrecking two cars in one day is not good for business. I just got my tail feathers chewed by Bear and Orly…well not Orly so much, but Bear gave me a good licking. I did remind them we were in the chase."

Alicia ignored the comment about Paolo being her boyfriend. "Yes, Paolo isn't too happy and I don't blame him. They have another car coming down from the shop. It should be here early tomorrow morning. Hey listen, they asked me to contact you. Remember I spoke to you about meeting Silas Biggs? If you were up to it, they were wondering if you could come up to the suite for the truck race in a little while this evening and meet Silas and his mom? That way we could keep an eye on you. By the way, you are on every highlight reel in the country right now."

"I'm okay, just a little sore. My pride is hurt worst of all. Is it a private suite? I don't want to have to stand around and sign autographs and do a bunch of interviews and answer dumb questions all night with a bunch of people."

"Yes, it's a private suite. Just us. Anybody from either team is welcome, but no one else. It is nice."

"No media?"

"No media."

"Will you pick me up?"

"Yes, I can do that. I suppose it falls under my official duties as the Blue Saber team representative."

Paolo was tired, and he was hungry. Somehow in

the course of the day, he missed lunch, and now it was going past dinnertime. Fatigue and hunger wasn't a good combination for him because it made him exceedingly irritable. Grouchy might be a better word. It was starting to get dark and getting a little chilly. He shrugged deeper into his jacket and hunched his shoulders. He was walking toward the motor home lot, but the aroma of food made him contemplate bagging a hotdog at one of the concession counters.

What a day, he thought to himself. *Two finely-tuned, hand crafted, race ready cars in the dumpster and now we have to start all over again.* Right after T.K.'s crash, NASCAR covered up the Blue Saber car and loaded it into their own Hauler. They wanted to take it back to their facility, and go over it with a fine-tooth comb. Do some tests and whatnot to see how the safety equipment held up and so forth.

In Paolo's mind, the stuff worked pretty good. T.K. was up and walking around, wasn't he? The Orly Mann shop built good stuff. He said he was gonna be sore but for crying out loud, who wouldn't be after a ride like that? The big issue was whether T.K. screwed up and lost the car or if something broke. That was a question that probably wouldn't get answered. At least not this weekend, anyway.

In the meantime, they were still in the chase with a race in front of them, but now they really had their work cut out. The back up car to the back up car was on its way from Charlotte. Paolo laughed out loud at that term…back up to the back up.

They had made arrangements with one of the local Chevy dealers to open their shop at 4:30 AM tomorrow morning. Hopefully the truck would be here right about then after the all night run from Charlotte. They would bag what parts they could from the hauler at the track so they would have all the spare pieces they might need.

That would give him and the crew a little time to fine tune the thing until NASCAR opened the garage at the track. They would work on the car until the last minute, then throw the thing back on the small Hauler and get it back to the track. As soon as the garage was open, they would run the car through tech inspection and hopefully get their competition sticker.

NASCAR would be tough on them in "the room of doom", but that was okay. They were legal. It was a logistical nightmare, but hopefully they could make it all happen. Then hopefully they would be ready for the first practice at 8:45 AM.

Paolo wiped his brow and put his hands in his pockets. Man, that was a lot of "hopefullys". At least the car was wrapped, and that was a good thing. They wouldn't have to worry about signage or decals. But in any case, there would still be a lot of stuff to check and double check and possibly change for the practice session. The guys at the shop didn't have time to do much because they needed to get the thing on the road.

He was still walking with his head down and deep in thought when a hand reached out and took his arm. Paolo was startled and turned around to face a big, bulky man wearing a cowboy hat.

"Hey Pelegrimi, remember me?"

Paolo replied, "It's Pelegrini not Pelegrimi. Yeah, I know you. You're the guy that has been hounding my driver. What do you want?" His tone was less than friendly.

"Lighten up, boy. Here, let me buy you a hotdog or something. I just want to talk with you for a minute."

"No thanks. I'm careful who I eat with and I'm not sure we have anything to talk about."

"Listen. Just hear me out for a second. Things might not be the way you think they are. It might be worth your while just to listen. I been watching you and I bet you are just plumb wore out. That kid knows how to tear up equipment, don't he." This last comment was made as a statement rather than a question.

"I remember when I was paying his bills, he could go through stuff faster than green grass through a goose." Williams took his hat off and dramatically wiped his head with his handkerchief.

He went on, "I'm the one that got him his start, you know. If it weren't for me, he wouldn't be where he is today. We had a deal. I got him started and then when he started winning, I fronted him the money to move up to the next level. I loaned him a bunch of money, even when I didn't have it. I sacrificed so he could pursue his dream, so to speak. I wanted him to be successful. He promised to pay me back every penny, but he hasn't paid nothin'!"

Williams stopped and put his hand on Paolo's arm again.

"You know I gave that boy everything he has, and he just treated me with the most disrespect. I wish someone would talk to him, and tell him how much I love him. I just wished he loved me..."

"Really. Is that why you abandoned him and his Mom and sister? Cut them off without a penny?" Once again Paolo disentangled himself from William's arm.

"You don't understand, boy. It wasn't me that left them. It was her that took off with the kids. She is a hard woman. You know, she has a little drinking problem, and I did everything I could to keep her on track, so to speak, but none of it worked. Then one day, she was gone. Just took off. What could I do? That was why I reached out to the boy and got him started in racing. I knew he needed something. Look where it has got him. I just wish he would pay me what he owes me. I need the money right now and I know he has it."

Williams looked at the ground and kicked his boot in the dirt. It was a melodramatic gesture. "Now this is how much I appreciate you and the Orly Mann bunch. If you were willing to speak to him and take my part, so to speak, I would be willing to pay you all a percentage of what he owes me. Could go right to you or the team and you could use it for whatever. I know you guys do a lot of charity stuff, helping people and whatnot. Just think of what you could do. All you would have to do is talk to him. It would be the right thing to do...you know it would. It is a fair offer. I want you to think about it. I'll catch you somewhere tomorrow. In the meantime, think about what I said. Especially when you are fixing the mess he made today."

With that, Williams grasped Paolo's hand and pumped it. Then he turned and strode away.

Paolo stood for a minute with both hands on his hips watching Williams walk away. Then he wiped his hand on his pant leg, put his hands in his pockets and walked toward the motor home lot. He didn't see T.K. step out of the shadows and head back into his coach.

- *O* -

Sometime later, Alicia pulled up in a golf cart in front of T.K.'s motor home. She tooted the little horn and a moment later, T.K. came down the stairs. She looked at him for a minute then laughed out loud.

"What? What are you laughing at?"

"I am laughing at you. You look like you are ready to go on stage with ZZ Top. No, I take it back. You look like Leon Russell. All you need is the bowler hat. I never saw such a bad looking beard! Where did you get that thing? It must be a foot long and white to boot, and the hair, oh my goodness."

"I borrowed it from Devin. I told you I didn't want to talk to anybody, so I am hiding out." T.K. said as he pulled up the hood on his jacket.

Alicia looked over at him, "If you are hiding out, why are you wearing your Blue Saber Team jacket that says T.K. on the front pocket?"

"It the only one I got with me, and I am cold. Besides, no one can see it in the dark. Come on girl, just drive."

- *O* -

The suite was like a muted oasis in the middle of the noise of the busy racetrack. It was warm and quiet, with one whole wall of windows that gave a bird's eye view of the pre-race activity of the pit lane below. The sound proof glass did a good job of keeping the noise outside, and the atmosphere was soft enough to carry on a normal conversation. In the middle of the room were a couple of buffet tables loaded with appetizing food and drinks that gave the room a nice smell and color. There were several television monitors located around the room, so no matter where one was sitting, they had a nice view of the track activity.

T.K. and Alicia made their entrance to the mixed greetings of the other team members. Alicia pulled T.K. over to meet Silas' mom.

"Hey T.K. this is Sarah, Silas' mom. Sarah, meet T.K."

Sarah looked at T.K. with a soft smile and said "My, I didn't realize race car drivers could be so…uh…hairy."

T.K. stammered and immediately pulled the wig off his head and the beard from his face. "Uh, sorry. I was just trying to hide a little. It's been one of those days, and it seems like everybody is after me." T.K. was stunned by her appearance. She wasn't spectacularly beautiful, but she projected an inner warmth and honest directness that made her incredibly attractive to him. He shook her hand, holding onto it a trifle too long as he smiled at her.

Alicia picked up on the chemistry immediately. "I'm going to leave you guys alone for a minute while I make a couple of calls. I think R.W. Coburn is going to join us along with some other people. Hey T.K., Silas is over in the corner with Orly. I know he wants to meet you."

"Alicia, you promised not a lot of people."

"It's okay, T.K., relax. It will be cool. Get the lady something to drink and settle down at one of the tables. If it gets too crowded, just put the beard back on."

- O -

Silas was sitting in a swivel chair with both elbows on the counter as he studied the pre-race action down below. Orly was slouched back in his own chair studying the boy beneath lowered eyelids. *The kid is sure thin*, Orly thought to himself. His hands were misshapen with oversize knuckles. Here he was complaining about his own burned hands, but they would heal. Silas' hands looked painful and swollen. He also looked like skin and bones. *There is hardly any meat on the boy*, thought Orly. He also looked like he was mulling something over in his mind. He glanced over at Orly and smiled sheepishly.

"You really are Orly Mann, aren't you."

"Yes, at least I was a minute ago, I guess I still am."

"That pretty lady sitting over there is your wife Hildy."

"Yup, Hildy is my wife, and she definitely is pretty."

"But you had another wife, and a little girl, right?"

Orly felt a stab in his chest. He paused, wondering if he could go there.

"Yes, I did. God saw fit to take them home to Himself and they died in a car accident." It was a difficult admission for Orly to make. It was not a subject that he could talk about easily, but he also had a sense that this conversation was going someplace, so he steeled himself.

Silas looked into Orly's face. "But you went on with your life and everything, didn't you. I mean you were sad and everything but …well, I mean…like you were okay, weren't you."

Okay? Orly thought to himself. Okay. That was a relative term. How could you describe the searing agony that came from loosing the two most precious things a man could have? Here one minute and gone the next. All due to another man who lost his job and saw fit to get drunk in the middle of the afternoon, then blast through a quiet neighborhood, ignoring stop signs and posted speed limits until he broadsided a mini-van, instantly killing a wife, a mother and her infant daughter. How did one describe the rending, crushing pain, the blind rage, the stifling grief that seemed to never end?

"Yeah, it took a while but it wasn't easy." Orly stopped as he saw a frown pass over Silas' face.

"Orly, are you afraid of dying?"

It was Orly's turn to frown. "Well Silas, to be honest, I don't think about it much. If I did, I wouldn't be doing what I do for a living. Racing cars is dangerous, you know that. Guys get hurt, look at me. If it wasn't for T.K., I might have gotten hurt real bad."

Silas wasn't going to let him get away with an easy answer. "No, I mean are you afraid of dying?"

Orly took a breath, "Silas, let me tell you something. When God allowed my family to die, or He took them home, I don't know which, I learned a great deal about living. At first I wanted to die too, but one day, all of a sudden, I realized how precious life really is. I decided after a while that I would do my utmost to live my life to the fullest with no regrets. I would make every day count for something positive for the Lord and His Kingdom 'cause I knew that was best for me. I think God has honored that. He gave me Hildy, and she is a most wonderful person. I am blessed and grateful that she is my wife." Orly paused.

"Now, if you are asking me if I am afraid of the physical process of dying, the answer is yes. I think every human being has that fear. It is put in us to make us respect the gift of life that comes from God. Now you and I both know what God's word says. We both know the Lord Jesus as our savior, right? Well, that means that when God calls us home we go to be with Him, and there certainly is no fear in that. It is a wonderful realization." Orly paused for a minute, studying Silas' face. "Whew boy, you are asking hard questions here. How come?"

"I told Dr. Miller that I wanted to talk with you because I thought you would listen to me and maybe help me, not because you drive race cars or you are famous and all, but because you…well, you know… you lost somebody, two people. I am what they call in the hospital somebody that is 'chronically ill', which means that I won't ever get any better, and I am just going to get worse." Silas stopped and looked into Orly's face. "They think I don't know, but I do. I spend a lot of time in the hospital with other kids, and kids hear stuff and tell each other things. We know more than the doctors and nurses think we do. I am not afraid of dying, in fact it might be better than hurting all the time."

Orly could see the tears forming in Silas' eyes.

"See, Orly, I am not afraid for me. I will be okay. Jesus will take care of me. I worry about my Mom. I am the only thing she has left. When I die, she will be all alone." Silas put both hands in the air with his palms out. "She doesn't have anybody else and it makes me very sad." Having said that, his thin shoulders slumped, and Silas began to softly cry. Tears rolled down his cheeks and dripped on his shirt.

Orly leaned over with his bandaged hands and wrapped his arms around Silas' fragile body. He slipped out of his chair and knelt next to the boy. He gently held him and patted his back while the boy sobbed with his head on his chest. Then, Orly spoke in a soft, quiet tone so only Silas could hear.

"Silas, we all die, it is a part of living. You know that. Your Mom will be sad, but she will be okay. God will see to that. In the meantime, you and I are alive. Tonight, right now we are breathing and living. Let's enjoy the moment. Tomorrow is a new day. We don't know what it will bring, but we know that our God is faithful to carry us through it. You are worrying about something that you can't control. You are a kid, be a kid. Let God worry about that other stuff. Mom will be fine and she will probably be dancing at your wedding some day. I want you to think of where you are. Hey man, you are in a suite at Texas Motor Speedway surrounded by a bunch of nice folks that think you are pretty special. We got a race to run on Sunday. We need your support up on that box. Now dry your eyes and let's get something to eat while we watch these truck guys go at it."

Orly sat back into his chair. "Oh yeah, and one other thing. I want you to know, Silas. I am your friend, and I always will be."

Sarah watched Orly and Silas from across the room. She couldn't hear their conversation, but she could see that it was serious. She was debating about whether to get up and go to Silas, and then Silas started to cry. She pushed her chair back.

"Wait." T.K. said, "Give him a minute. He is just being a man. Don't embarrass him. Orly will handle it. You can trust him, I guarantee it."

Sarah looked at him sharply, then her face softened. "Yes, I suppose you are right. If he wants me to know what is going on, he will tell me later." She paused for a minute. "How do you know I can trust Orly?"

"I just know. Some of us ...well, Orly is an easy guy to talk to."

- *O* -

Paolo and Doug rode the elevator up to the suite. The truck race was in full swing with the usual beating and banging that accompanied these hard charging drivers. They gave no quarter and asked for none.

The group in the suite was watching with a professional but detached perspective. This wasn't their gig, but at the same time, it was racing, and racing is always interesting. As a result, Doug and Paolo slipped into the room virtually unnoticed. They both headed straight to the buffet table and filled their plates with enormous piles of food.

Paolo dropped into a chair next to Alicia. "Hey girl, how you doing?"

Alicia started to answer when she was interrupted by a commotion at the door. R.W. Coburn rolled into the room accompanied by two young men who were obviously cowboys and most likely bull-riders.

His voice boomed across the room and shattered

the quiet calmness. "Howdy, ladies and gentlemen. We have come to pay our respects and to especially thank a couple esteemed members of the Orly Mann Racing Team for jumping in and pulling one of our cowboy bull-riders from the manure pile."

Paolo slumped down in his seat and kept eating while Doug grinned. He looked at Alicia. "Is there a back door outta this place?"

"Nope, you are stuck, Cowboy."

Coburn looked around the room and spotted Paolo. "There he is." He stood by Paolo and addressed the room.

"Ladies and gentlemen, we have a little something to show our appreciation for bravery above and beyond the call of duty, and also to welcome this young man into our fraternity."

One of the young cowboys produced a box the size of a dinner plate and handed it to Paolo. Paolo had no choice but to open it. He pulled off the lid and was greeted with a polished silver belt buckle fully ten inches across. It was covered in filigree and carried the PBR crest. Engraved on the buckle were the words:

Paolo Pelegrini
Genuine foot stompin', belly rubbin', afraid of nothin'
Bull Fighter

Paolo had no choice but to hold it up and show it to the room. There was a round of applause as he stood up and took a bow. He could see T.K. smirking at him. Coburn went on as the cowboy produced another box. "We have a second award for the young man that produced the pocket knife that allowed us to cut the rigging strap on the bull." They handed Doug the box. He dutifully opened it to find a belt buckle only slightly smaller than Paolo's. Engraved on it were the words:

MacGyver Award
For being ready in the midst of battle.

Doug stood up and took a bow, much like T.K. after his crash.

But Coleman wasn't done. He looked around the room and spotted T.K.

"Ladies and gentlemen, we have one more award. After the events of this day and the wild ride that this young man took this afternoon, we thought it was appropriate to award him with this presentation."

The other young man produced a box equal in size to the one given to Paolo and Doug, and laid it in front of T.K.

T.K. opened it and saw that it was indeed a beautiful silver belt buckle. Emblazoned across it were the words:

T.K. Kittridge
Best "Getoff"
Texas Motor Speedway

Coburn went on. "Now for you uneducated folks, a 'getoff' is a dismount from the bull. It is what a cowboy does, hopefully after eight seconds, when his ride is finished, or finished for him. He gets off, so to speak. Considering the circumstances, we thought T.K. here,"

Coburn patted T.K.'s shoulder, "had the best 'getoff' we have ever seen here at Texas Motor Speedway, and we wanted to award him accordingly."

Before Paolo, Doug and T.K. could say or do anything, they found themselves standing side by side in front of a photographer, holding their buckles and grinning foolishly for the camera.

As they headed back to their tables, T.K. leaned over to Paolo and said for his ears only, "So what kind of deal did you make with Willy? I saw you talking with him by the motor home lot."

Paolo's eyes flashed. He smiled a toothy smile for the room then said in a quiet voice "Let's step outside this room and I'll tell you. Then I am going to break your butt into six pieces. I have had it with you, Jerk! "

They both headed for the door with shoulders hunched and frozen faces. The exchange was not lost on Bear. He looked at Coburn, who nodded as they headed for the door as well.

Chapter Nine

"Remember, if life was perfect,
you wouldn't need roll cages in race cars."
Buddy Baker, retired NASCAR Driver.

Orly sat quietly in his motor home, watching the sun come up. He liked this time of day best. It was peaceful, and it gave him a chance to think and pray before the activity of the day. He had always been an early riser, even when he was a kid. He seldom if ever slept more than six or seven hours. He poured himself another cup of coffee and pondered the events of last night. His conversation with Silas had been sobering. The odds of the boy living to adulthood were slim.

He could be on borrowed time right now. He knew it. Orly knew it, and most certainly his Mom knew it. The reality was that it was in God's hand, and Orly was honest when he told the kid to live everyday and consider life a gift. It still didn't make it any easier to accept facts. Orly's reverie was interrupted as he heard Hildy get up and head to the bathroom. A few minutes later, she came staggering out, looking pale and drawn.

"Hey Babe, what's the matter? You sick? You don't

look so good."

"Yes, I'm a little sick. I knew I shouldn't have eaten those cucumbers last night. They didn't sit well."

"I am sorry, Hildy. Is there anything I can do for you?"

"No, I'm okay. I just need to sit for a few minutes." Hildy curled up in one of the overstuffed chairs, pulling her robe around her.

"So how did it end up last night? Did anybody lose any teeth? Personally, my money would be on Paolo." She was, of course, referring to the altercation between Paolo and T.K. in the suite during the truck race.

"Well, I didn't see much at all. I was watching the truck race with Silas. The next thing I know, Paolo and T.K. are heading to the door. Bear is right behind them, and old Coburn was right behind him. I figured that was enough so I stayed put. It all started right after you left. After awhile, Coburn and Bear came back, so I assumed it wasn't much, but I was wrong."

Orly got up and walked over to Hildy while he talked. He very gently felt her forehead. "You don't seem to have a fever. You sure you're okay? Seems like you've been sick a lot lately. Is that why you left so quick last night?"

"Yeah. I wasn't feeling very well. I'm better now. Go on, what happened next?"

"Well after we got Silas and Sarah home, I had a chance to talk with Bear. He said the guys were just about to tear into each other in the lobby when Dr. Miller walks right into the middle of them. He chews their tail feathers a bit, and that gave Coburn and Bear a chance to get between them and pull them apart. Bear took Paolo, and Coburn grabbed T.K. and settled things down. That's all I know for now. I imagine Paolo and Bear are working on the back-up car this morning, and T.K. will be getting ready for the happy hour practice session and the Nationwide race later on."

"So what was up with Silas? When I left, you two were in what appeared to be a very deep conversation."

"Yes it was heavy. The bottom line was that he knows he is dying and he is afraid to leave his Mom. He wanted to know how I got through the loss I suffered, and if he dies, will his Mom be able to carry on, so to speak."

Hildy stared at Orly with her mouth open. "How old is this boy again, and what is his prognosis?"

"He's thirteen, and he more than likely won't live past his early teens."

"According to Dr. Miller, and he should know, the kid has a disease called Juvenile Idiopathic Arthritis. There are three types, and Silas has the worst type. It's called systemic JIA. It works not only on the joints, which you can tell just by looking at him, but it works on the soft tissue as well. Internal organs, I guess. It has a lot of symptoms, and is pretty painful. One thing it does is cause inflammation, and that results in fevers, which put the kid down. That is why they worry about him getting enough rest."

"So what did you say to him, Orly?"

"Well, we talked about the Lord, and I essentially told him that life was a gift and to enjoy every bit of it. Which, when you think about it, is not so easy when you are in the kind of pain that he is. He is a solid believer though, and he trusts the Lord to carry him through. I built off of that to assure him his Mom would be okay. I did share with him that it took me awhile to get over the shock and the initial pain of what I lost, but I am able to deal with it in a healthy way. The pain is still there. I didn't tell him that, and I suppose it will always be there, but it happened and…well, life goes on. I have you now and that makes things a whole bunch easier."

"Are you okay, Orly Mann?"

"Yes, I'm okay, Hildy. You know I am."

"If I told you a secret, would you be okay then?"

"Hildy, what are you talking about? A secret? What kind of secret?" Then it hit Orly like a brick. The morning sickness that sometimes lasted all day, the mood swings…Hildy was pregnant. "You are pregnant, aren't you? You're going to have a baby."

"Yes, Papa, we are going to have a baby."

Orly fell into the chair, then immediately got up and walked over to take her in his arms. "Hildy, I am plenty okay. I couldn't be happier. I can't think of any greater joy! How long, I mean when, well, when is he or she due?"

Hildy smiled. She couldn't have asked for a better reaction. "I see the doctor on Monday when we get home. I will have a better idea then, but early May probably. Hey Orly Mann…you know twins run in my family."

- O -

The early morning darkness had given way to a brightening sun. The Blue Saber crew had already been hard at it for two hours. Paolo studied his laptop. He had a little bruise under his left eye from last night. A part of him was deeply engrossed as he peered at the setup notes and numbers. Another part of him was still angry over the confrontation with T.K. He should have broken the guy in half. He certainly could have. After T.K. threw that wild first punch, he could have nailed him in the solar plexus with a left hook and then taken his head off with a right cross. He didn't, though. Maybe he should have. *Heck of a way to start a Saturday morning*, he muttered to himself.

Bear was looking over his shoulder. Because he was much shorter, it was difficult. There was just too much to do. Paolo reached behind him with his right hand and gently pushed Bear backwards.

"For crying out loud, Bear, quit crowding and stop breathing on me. You ate too many of those garlic appetizers last night, and you're about to do me in." Bear ignored Paolo's comment.

"I think if we put a packer in the left front, we can always pull it later. It would give us some more adjustment. I also think we ought to go with the J7 left front shock. What do you think?"

Paolo didn't say anything for a minute. *He is really asking my opinion*, he thought to himself. Paolo turned and stared at the Blue Saber car. The crew had it up on jack stands with the wheels off, and two guys were laying on the floor underneath it, checking the bolts on the drive train. Two more guys were under the hood doing the final check on the recently installed engine. A fifth guy was wedged up under the right rear wheel well making adjustments on the track bar. There was little conversation. The only sounds were wrenches on bolts.

These guys all knew what they were doing. They had been working around and on top of each other for the better part of the season, and everybody knew what was supposed to be done. Besides, the coffee pot was empty, and the goal was to get done and get the car back to the track for tech so they could eat breakfast.

"Well, ordinarily, I would agree with you, but I have a hunch the track is going to change some. If we go with the J6 shock, it gives us more latitude later. The last thing I want is T.K. screaming in my ear." Paolo looked at Bear through tired eyes, "How long is that last session?"

"One hour."

"Not a lot of time to make changes. He needs the track time, so I can't keep bringing him in the garage. We both know he's going to be sore today. Not only physically from yesterday, but he is so mad at me, he can't see straight, and quite frankly, I wouldn't care if he fell off a bridge. No matter how we slice it, he's going to start at the back of the field. He needs handling to work his way through the pack. We need to dial him in for speed later in the race, but sheer speed isn't going to get him through the pack, but at the same time, we're going to need that speed later. We have to factor all that in. We also are going to have to hold him in check a little, so he doesn't kill the car initially and wear it down."

Paolo folded his arms. "Great Bear. You got a gimp for a driver and I have a hothead maniac. This ought to be a very interesting race tomorrow."

Just then Bear's cell phone went off in his shirt pocket. He looked at the number, then put it to his ear. "What do you want this early in the morning?" He looked over at Paolo and mouthed the word "Orly".

"Whaaat!? No kidding. Well, you sound pretty stoked. Congratulations! I am very pleased for you, Orly. What a blessing. Well, thanks for the call. Thanks, Orly." Bear clicked the phone off. "Make that a gimp whose wife is expecting a baby."

Paolo was deep in thought. "Yeah, let's go with the J6. I think that's best...Say what? Who? Orly?"

- O -

Sarah sat curled up in the big overstuffed chair beside the queen size bed in the back bedroom of the motor home. She was watching Silas sleep. He looked so small and frail in the middle of the oversize bed. He was lying on his side with his "blankie" clutched in his right hand. Even though he was thirteen, his blankie went everywhere with him. Particularly when he went to the hospital.

Some might think it odd that at his age he still had a so-called security blanket, but considering what he had been through, and what he still had to deal with, it was understandable. He never talked about it, but when he started feeling really bad, he looked for it. It was her job as his Mom to make sure it was available. It was part of the understanding that they had with each other. She knew that he relied on her a great deal and that was plenty okay. He always had, and she was more than willing to be there for him.

But now he was heading into adolescence with both feet, and he was seeking more and more independence.

It made her job increasingly difficult, but she was willing to give him space. *Being the single parent of this special young man has its challenges*, she thought to herself.

She shifted in the chair and checked her watch. Early morning. She was so glad he was having the time of his life. Everyone was bending over backwards to make this weekend so special. Actually, she was having a great time herself. She hadn't expected to, but she was enjoying the friendship and openness of the Orly Mann team. Especially a guy named T.K.

By the time she got Silas back to the motor home, it was late. Then even though it was late, T.K. dropped by and introduced himself to Silas. After the confrontation with Paolo, she was surprised to see him. But he told her that he had promised to meet Silas, and here he was. All three of them hit it off right from the get-go. Silas warmed to T.K.'s gentle kidding and easy laugh and so did she. She was surprised at her own reaction to this tall, handsome guy.

After she shooed Silas off to bed and got him settled, it seemed only natural to invite T.K. to stay for a cup of coffee. Silas was not the only one who found T.K. charming. They talked and talked and then talked some more. Then she fixed a late night snack and they continued to talk. It had been a long time since she had such a relaxing time with a man. The laughter was frequent and came easy. It was close to four in the morning before he drifted off to his own motor home.

He is handsome, she thought to herself. He was also attractive. He was just a few years younger, but to her, it seemed that he was very mature and that they had a great deal in common, home background and whatnot. She shook her head, and reminded herself that she already had a young man. Taking care of him was nearly a full time job, and she was committed to doing it the best way possible. She tucked the blankets around Silas, making sure to keep the blankie in his hand, then headed off to her own bed. She was just getting settled when her cell phone rang. It was T.K.

"I just wanted you to know that I really enjoyed spending time with you tonight." He hesitated. "You're easy to be with, and I like that a lot."

"Thanks, T.K. I enjoyed the time myself. Shouldn't you be in bed? I mean, don't you have a full day ahead of you?"

"Yeah, but I just wanted to hear your voice one more time. G'night."

"Good night, T.K." Sarah smiled as she closed her eyes. "T.K., what time do you have to be in the garage?"

"Couple of hours, I dunno, maybe three."

"Come by here in two hours and I will cook you breakfast."

- *O* -

Slick Willie got up, scratched, and stretched as he greeted the day. He looked around the messy motor home and contemplated making coffee. "Nah," he muttered out loud. He pulled his clothes on, and splashed water on his face and headed out the door. They had good coffee at the TxArm tent, and more than likely even had a couple or three donuts to go with it. Besides, it was free. He knew Miller wasn't serious when he told him not to come around.

A few minutes later, Willie was settled down at one of the white plastic tables under the tent with an extra large cup of coffee and a handful of donuts. A few feet away from him, Big Sam was sharing the morning devotion.

"Now folks, there are a number of things we can take away from this passage. God tells us through Luke (Luke 19:1-10) that Zaccheus was wealthy, a rich man. He had all he needed plus more in terms of worldly gifts, but he still lacked one thing. The most important thing a man needs, and that is a relationship with Jesus. Here was Zaccheus, a middle-aged man willing to climb up a tree to get a glimpse of the Savior. And you know what? The Savior responded. In fact, the Savior even came to his house for a meal. Pretty powerful stuff."

Blah, blah, blah thought Willie to himself. Willie was just gulping coffee when a well-dressed older man with a pure white Stetson hat sat down across from him. He reached out his hand.

"Howdy, R.W. Coburn here."

Willie took the hand and put on his best smile. This guy looked prosperous. Maybe he could sell him a car or borrow money, or sell him that ratty motor home or something. He was immediately sorry that he didn't take more time cleaning up before he claimed the free coffee. Should've shaved at least. "William Williams here. Glad to meet you. Where you from?"

"Oh mostly out of Oklahoma. I'm a stock broker... you know, rodeo stock."

Williams's eyes lit up. "So how is business in this lousy economy?"

"Fair to middlin'. We're holding our own for the

minute." R.W. looked over William's shoulder and could see that Sam was closing out his group with prayer. R.W. motioned for Williams to be silent for a minute.

"You don't believe all the righteous religious stuff do you? Successful business man like yourself."

R.W. looked across the table into Williams's eyes. "Yes I do, Slick Willie, and if you had any sense, you might stop and take stock of what God is saying to you. Yeah, don't look so surprised! I know exactly who you are and what you're up to. I spend a lot of time in the Phoenix area and everybody knows your reputation. It's time for you to make some changes. Big Sam there is talking about Jesus coming to Zaccheaus' house, and let me tell you something. He is knocking on your door. There are other ways to solve your problems, instead of hassling T.K. and trying to grab what isn't yours. If I was you, I would be very, very careful because you could just wind up back in the pokey. I imagine you think you're pretty clever, the way you have been talking to everyone and making your empty promises. My hunch is you are desperate and trying to work your situation out by whatever crooked way you can. I don't think it's gonna happen."

R.W. took a minute to sip a little coffee, then looked back at Williams.

"You see Willie, God has got your number, and all these folks you see gathered around here have been and will continue to pray for you. I can testify from my own life that prayer is mighty powerful. Yes sir, that is a fact."

Williams slid his chair back, and as he did so looked around the seating area under the tent. There were a number of people sitting at the white plastic tables, and many of them were looking directly at him. "I have to go," he said as he knocked over his chair and abruptly headed for open space.

"Let me tell you how it works, Willie. You can run from God but you sure can't hide," R.W. said to his back.

- O -

Bear was glad to be back at the track. The garage was open, and the place was rocking with activity. He stood in the background as he watched Paolo and the crew work the new car through tech. It was obvious Paolo knew what he was doing. Alicia was standing just off to the side with the proper paperwork on the clipboard and was quickly able to produce whatever was needed.

The NASCAR official was in Paolo's face saying, "Now boy, you know we are going to be watching you guys pretty careful. Also remember that we might be tearing you down after the race, so be prepared."

Paolo flashed a smile. "You bet. We understand. We're okay, everything is legitimate."

"Yeah, I've heard that before," said the official as he put the sticker on the car.

Paolo breathed a sigh of relief. Finally they were through the "room of doom" and they could push the car into their stall in the garage and act like real racers. At least they were back to square one, with a race car, anyway. Just how good it was remained to be seen.

A few minutes later, Bear and Orly came striding up

to Paolo in the garage area. Bear's face was cloudy with anxiety. He leaned over and said for Paolo's ears only,

"We got another little problem. Orly and me just come from the NASCAR trailer. T.K. is not going to be happy. Not happy at all. Devin has been suspended. He failed a random drug test. Somebody turned him in, they tested him and he failed. Bingo. They wouldn't say what he tested for but the test came up with an anomaly, and until they get it sorted out, he is in violation of section 12-1 of the rulebook. Guilty until proved innocent. That means he can't spot for T.K., and in fact, they won't even let him stay on the property. If the test shows a 'banned substance', then he loses his license for good and can't be reinstated until he completes a rehab program to NASCAR's satisfaction." Bear jammed both hands into his pockets. "Boy, I tell you Paolo, if it ain't one thing, it's something else."

Paolo said nothing and ignored Bear's obvious statement. He was surprised, but at the same time, he wasn't. Devon was a strange dude. He wasn't a racer. He didn't hang with anybody on the team and pretty much kept to himself. Nobody saw him during the week, and Paolo wasn't even sure where he lived. He just showed up at whatever racetrack was on the schedule and went to work. Apparently he and T.K. were kin. Family. T.K. wanted him to spot for him, and Bear acquiesced. Rumor had it that it was even in T.K.'s contract. Done deal.

The issue now was who was going to spot for T.K. this weekend. Spotting wasn't easy. More importantly, it had to be somebody who knew what they were talking about and it had to be somebody that T.K. trusted. A spotter was literally the eyes of the driver and couldn't afford to make a mistake in the heat of battle. When the spotter said "go low or go high" the driver had to respond instantly. Particularly when a race car was traveling near 200 miles per hour.

"Well, you guys know we only have one choice, and that's Doug. The big issue is whether he and T.K. can communicate. Gonna be tough enough for him and me to work together, let alone Doug, although he and Doug don't have the history I have with him."

About that time, Doug and T.K. came sauntering into the garage area. Doug had his laptop under his arm and a cup of coffee in the other hand. He was listening intently as T.K. was talking into his ear. T.K.'s conversation was punctuated with hand gestures for emphasis. Doug was nodding his head, indicating that he understood what T.K. was communicating.

As they got closer, Paolo heard T.K. say "That's what I need you to do. I think it will work. I trust you. You're a pretty savvy guy."

Bear listened for a minute then spoke, "I'm going to assume you have heard from Devin."

"Yeah I did. Early this morning. It isn't what you think. He took some cold medicine and it messed up the test. He also takes stuff for his asthma. Devin doesn't do drugs. I guarantee you they'll sort it out this week and he'll be back for Phoenix next week. We all know who turned him in. If NASCAR gets what they think is a legitimate tip, then they have to act. It only makes sense. In the meantime, I asked Doug here if he would spot for me. I think Doug is sharp, and he knows what he's doing. If you say it's okay, Bear, he'll do it."

Bear cleared his throat. "Uh hum, I don't have a problem with it, but I think you better clear it through your crew chief there." He motioned to Paolo, who stood with his arms folded.

"Yes, you're right. Excuse me, Paolo, I didn't mean to go around you. Hey listen, I want to say a couple of things right here, right now, in front of everybody. First, I want to apologize to you, Paolo, for last night. I spoke out of turn. I felt like an idiot after wrecking two cars and the way Willie has been hounding me…well, I just cracked and ran my mouth. I'm sorry I said what I said and I also am sorry I threw that punch. I'm awful glad you didn't hit me back. You might have killed me." T.K. stuck out his hand.

Paolo unfolded his arms and took the proffered hand. "No problem man, we are all a little beat from the schedule, and the way things have been coming down. Apology accepted."

Paolo dropped T.K.'s hand and looked him in the eye. "Hey T.K. I want you to understand something. We are a team. We are in this together, and I am the crew chief and I have got my driver's back. I will do everything I can to take care of him…and that's you. All of us understand the crap you have been dealing with and all of us have been doing our best to protect you. We are on your side." Paolo stuck out his hand again. "Now driver, we have our work cut out for us. Climb in that car and tell me what we have for tomorrow and what changes you want us to make." Paolo's words were punctuated by the sound of high-powered engines thundering to life as the crews started warming the cars for the final practice session.

Bear and Orly headed for the Speed King car. "Man, that is a turn-around," said Orly into Bear's ear. "What got into that guy? Talk about an answer to prayer."

"Yeah, I'll say. I think a lady named Sarah has a lot to do with it."

"No kidding," said Orly as he carefully placed his injured leg through the window and worked himself into the car.

Ten minutes later, T.K. was smiling to himself as he exited turn four into the dogleg. The car was good. No, excellent was a better word. They made a few minor tweaks and the thing got even better. That in itself was very encouraging. Sometimes you could adjust all day on a car and it wouldn't or couldn't get any better. They would have their work cut out for them tomorrow, coming from the back of the field, but if he was patient and chose his openings carefully, they could do it.

Doug's voice echoed in his ear. "Lap 15 on this run. Times are looking good. High 28's low 29's, which pretty much puts you at the top of the leader board."

"Check."

"If you're ready, T.K., bring it in. No sense in wearing it out. We want to check fuel mileage, anyway."

"Check. I'll bring it in. I'm happy." And indeed he was happy. Ecstatic might be a better word. The boys had done a great job. Now if he could just do his part and keep things clean, they just might be okay.

Orly and Bear in the meantime were also pleased. Orly was satisfied with the Speed King car's performance. He and Bear had decided that the best strategy for tomorrow would be to try to stay up front as long as they could. Maybe, if the opportunity allowed, even lead for a while and stay out of trouble in the clean air. That was the plan, anyway. Sometimes things happened, but then, that was racing. After a ten lap shakedown run, they brought the car into the garage and covered it up.

- O -

Silas was watching the practice session on the big screen TV in the motor home with his radio earpiece monitoring T.K. and Orly. Finally the practice session finished.

"Silas, how are you feeling?"

"I feel good Mom, stop worrying. I'm fine." It was a lie. Actually he didn't feel very good at all. He felt a little flushed and just a tad bit achy, but he wasn't going to tell anybody. Orly and Hildy had promised to watch the Nationwide race with him, and maybe even Bear, and he wasn't going to miss that. Besides, the Cup garage closed at 1:30 and nobody could work on their cars after that.

"Are you sure you're okay?"

"Mom."

"Okay, okay. Well, I wanted to ask you something. T.K. has invited me to go with him to a ranch in Pilot Point that is owned by a friend of Mr. Coburn for a barbecue this afternoon. Apparently, a number of people have been invited. You could come with us or you could stay here with Orly and Hildy and watch the race. Or I could just stay here with you."

The truth was Sarah was feeling guilty about leaving Silas, but being with T.K. for the afternoon in a social setting with other people seemed so attractive. It had been a long time since she had gone out on a date.

Silas stopped looking at the TV and turned to his Mom. "You like T.K., don't you Mom."

Sarah was taken aback. "Well, he is fun to be around and he likes you, too. It is just an afternoon thing with a bunch of other people. Like I said, you could come with us."

"Nope. You go Mom. I will be fine. I want to see this race." Silas smiled, "and hey Mom, I like T.K., too. He is a good guy."

Sarah smiled. "You're sure you will be okay? You can call me. I don't know how far it is, but I'm sure I can be back in a short time if you need me."

"Mom."

- O -

"So I was wondering if you were real busy this afternoon? I mean there are a lot of things we could be doing around the racetrack. Going over stuff and what not."

Paolo was talking with Alicia on his cell, and he was nervous. He wasn't quite sure why he was nervous, and he didn't have any reason to be nervous, but somehow, he was. They had been friends for a long time, but just lately, things had changed. The step up to a crew chief position, even though it might not be permanent, had changed his perspective on things.

"Are you suggesting that we get together and work this afternoon?"

"No, Alicia. I'm not. That isn't at all what I had in mind. T.K. and Sarah have been invited to a barbecue

205

out in Pilot Point, wherever that is, and he has asked me to come and bring somebody. I was wondering if you wanted to go. I mean there is a lot of stuff that I could be doing….but I don't want to. I'm tired, and I want to get away for a while, so I was wondering…"

"Why, Paolo, are you asking me out on a date?"

"Yeah, Alicia, I am. I can't think of anybody else that I would like to spend the afternoon with. No racing talk. Just you and me. So how about it?"

- O -

Slick Willie sat casually in a lawn chair across the street from the competitor's motor home lot. He was waiting for inspiration. He was innocuous in the crowd of people that hung around gawking at the lot. Everybody wanted to get a glimpse of their favorite driver or celebrity. He was interested in only one.

There had to be a chink in the armor somewhere. He thought he might have been able to work with Devin, but that had gone nowhere, even though he threatened the guy. (In a nice way, of course.) Then just like he promised him, he made an anonymous call to NASCAR and they followed up with a test. The TxArm people were no help. They were more of a hindrance, especially with all that prayer garbage. That guy Coburn was pretty heavy weight. Boy, he misjudged that guy.

So far nobody on the Orly Mann team was willing to even listen to him. One crew guy even threatened him and told him to quit hanging around, acting like he was connected or something. There had to be a way.

There was a stir in the crowd as Paolo and Alicia

pulled up to the gate in a golf cart. The security guard let them in and they motored down to T.K.'s coach. He came out the door, and then they stopped at another coach. Willie watched as the attractive lady came out the door, smiling. She climbed in the cart beside T.K. and they were off. Once they were out of the gate, they headed to the helicopter pad. thought Willie to himself as a plan began to form. *There might be a way after all.*

Chapter Ten

"Yes we spend a lot of time traveling. Is it fun? Well sort of, but after a while even private airplanes get pretty cramped. Every so often I wake up in a hotel room and have to remind myself what city I am in."

Alicia Chen, Publicist for the Orly Mann Team.

When Sarah climbed into the golf cart, she had no idea where exactly they were headed. She still had misgivings about leaving Silas, but he kept reassuring her that he would be fine. Orly and Hildy showed up ten minutes before they were to leave, and they too reassured her things would be plenty okay.

The suspense was killing her. Finally Sarah leaned over to T.K. and said "where are we going? I thought we were off to Pilot Point to a barbecue. Are we going there by golf cart?"

"We are, sort of." T.K. laughed "We're headed to the chopper pad to catch our ride."

"You mean we're going there by helicopter?"

"Yeah, sure. I was told that it's just a short jump. No traffic. Easy as pie." T.K. felt her stiffen beside him. He looked over at her. "Don't tell me you've never been on a helicopter or that you're afraid of flying?"

"Yes, or I mean no, I have never been on a heli-copter, and no I am not afraid of flying, although I haven't done much of it. I'm used to getting in the car and driving myself somewhere."

"You will like it, I guarantee. See, there it is waiting for us. Looks like a Bell Long Ranger. A six-seater. They're pretty comfortable. It'll be a nice flight. Helicopters aren't the smoothest things in the world, but you get used to it. " T.K. put his arm around her shoulders. "Look, we fly all the time. With the way we travel, we have to. It's no big thing."

Sarah disentangled his arm. "Maybe for you."

T. K. was embarrassed. "I'm sorry Sarah. I didn't mean to be crowding your space. I was just trying to reassure you. Here, let me hold your hand instead."

Sarah reached out and took his hand. "Sorry, this is all so new to me. I'm not used to what you folks do and how you travel so much. By the way, how are you feeling? No residual injuries or anything?"

"No, nothing but the regular aches and pains. Actually I'm just a little sore, but nothing unusual."

Alicia leaned over the seat. "I know exactly how you feel, Sarah. It took me a long time to get used to living out of a suitcase. It really makes you appreciate the time when you're not on the road."

Paolo parked the cart and they hopped out. He put his arm around Alicia as they headed to the chopper and said something in her ear. She laughed and punched him gently in the shoulder. Even though there was a great disparity in their size, Sarah was struck by how natural they looked together. There was an easy familiarity between them.

"Have they been a couple for a long time?"

T.K. responded "Yeah, practically forever. He just hasn't figured it out yet."

- *O* -

Doug was back in the hotel room that he shared with Paolo. It seemed like he shared everything with Paolo. They lived together in Charlotte in a very sweet condo fairly close to the shop.

He was deep into his laptop watching video of the past Texas races. In the meantime, the butterflies were doing barrel rolls in his stomach. He was trying to assimilate as much information as he possibly could. He hadn't spotted much in his career, even though he grew up in the stock car world.

The practice session went okay and T.K. seemed satisfied, but that was practice. Tomorrow would be a race with forty-three aggressive drivers pushing and shoving and fighting for position. Twelve of those drivers were in the chase and absolutely desperate for points. This would more than likely be a very aggressive race with a lot of contact and risk taking.

Doug was having a hard time staying focused. His mind kept returning to Paolo. Yeah, they were best friends and had been for a number of years ever since they met at Sears Point, (which they now call Infineon). He probably knew Paolo better than anybody, even though they were radically different.

Paolo was west coast all the way while Doug was a good ole' southern boy that grew up in North Carolina.

They even looked different. Paolo was a big guy, thick through the shoulders and strong as an ox. Doug, on the other hand, was thin and tall. When Paolo and T.K. got into it last night, Doug was certain there was going to be blood and mayhem. Paolo was really angry, and if he ever got his hands on T.K., the guy would have gone home on a gurney.

Fortunately, Paolo got a hold of himself when Bear and R.W. Coburn stepped between them. *Thank goodness,* thought Doug. The responsibility of being a crew chief had already begun to change Paolo, or maybe it was just part of the aging process. Growing up and all that rot. Doug didn't know and didn't care all that much. He just knew Paolo was different than he had been just a few days ago.

He got back to thinking about the issues at hand. With only three races to go in the Chase, it looked to Doug's experienced eye like the Chase was narrowing down to five teams. The point spread for sixth on back would make it difficult for those guys to catch up. There just weren't enough races left, even if they won all three.

But those five teams with a chance of winning all the marbles would be pushing the limits in every way possible. It was going to be tough, especially considering that two of those teams were coming out of the Orly Mann shop.

Doug knew the "racin' bidness," as Bear liked to say, and he also said that Doug had an intuitive streak in him that was amazing. He could almost predict the outcome of a race before it was run. Doug wasn't sure that was right, but he did have a good feel for what was going on. He was an observer by nature, and he had trained himself to keep track of everything during the course of a race. He could generally tell you who had stopped for fuel and who needed to, who was in need of tires and who was pushing way too hard and wouldn't be able to keep up the pace.

A race was like a good book. It had a beginning, a middle and most of all, an exciting conclusion. Maybe his ability to keep track of everything would help him in spotting for T.K. He sure hoped so.

Stock car racing was second nature to Doug. His father was a long time crewman for Orly and Bear, and had been with them practically as long as they had been in business. Doug grew up around the racetrack and the shop.

He had been knee deep in race cars and stock car racing his whole life. After high school, he took a break and went off to college to get his degree, but it seemed only natural to come back to work for the Orly Mann team full time. Bear was like an uncle to him.

Doug's Dad was retired now and didn't travel much. He was fighting a tough battle with cancer. Doug's Dad still had all his marbles, as he liked to say about himself, but there wasn't anybody, except maybe Bear, that knew more than his Dad did. He checked his watch. He would give him a call later on and pick his brain a little. Maybe he could give him a couple of tips about dealing with T.K.'s volatile personality.

In the meantime, Doug was practically living in Jimmy's pocket. Jimmy was Orly's spotter, and he too had been around the business a long time. He was a slow-talking Texan and seldom if ever got rattled by anything. That was why Orly liked him to spot for him.

But Orly's style and T.K.'s were radically different.

Orly was a guy who drove with his head and seemed to know what moves to make a long time before he made them. T.K., on the other hand, was what one might call "intuitive". He made the move, then thought about it. Doug was going to have to stay on his toes to stay ahead of this guy.

His stomach lurched again. *Time to take a break*, he thought to himself. He slammed the laptop shut and got up and walked around the room. Maybe he should have gone with Alicia and Paolo to the barbecue. Nah. No way. He was tired of being a third wheel or whatever they called it. He wasn't going to play that gig anymore.

Alicia was in love with Paolo, and he was in love with her. Pure and simple. Doug had known that for years and had been telling Paolo at every opportunity. Then one day, Paolo unloaded on him, and threatened to tear his head off if he didn't shut up. Doug could see that he was serious so he shut up. Last night was different.

Everybody's emotions were high and when they finally got back to the room, he cut loose and let fly. He flat out told Paolo to get with the program and get serious or he was going to lose Alicia one day soon. Some guy was going to come in and sweep her off her feet, and she would be gone. Paolo better make some decisions about what he was going to do with the rest of his life. He was fully prepared to have Paolo beat him to a pulp, but he didn't. Paolo didn't fire back at him and tell him to shut up or pound salt or mind his own business like he had every other time he said something.

Paolo got a pensive look on his face and simply

replied "yeah, you're right." Then he called her up and invited her to the barbecue. *Could have knocked me over with a feather*, Doug thought to himself. His intuition told him that he might be looking for a new roommate one day here pretty soon. In the meantime, he was going to head over to Silas' motor home and watch the Nationwide race with Bear and Orly. They might learn something for tomorrow.

Doug checked his watch then picked up his cell phone.

"Hey Dad, how you feeling?"

- O -

Silas sat huddled in the big overstuffed chair with a blanket wrapped around him. He was having the time of his life. Orly was sitting on the couch close to him. Bear was pacing back and forth. Everyone's attention was on the Nationwide race, which had turned out to be one of the most competitive ever. The big screen TV gave them a bird's eye view of the broadcast. Bear had brought a scanner so they could copy the conversations between the drivers and the crews. Doug was sitting on the floor next to Silas' chair.

It was down to crunch time with twenty-five laps left. Somebody had cut a tire and left some debris on the track, bringing out a much needed yellow. The field was currently idling behind the pace car, waiting for the pits to open.

"What do you think, Bear? Do we come in for tires as well as fuel or do we just take a little splash and go? Seems like everyone up front needs a little gas to finish the race so everyone has to pit. Might just get two. Depends on how your car is handling."

Bear replied, "Yeah, if you're tight, two tires might make you more tight. Don't know. Hey Doug, what do you think, being as you are a big time spotter now?"

"I would just tell my driver to pay close attention to whatever the crew chief decides." In the meantime he nudged Silas and held up nine fingers and mouthed the words "no stop needed."

"Nah, uh, not everyone has to stop. The nine car just came in a few laps ago and got fuel and tires. He has enough to finish the race. He could stay out and hold his track position, and if nobody else gets tires, he might have a big advantage with fresh rubber. Twenty five laps is a lot." Silas smiled as he spoke. Both Bear and Orly looked at Doug, who did his best to look innocent. Silas laughed.

"Boy, I tell you Bear, this kid here, Silas, is getting pretty smart. We better keep an eye on him."

Hildy was in the kitchen bustling around, replenishing the snack supply. While everyone else was watching the race, she was watching Silas. She didn't like what she was seeing. His cheeks were pink, and he kept hugging the blanket around his thin shoulders like he was cold.

Sarah had left explicit instructions along with the little medical bag and his meds. She rummaged around until she found the digital thermometer. She took the tray of goodies out and sat it on the table, then casually walked over to Silas. She pushed the hair off his forehead and put her cheek next to his skin. At the same time she touched the thermometer to his ear. Yes, he did indeed feel warm. She waited for the instrument to beep.

She spoke softly to him. "You okay, Silas? Are you getting a fever?"

He looked up into her eyes. He could have lied, but it wasn't in his nature to do so. Besides, he liked Hildy a lot and felt that he could trust her. He too spoke softly. "Yeah, I think one is coming, and it feels like a big one. When is my Mom coming home?"

"In a couple of hours, but if you want, I could call her and she could come sooner."

"No, don't do that. I'll be okay."

"Are you sure?"

"Yes."

"Here comes the restart. Silas, you were right. The nine car stayed out. Look at him, he has taken the lead, and pulled out from the pack. How did you figure that out?"

"Just smart, I guess. I want you to remember this, Bear, when I come looking for a job in a few years."

- *O* -

Sarah was having a great time. She couldn't remember when she had a better time. The helicopter ride was, if nothing else, exhilarating. It was an experience to see the whole of the Speedway and truly get a picture of just how many people were camped around the track. The crowd was starting to funnel in for the Nationwide race and she could see the race cars lined up in the pit lane. T.K. was pointing out various landmarks to her, and she found herself enthralled by the spectacle of it all. What an experience, flying through the air above everything.

When they landed, R.W. Coburn and the owner of the ranch greeted them. R.W. was his usual, effusive self. Come to find out, the barbecue was a small affair with just essentially the four of them as guests. R.W. had seen to that. They started out with a horseback ride along a beautiful trail out into the backcountry. At first Paolo, wasn't going to get on the horse, but they talked him into it. After ten minutes, he was learning to let the horse lead and stopped trying to steer it.

Sarah was delighted to be on a horse again. It had been a long time and she had forgotten how relaxing and fun it could be. T.K. and Alicia were natural riders and looked comfortable from the get go. By the end of the ride, they were ready to eat, and the steaks were melt in your mouth perfect. It couldn't have been a more beautiful afternoon. Even the Texas weather cooperated. They were ready for dessert when her cell phone vibrated in her pocket. She excused herself to answer it.

As she fumbled with the phone and saw the number she felt an overwhelming sense of guilt.

"How high is it, Hildy? Okay, that isn't too bad. How is he feeling? I mean is he lethargic? Is he still talking?" She listened intently to Hildy's description trying to evaluate Silas' condition over the phone. "Okay. Sometimes they just come and go. Give him that one med I showed you and wait a half hour or so, then check him again if you don't mind." Sarah checked her watch. "I will call you back in thirty minutes. I don't know what our time frame here is, but I will find out."

She put the phone back in her pocket as her eyes

clouded with tears. *I probably shouldn't have left him. I just wanted to have a little fun for a few minutes. Why Lord oh why?* She dried her eyes on her sleeve and gathered her wits as she started to head back to the table. Just then her phone vibrated again. Thinking it was Hildy, she snatched it out and answered it quickly with thoughts that Silas' condition had suddenly deteriorated.

"Hello."

"Is this Sarah Biggs?"

"Yes, who is this please?"

"Ms. Biggs you don't know me, but I would like a few minutes of your time. I feel that I need to impart some information to you and then perhaps you might help me procure something."

"Help? How can I help you? What kind of information? What are you talking about? Who is this please?"

"I'm going to come by your coach this evening at 11:00 PM. I will knock twice, and I think it prudent that you let me in. It would also be wise that you tell no else about my visit."

"I will do no such thing. If you show up, I will call the police. Now who is this, and what do you want with me?"

"Now calm down, Ms. Biggs. It has come to my attention that you have been consorting with a certain T.K. Kittridge. Mr. Kittridge is not at all who he might appear to be, and in point of fact, he is a dangerous individual with a checkered past. You would do well to protect yourself while in his company. I also happen to have film of him leaving your motor coach at approximately, actually, exactly at 4:37 in the morning. I wonder what might happen if that film was passed on to the Reverend of your little church and several others in key leadership positions? Particularly when it is coupled with the facts of Kittridge's background. I am sure that certain senior ladies of the congregation might be a little disappointed in your behavior."

Sarah felt her anger rising. "Listen, you jerk! What are you doing spying on me? And oh, by the way, welcome to the 21st century! It is none of your business whether Mr. Kittridge and myself are 'consorting', as you say and, 'in point of fact' nothing happened between us. If you knock on my door, I will have you arrested."

"Have it your way, Ms. Biggs. I understand that you have a young son, born out of wedlock, no doubt, who is quite ill. Perhaps a call to the Child Protection Agency in your hometown might be prudent. I am sure you are doing all that you can, but a thorough government inspection might be in order. You see, Ms. Biggs, I think it is important that you talk with me."

This latest threat took the air from Sarah's lungs and left her speechless. She was the best mom to Silas that she could possibly be. She had educated herself to help him with his disease and knew more about practical nursing than a good deal of medical people. But, she was still a young, single Mom doing her best to support them both. In this day and age, these kinds of threats were terrifying. When he was young, there were indeed those who questioned her ability to give him the kind of care he needed.

"Until 11:00 this evening then. Thank you for your time."

The phone went dead. Sarah quickly looked for

the number but found only "unknown caller" on the message screen. She was shocked by the call. At first, the threats were overt, but then the caller had gotten specific.

What was up with that? Did T.K. have a dark side? She really didn't know much about him. She felt a knot of fear building in her stomach. The longer the man talked on the phone, the more threatening he became. The only things she knew about T.K. were what they had talked about last night. Who knew if he was lying or not? That and that Silas might be developing a fever overwhelmed her. Sarah had to get her priorities straight.

Suddenly, she felt an overwhelming sense of urgency to get back to Silas as quick as possible. She probably shouldn't have come anyway. Sarah fought the feeling down and prayed a quick prayer. She knew Silas was perfectly okay with Hildy and Orly. They would take good care of him. She took a few deep breaths, then camouflaged her feelings and did her best to pull herself together. Then she headed back to the table.

T.K. and Paolo were sharing some sort of joke, both of them laughing softly. Alicia was looking fondly at Paolo. She turned and glanced at Sarah as she slid the chair back and sat down. Sarah saw her brow furrow as she studied her with her dark eyes.

"Everything okay?" she asked.

"Uh, yeah. It was Hildy, and maybe Silas is developing a fever…but I had her give him some medicine to see if that helps. I'll call her in a little while to see how he's doing."

"Hey, she didn't say who won the Nationwide race,

did she?" T.K. asked.

"No, she didn't say a word. Is that all you race car drivers think about? Racing, I mean?" There was a slight edge to her words. She excused herself and headed to the Ladies room.

She was standing at the sink splashing cold water on her face when Alicia came in and stood beside her. "Sarah, what's going on?"

"Nothing. I am just worried about Silas, that's all." Sarah paused for a minute, then swallowed and took a risk. "Alicia, can I trust you?" She looked at Alicia's reflection in the mirror.

Alicia looked back and said simply "Yes."

"After I got the call from Hildy, I got another call from a man. I don't know who he was. He said he wanted to talk with me, and that there were certain things I needed to know about T.K. He wants to come to the coach at 11PM tonight. Then he threatened me, and quite honestly, I'm a little afraid."

Alicia smiled. "Yeah, I wondered when he would get to you. He sure didn't waste much time. Did he sound like maybe he was in his fifties, and did he start out smooth and then get rougher as the conversation went on?"

Sarah thought a minute. "Yes, that is exactly what he did. Do you know this man?"

"Yes, we all do. His name is William Williams, better known as Slick Willie. He is firmly convinced that T.K. owes him a pile of money…well it is a long story. He was T.K.'s sort of stepfather, but he abandoned the family when T.K. was a teenager. He was incredibly abusive, and now he has a shady auto dealership or something in Arizona. He has tried to work practically everybody on the team to cooperate with him in pressuring T.K."

"Is he dangerous?"

"I don't know, how do you judge? I don't think he would actually hurt anybody physically, but who can say. At any rate, we need to put him out of business. Don't do anything or say anything to anybody yet, especially T.K. He will go crazy and that won't help right now. When we get back to the track, I'll make a phone call. I know two guys that will take care of this once and for all. This has gone on long enough and this guy is going down!" Alicia patted Sarah on the back. "Dry your eyes and put a smile back on your face. We will fix this, trust me." Alicia was getting angry.

"Alicia, is there anything that I should know about T.K.? I mean, well, you know what I mean. That guy said…"

Alicia interrupted. "Let me tell you something, Sarah. T.K. is exactly what he appears to be. I have known him for a couple of years and he is the nicest, sweetest guy that you would want to meet. Sometimes, he is cocky and he can be arrogant, but underneath it all, he is genuine. I like him a lot, and I think he has fallen head over heels for you in a very short time. He thinks you're very special, and I don't know what you guys talked about all night, but it had a profound effect on him."

Alicia paused, considering her words. "I am jealous of you. If I wasn't meant to be with Paolo, I would give you some competition."

"I don't know what to say. I just met the guy and

we sort of instantly hit it off. He listened when I talked, and he seemed genuinely interested in me. I listened to him, but he really didn't share all that much. I want to know more about him. What makes him who he is. We mostly laughed and talked."

Sarah wiped her eyes. "He seemed to have genuine empathy for Silas and for me taking care of him like he really understood what was going on. I felt like he liked me for who I was. For me, that was unusual. Usually a guy takes a look at Silas and hits the road." Sarah started to cry again.

"Alicia, you people don't understand. You travel all over and go here and there. You live in nice places, and you have exciting lives…We can't do that. Silas needs to be close to his doctors and the hospital that knows how to treat him. Besides, I don't know how much time he has left, and my job is to do my best to care for him. I don't know why God gave us this burden, but he is my child, and he has to come first."

Sarah wiped her eyes, and blew her nose. "I probably shouldn't have even come today, and now I have some maniac that is coming to my house tonight."

"All right, Sarah, that is enough of the pity party. Suck it up! You had a good time, didn't you? Sure, you did. You know as well as I do that God never promises any of us more than one day at a time."

"Yes, I know that, and that is what T.K. and I mostly talked about."

"Well, maybe you can finish that conversation soon, but in the meantime, we have to take care of the 'maniac', as you call him. Rightly so, I think."

Thirty minutes later, Sarah was on the phone again

to Hildy. "So how is he doing?" She listened as Hildy explained that he was about the same. He wasn't eating anything, and his cheeks were still flushed, but his temperature was about what it was before.

"Okay. We're heading back in a little while, so I will be there pretty soon. Thank you, Hildy, for keeping your eye on him. I really appreciate it."

Chapter Eleven

"It has been said that we need three things to make our lives complete: something to do, something to look forward to and most of all, someone to love. I got all three in bushel baskets. I couldn't be happier."

Paolo Pellegrini, NASCAR Crew Chief

Paolo and Alicia dropped T.K. and Sarah off at her motor coach.

"Where do you want to go, pretty lady?" Paolo said.

"I probably should head over to the media center and pick up some stuff, then I need to meet Carol a little bit later and get set up for tomorrow." Alicia said as she brushed her hair out of her eyes.

"Did you have a good time today, Alicia?"

"Yeah, Pally, I really did. It has been a long time since we were on a date."

"I know, way too long. I don't know what's going on with me. Maybe being a crew chief has made me see things differently, I guess. All of a sudden, I feel like I've turned a corner or something. I dunno, hard to say." Paolo pulled the cart over next to the gate to the media center and shut it off.

"Alicia, I want to say something to you. I think I've always taken you for granted. I'm sorry for that. It wasn't fair to you or to myself, either." Paolo looked into her face. "I just want you to know that I think you are incredibly special, and I had the best time today because I was with you."

Alicia smiled. *He is doing it to me again. Just one look, the right combination of words and I fall in love with him all over again, she thought.* "Thanks, Pally, I had a wonderful time myself. We always have a good time together. We always have and I hope we always will." She started to gather her stuff to get out of the cart. "I have to go."

"Yeah, I know. It is the 'will' part I want to talk about. The future." Paolo gently put his hand on the side of her face and softly kissed her on the lips. It wasn't their first kiss, by any means, but it was by far the most significant. "I love you, Alicia."

Alicia put her arms around his neck and whispered in his ear, "I love you, Paolo. Let's get through this weekend, then we can talk." Then she kissed him quickly on the lips once again and slipped out of the cart. "See you later."

He watched her walk up to the gate. It was like seeing her brand new or for the first time all over again. She turned and gave him a smile with a little wave.

"Stay a while." Sarah said to T.K. "I had a wonderful day. It has been so long since I was on a horse. I really enjoyed it."

"I'm glad you did, Sarah. I had a good time as well. Gave me a chance to relax a bit and not think about race cars and the Chase, and the whole racing thing."

"Is it hard, racing cars? I mean, what is it like? Will you be nervous tomorrow after crashing like you did?"

"No. You just have to put it out of your mind. I'm still alive, I mean here I am, all in one piece. I don't think about that part of it much. If I did, I probably wouldn't do it. Just part of the game. I think about winning and what it would mean to the team and me to win the Championship. It would be something that no one could ever take away from me. To be the best… You know."

Sarah didn't know, but she was doing her best to try to understand. "So if you win the championship, what will that mean to your future?"

"It will mean a lot of things. It will mean that I am one of the best drivers out there and all that, but it will also mean millions of dollars and everything that goes with that. The appearances, the endorsements. All that stuff."

"Don't you already have a lot of money? I mean I'm just trying to understand why you would risk your life for more."

Before T.K. could answer, Silas came out of the back bedroom where he had been resting. "Hey Mom, I have to get ready to go now."

T.K. could see Sarah shifting focus. "Silas, you know better. You aren't going anywhere. It is really starting to cool off, and you shouldn't be out there in the wind."

"Mom, you don't understand. I have to be there. My car is the fastest and they are going to start the racing in fifteen minutes. Please Mom, let me go." Silas was pleading with Sarah while T.K. stood by and said nothing.

"Silas, I know this is important to you. But listen to me. If you're going to watch the race tomorrow from Orly's pit box or whatever they call it, you have to rest. You know how these things work. You have a little bit of a fever, and we don't want it to get any worse."

Silas did indeed know how these things worked. He knew that he probably shouldn't go. He was really starting to feel rotten, but he had worked long and hard on the pinewood racer. He had it painted up real nice in Orly's colors and he was sure that it was going to be a winner. It was traditional for TxArm to run a pinewood derby on Saturday evening with trophies for the winner and everything. This was a chance in a lifetime. It was worth being sick a little to compete...but Mom was having none of it. Then he had an idea.

He turned to T.K. "T.K., you are a race car driver right?"

"Yes, I suppose I am."

"Well, if Mom won't let me go, how about if you go over to their tent and run my car for me? I could be the owner and you could be the driver. Then when my car, wins you could get the trophy for me."

"I don't know, Silas. I've driven a lot of race cars but I don't think I have ever driven a pinewood car." T.K. winked at Sarah. "Do you think I could handle it?"

"Yeah, you really don't have to do anything. You just give the car to Mr. Sisk and they do the rest. You could do it. Easy-peasy."

"Do you think Bear will mind? It might be in violation of my contract or something."

"You just tell Bear to talk to me if he has a problem

with it.

This is important."

"Okay, but say...what is my percentage of the purse?"

Silas never missed a beat. "I will keep letting you spend time with my Mom."

"Fair enough. That is more than a generous offer. I'll take it."

Five minutes later T.K. was heading to the TxArm tent with Silas' car safely tucked under his arm.

- O -

"So Dude, how was it?" Doug and Paolo were ensconced in T.K.'s motor home. He had graciously offered to let them chill there for the evening. It saved a trip back to the hotel.

"It was great. Very relaxing. It was really good to not think about race cars and pressure and the Chase for a while. We went horseback riding and ate until we were stuffed. Great food. It was mostly just the four of us. It was cool."

Paolo was flaked out on the couch. "You know Doug, I had forgotten how special Alicia was. I've sort of been taking her for granted all these years. What you said to me got my attention. Hildy and Orly having a baby... you know life is going by. I think I really do love her. No, I don't think... I *know* so. I love her to pieces."

Doug laughed out loud. "Dude, you got on a horse? I don't frickin' believe it. Did you get a picture? Coburn would be proud of you." Doug got serious.

"Hey Pally, I only told you what you already knew

in your heart about Alicia. Look at you, man. You got that chick-flick-lovesick-dreamy look on your face."

"Yeah, maybe. I'm going to take it to the next level. We have a date next week when we get back to Charlotte. I might stop by and see a jeweler when I get a chance. I think we're both going to take a little time off after Homestead at the end of the season and maybe go to California. You know, see the folks during the off-season. Are you going to be around somewhere in case things progress the way I hope they might?"

"Dude, what are you saying? Are you going to ask her to marry you?"

"You never know. We will just see how the Lord leads us."

"Cool." Doug was stretched out on the plush carpet. He wasn't surprised. The boy was beginning to see the light. It was funny how everybody else could see it, but Paolo had a tough time when it was right in front of his face. About time.

What did surprise Doug was the reversal in T.K.'s attitude. "So what brought about the change in T.K.? I mean the turnaround was pretty sudden. One minute you and him are pretty set on ripping each other apart and the next day you're double dating. What happened?"

"Yeah, pretty strange. He spent practically the whole night talking with Sarah in the coach. I guess they really hit it off. By the way, she is way cool. She is a lot younger than you think. I guess she had Silas when she was in high school or something. She was really young. But Alicia told me that Sarah pretty much told T.K. he needed the Lord. She told him that was the only way she made it. Without God's help, she would have thrown in the towel a long time ago." Paolo sat up.

"At any rate, it had an impact on him. Next thing I know, he is shaking my hand and apologizing."

Paolo got up and went over to the enormous refrigerator. "He left me no choice. I couldn't stay mad at him. Besides, you know how I am. I get really ticked and then I cool down. Must be my Mediterranean background. Besides, Dude, he is driving my car, so like it or not, I have to work with him. He really isn't a bad guy."

Paolo changed the subject. "So what time do we hit the TxArm tent tonight?"

"Dr. Miller said about 9:30 would be cool. In the middle of the concert, I think. They have that cool band again. I think it was the one that was at Talledega. No let's see, maybe it was Charlotte. This time of the year, everything seems to run together. Hey, we ought to invite T.K. to go with us."

"Yeah, sure. I don't know if he will come, but it might be worth a try." Paolo changed the subject yet again. "All right, let's get serious. What did you learn watching the Nationwide race today? Anything we can use?' Paolo rummaged in the refrigerator.

- O -

Slick Willie sat in his motor home in the dark. His face was partially illuminated by the cell phone in his hand. He was staring at the number in his voice mail. He knew exactly who it was, but he wasn't going to call them back until he was ready. He was too scared. For the past two days, they had been calling him every three hours around the clock. He was desperate. The wolves were circling. His creditors were getting impatient and moving in for the kill. He had to do something and do it fast.

The dealership in Arizona was going belly up. Willie didn't care much about that. He'd already gutted it and gotten everything out of it he could. He could always start another business. The best way was to go bankrupt and leave the employees and the supply houses hanging. He'd been there and done that. No big thing, except this time it wasn't an option. He had already borrowed all the money he possibly could from legitimate sources with no intention of paying it back. But he still needed money.

In desperation he turned to less savory options, but you didn't stiff these guys. When he borrowed it, he had several deals going, and he knew success was just around the corner. He was sure he would be able to pay them back, no sweat. That wasn't the case, however. Things in the economy went from bad to worse, and people were just not buying anything.

That's what he told himself, anyway. The truth was his crooked business practices had finally caught up with him. His reputation was shot. This was a guy who boasted that he could sell down jackets to polar bears, but not any more. Everybody from the Better Business Bureau to the Chamber of Commerce, to the guy on the corner, knew he was a shyster and crook.

Plus, there were several judgments pending against him and he had to get out of town quick. Pass the butter, he was toast and he knew it. His time in jail hadn't helped either. Jail itself hadn't been too bad. He had to admit that he slept good there. There was something comforting about having a locked door between you and your enemies. But going back to jail wasn't going to protect him this time.

He had to pay these guys off. They didn't play nice. Jail wouldn't stop them. They could reach out practically anywhere. T.K. had what he needed. He had the money. In fact, he knew that the kid had to be worth millions with all the product endorsements and the big contract with that Orly Mann Team. That didn't take into consideration the purse money that he had picked up this year. Flying around in airplanes and driving fancy cars and motorcycles. He had that place outside of Charlotte on Lake What's-its-Name. A big share of that pie belonged to him, William Harold. If he got what was rightfully his, he could pay the lawyer off and still have some left to start over someplace else. It had to happen. He didn't want to consider the alternative. It wouldn't be so good for his health.

Getting his hands on T.K.'s money, which was rightfully his anyway, was all about leverage. He just had to find the right person…and maybe this time he had. He closed his eyes and went over his script in his mind once again.

- *O* -

T.K. wasn't sure what to expect. He didn't know much of anything about the Raceway ministries group. He'd heard a little about it listening to Orly and Bear talk. He knew Paolo and Doug were probably involved. They went to Chapel every Sunday before the race. They were basically nice guys. They didn't party too hard, at least not from what he'd seen. They were fun to be with. They knew how to have fun and joke around, but they weren't crass or crude. Apart from that, he didn't know much about them or TxArm.

It was a nice early evening, so on a whim he decided to walk from the motor home lot through the campground to the TxArm tent. He was halfway there when it dawned on him. There were tons of people all over the place. If somebody recognized him, he might get trampled to death or cause a riot or something. He had been the object of a crowd's affection before and it wasn't a fun thing. He hunkered down inside his jacket. Then he saw the guy directing traffic on the entrance road. He was wearing a bright yellow jacket that said STAFF and a Texas Motor Speedway hat. He sauntered up to the man, keeping his head down,

"Hey buddy, my name is T.K. Kittridge. I wonder if I might ask you something?"

The man took a long look at him. "You sure are T.K. What can I do for you?"

"How about if I give you this Blue Saber jacket and you give me that yellow jacket you're wearing and your hat? I'm trying to be a little less recognizable, if you know what I mean."

"Yeah, I can imagine. You might get mobbed if you aren't careful." The man looked around. "Listen, I am not comfortable giving away stuff that doesn't belong to me. The hat is mine. The jacket doesn't belong to me. It belongs to the track, and I need it to do my job, so I can't give it to you. But I'll tell you what. My stuff is right over there at the base of that pole. I've got a nice Dallas Cowboys windbreaker lying there. I'll swap you for that."

"Done." T.K. left a couple of twenties in the jacket pocket as he made the swap.

A few minutes later, he was walking through the campground looking just like any other fan.

He was surprised at the number of people gathered around the sloped racetrack under the tent. It looked like things were just about to get going. He gently elbowed his way through the crowd until he could reach the man that was testing the release gate on the track.

"Are you Mr. Sisk?"

"That I am." He didn't look up.

"I have a race car here that belongs to Silas Biggs. He couldn't come tonight. He's not feeling so good. Is there any chance you can put it in the mix and give it a run?"

"Been looking for Silas. I had a nice visit with him yesterday. I'm really sorry he can't be here. Yeah, you bet we'll put his car in the mix. Give it to me and we'll weigh it out and get it lined up."

As T.K. handed over the car, a soft voice spoke over his shoulder. "So Silas isn't doing well? How bad is he, T.K.?"

T.K. turned to see Dr. Miller standing beside him.

"I don't know, Dr. Miller. I'm not a good judge. Sarah seems concerned though."

"I wonder if she needs our medical people to stop by. I'll give her a call in a few minutes and see."

"I'm sure she might appreciate it."

"I need to call her about another matter anyway." Miller changed the subject. "Hey T.K., how about I introduce you to the folks? Several people have recognized you, and it would be best to get you up front and out of the crowd."

"Yeah, sure. I could sign a few autographs, if you like."

The Pinewood Derby went off without a hitch. Miller introduced T.K. to the crowd, and he signed autographs until his hand was tired. As he thought about it later, he really did enjoy himself. This was a great bunch of people, and they did an excellent job of serving the fans. Silas' car didn't win the race, which was done in a series of runoffs. He did garner an award for "best painted". He called Sarah to give her the news.

"So how is he doing?"

"Actually, he seems a little better. He wants you to get back here so he can see the trophy."

"Okay, I'll drop it off. Then I have to go. Carol is looking for me, and I have to get the schedule for the morning. I'm supposed to make a couple of appearances before the race. Sponsor things. Then I want to meet with Paolo and Doug and go over some things for the race."

"Do you feel good about tomorrow? I mean, can you win? I don't know much about how these things work, but I know you're starting at the back."

"Yeah, we can win, I think. Lots of variables."

"I will be praying for you."

- *O* -

The three young men were sitting around the table discussing strategy with Bear. They had been going at it for an hour. Bear was pleased. These guys were working together with a lot of give and take, and there seemed to be a bond developing between them. They were actually listening to each other, which was a good thing. Nobody won a Cup race by themselves. It was a team effort, and the better the team gelled, the better the effort. These guys were gelling.

Paolo looked at his watch. "We better wrap it up. Doug and I promised the TxArm people we would be at the concert tonight and maybe share a little. Well, I guess I'm sharing a little. Doug doesn't do crowds."

"No way, Dude. That's your gig, not mine."

"T.K. why don't you come with us? It will be fun. We won't be there long, then I am heading back to the room to crash. I'm beat."

T.K. thought about it for a minute. For some reason, he didn't want to be alone right now. Maybe he was just missing family, such as it was. "You know, that sounds kind of fun. I had a great time this evening. Did I tell you Silas got a trophy for best paint? His car looked just like Orly's. Yeah, I'll go with you, if you don't mind."

- O -

"So Mr. Race Car driver, how you doing? You look pretty pensive." Hildy spoke from the kitchen of their coach. Orly was sitting in the overstuffed chair with his legs elevated.

"Doing okay. Just sitting here thinking about our baby. Thinking about Silas. Just wondering about a lot of things. What will we do if there are complications or the baby isn't healthy? What are we going to do then?"

Hildy came around the counter and walked over

to Orly. She took his face in both hands and kissed his forehead. She looked into his eyes.

"We will just deal with it as it comes. Just like Sarah does. We will get our strength from the Lord as always. Now quit worrying. It's time for me to change the dressings on your hands. How is the leg feeling?"

"Okay. I think it will be okay. Yup, I got to quit worrying and go out there tomorrow and make some money. Baby might need a new pair of shoes."

The evening had turned cool but that didn't slow the crowd any. It was a noisy bunch that rocked out to the tunes blaring from the speakers. The band was good and they were "making it happen" from the stage on a flatbed truck trailer. Dr. Miller was pleased with the turnout as he surveyed the attendance. He watched as Doug, Paolo and T.K. approached.

"Hey guys, good to see you. Thanks for taking time to come out. T.K., good to see you. How is Silas doing?"

"Sarah says he is doing better. She has him tucked in, despite his best efforts at staying awake."

"Good. Paolo, I will introduce you after the band finishes this set. Looks like a pretty lively group."

- O -

"Got it. I think we're ready."

Miller introduced Paolo to the crowd, and they responded with wild applause. The Orly Mann Team was a popular one.

Paolo began by sharing how he and Doug met at Sears Point while he was working the Chicken Shack for his uncle Rollie. One thing led to another and he made it to the Orly Mann team. Now all of a sudden, he found himself the crew chief of the Blue Saber Team and deep into the hunt for the championship.

"I have to tell you, ladies and gents, I never expected to go up the ladder so quick, but I guess God had different plans. Throughout the course of my life, I have seen the Lord do wonderful things. That doesn't always mean that things go the way you want them to, but there is that realization that no matter what comes down the road, the Lord is with us." Paolo paused for minute.

"You know, my friend Doug here is a great guy. I couldn't ask for a better friend. I know he didn't expect to be spotting tomorrow but he has stepped up to the plate. Let's give him a round of applause."

Doug waved his arm to thunderous applause.

"Standing next to him is one of the best race car drivers in the world, and I call it a great privilege to be his crew chief. How about giving my driver T.K. Kittridge a greeting?" The place came apart as people whooped and yelled their appreciation.

"Let me tell you, folks. We're praying for our race tomorrow. No we aren't praying for a win, like some might think. We're just praying that we might do our best and be a solid testimony to the God who loves us. Now, I want you to understand something. My father is Portuguese and my Mom is Armenian, which means I am a pretty passionate guy. Before I quit, I saw a very special lady join us. I would like to introduce her to you. Alicia, I see you out there. I wonder if you could come up and join me?" The crowd turned to see where

Paolo was pointing.

Alicia was taken aback. She just thought she would slip in the back of the crowd and listen, and then maybe catch a ride with Doug and Paolo back to the hotel. The crowd opened up before her, making a path for her to get to the stage. Dr. Miller helped her up the stairs. She stood next to Paolo with a puzzled look on her beautiful face.

"Alicia, how long have we been friends?"

Someone handed her a microphone. "Uh, I don't know exactly, but a good long time. We met at church when we were kids. Pally, what are you doing?"

"I think I loved you the very first time I met you. I just didn't realize it. Well, I realize it now. In front of God and all these witnesses I want to ask you something." Paolo got down on one knee.

Alicia felt her face flush and her stomach go numb.

"Alicia, I love you very much. More than words can describe. Would you marry me? I don't have a ring yet. I want to get the one you want…if you'll have me."

The crowd went dead silent. There was a hush as everyone in earshot waited for her answer. People in the campground that could hear the speakers from the compound came out of their tents and RVs to hear better.

Tears came to her eyes. She looked down at this big broad shouldered young man with such an earnest look on his face. Her heart melted. "Yes, Paolo, I will marry you."

The crowd went absolutely bananas. Paolo got up and took her gently in his arms. He kissed her long and slow in front of God and everybody.

Dr. Miller took the microphone.

"Well folks, that is the TxArm ministry. You never know what is going to happen around here. Enjoy the rest of the concert."

- *O* -

Sarah sat nervously in the overstuffed chair, waiting impatiently. She looked at the clock once again. It was 11:15. Maybe the guy wasn't coming, which was okay with her. She wasn't sure how wise it was getting involved with this clown. Silas was asleep, and that was good. She turned the TV on but kept it down low. Finally, when she couldn't sit still any longer, she got up and paced the floor. At 11:25 there came a soft chime on the intercom announcing that someone was at the door. She picked up the remote, said a soft prayer and opened the door.

He slowly came up the stairs. He was a burly man with a handlebar mustache. Probably late middle-aged, nicely dressed and looking pleasant enough.

"Ms. Biggs, I presume."

"Yes."

Williams extended his hand. "My apologies for being late. I had a little problem getting through security at the gate. Apparently the rich value their privacy." What he didn't say was he thought he could bluff his way past the guard at the gate, but the guy didn't go for it. He finally managed to stow away on the back of a water truck that was topping off several of the coaches. It was inconvenient, but it worked. He was here now.

Sarah ignored his proffered hand.

"I assume young Silas has retired for the night?"

"Yes."

"And what is name of the malady that he is suffering from?"

"Juvenile Idiopathic Arthritis."

"And his prognosis?"

"That's enough. What do you want and why are you here?" Sarah was out of patience.

"May I sit down please? I am a little winded after my…uh, adventure." Willie dramatically pulled a handkerchief from his pocket and mopped his brow as he collapsed into a chair. "Perhaps you might offer me some refreshment?"

"No, I don't think so."

Willie could see that the sympathy tack was going nowhere. "All right Sarah, have it your way. My name is William Williams and I am T.K.'s beloved step-father. I raised the boy and his sister and did my best to give them a stable environment until their mother's drinking made it untenable. I got the boy his start in the racing world. I financed his early years and took care of him until he made enough to become self-sufficient. I did this at great sacrifice to my own financial well-being, I might add." Willie paused. "Are you sure you can't offer me at least a small drink of water? I'm told that those of your religious political persuasion reap a blessing by doing so."

Sarah said nothing. She simply went to the kitchen, pulled a glass from the cupboard and filled it with water. Then she handed it to Williams.

He caressed her fingers as she offered the glass to him. "Such beautiful hands." Williams refocused.

"As I was saying, I was pretty much responsible for getting the man's start in the racing world. Now I find myself in a rather precarious financial position, and I need his help. The economy has decimated my business…and my health, I might add." Williams coughed into his handkerchief.

"But T.K. has consistently rebuffed my pleas and my desire to re-establish a relationship with him. I love that boy." Williams paused for dramatic effect.

"The sad part is I know why he won't maintain any contact with me. You see, Sarah, all that success has gone to his head. This is what I alluded to when I called you on the phone. He has surrounded himself with the wrong kind of people and may I say it…the wrong kind of vices. I am afraid that his world will come crashing down if he doesn't get help. Are you aware that his spotter Devin Hester failed a drug test and has lost his NASCAR license?"

Sarah said nothing. She simply stood with one arm across her stomach and the knuckles of the other one pressed against her chin.

"Well I can see by your expression that you were not aware of that fact. Now, it has come to my attention that you and T.K. have spent a good deal of time together these past two days. Judging from your carefree attitude when you returned from the barbecue, you seemed to enjoy the outing very much. Maybe you're developing feelings for T.K. I'm wondering if perhaps you might be willing to work with me in accomplishing my goal of helping the young man disentangle from a destructive lifestyle before it engulfs him?"

Sarah said nothing for a minute, then she put her

hands on her hips.

"I don't get out much, Mr. Williams, but I have to say that is the biggest load of garbage that I have heard in a long time. You are a liar, and most likely a cheat. What you are attempting to do is not only dishonorable but dishonest as well. I think it is time for you to leave."

Williams transformed before her eyes. His frustration and rage boiled to the surface. He threw the handkerchief down on the floor and stood up to his full height. His eyes narrowed, and he balled his fists. His voice took on a steely grating edge. "All right lady, I thought it might come down to this. This is what you're going to do. You're going to help me get to T.K. and get the money he owes me, and this is what will happen to you if you don't."

Williams took a step toward Sarah. "First of all, I know that you do accounting work from your home to support yourself. I wonder what would happen if several of your clients received anonymous tips that your own personal finances were not in order because you've been juggling certain people's books to benefit yourself. I'll start there." Williams took another step toward her.

"Then I will place a call to the Child Protective Services people and, like I told you earlier, tell them that there are some concerns in regard to your ability to care for the sickly boy that was born no doubt as a result of a promiscuous lifestyle. Then I will contact your church, as I promised and I-"

Williams was interrupted as R.W. Coburn flanked by the two young cowboys stepped out of the bedroom.

"Time for you to shut up there, Willie. I think we have enough here to put you back where you belong."

Coleman flashed the tape recorder. "Yeah, these coaches have a beautiful sound system. It plays and records. In fact, it records so good you can hear every word."

Slick Willie looked like he had swallowed a jalapeño pepper whole. He turned to Sarah. "You set me up, didn't you?"

"Yes."

Coburn reached out and gently took Sarah's arm and pulled her behind him, so he stood facing Willie.

"Willie my boy, you are caught. I have a record of everything you said. I got three witnesses here. Tomorrow morning, I am going down to file charges against you on behalf of several people. My advice to you is that you might consider getting your affairs in order because I don't think this next stint in jail is just going to be three months."

Williams raised his finger to bluster but then realized the futility of protesting. He was caught. He headed down the stairs and out the door.

Coleman turned to Sarah. "You okay?"

"Yes I'm okay. What an evil man. It must have been a blessing when he abandoned the family."

"Yes, I expect so. You know some folks just don't have the sense God gave a duck. How could that feller think he could accomplish anything by threatening practically everybody? Makes no sense at all."

- O -

Twenty minutes later, Dr. Miller was sitting under the TxArm canopy at a table drinking a late night cup of tea. The concert was over and the campground had pretty much quieted down. Miller looked up to see Willie's RV headed down the access road toward the exit. He was wasting no time. Miller smiled. "Yes sir, Lord, you certainly do work in amazing ways."

Chapter Twelve

"I love this kind of racing, but these guys sure change their personalities in race mode. They're like Doberman pinschers with a hand grenade in their mouths."

Road Racer Boris Said on NASCAR drivers.

There is a certain vitality that fills the pre-dawn darkness on race day. The waiting is over. This is it. Late in the afternoon, a winner will be crowned and the rest of the field will be considered "also ran". The parking lots start filling in the early morning darkness as the fans start moving around, hunkered down in their jackets and hoodies.

There was a solid line of headlights on 30W and the other arterial roads moving toward the track. Every intersection was shepherded by the traffic controllers directing the fans toward the ticket lanes. It was race day. Everything else was window dressing. Yesterday's Nationwide race, though exciting, was simply an appetizer. Today wouldn't be the frosting on the cake, it was more like the whole gourmet meal, including the expensive wine and the tiramisu chocolate dessert. The race for the Chase was tight with just a few precious points separating the leaders. The drivers in the mix were popular. Ford, Chevy and Toyota were punching it out. It was the big multi-car teams and smaller two-car teams vying for the title.

It was a day for questions, and it would be a day for answers. One Chase contender was recovering from injuries suffered in a testing crash. Could he man up and win this thing? One was starting dead last after the most horrific one car crash in qualifying history. Could he come through the pack in an untested car? A new crew chief, theoretically young and inexperienced, was tapped to step into the scene to guide him. Would this guy have what it takes to call a winning race?

The day reeked of competition. It was in the air like the smell of freshly brewed coffee and the sizzle of early morning breakfasts from the tailgaters. All the elements of drama were in place. Today just might be a record crowd for Texas Motor Speedway. In a few hours, the battle would be joined. No quarter asked and no quarter given. At the end, there would be one winner standing in the Victory Circle celebrating and forty-two otherstallying their points and licking their wounds.

- *O* -

Silas lay awake in the great big bed. He felt okay. God answered his prayer. He didn't feel feverish at all. He was the most excited he had ever been in his whole life. To think that he was going to watch the race from Orly Mann's pit box with Bear and everybody was beyond belief.

It was really going to happen. What a special gift...
Thank you Lord, he thought to himself. Wow!

He looked at the clock. It was still way too early to
get up. It would be awhile before they came to get him
for the driver's meeting, and then the Chapel. Then just
a little while to the time when the pre-race stuff would
start. Texas most always brought in a big name enter-
tainer to do a concert before the race started. Everybody
liked that. Then the flyover and the National anthem,
and the prayer and all that stuff, then it was "gentlemen
start your engines" and the race was on.

Orly was up front, but T.K. had to start last. That
was tough. Could he make it through the field? *I
think he can*, Silas thought to himself. With Paolo and
Doug, and even Alicia and his good pit crew, he might
be able to.

Now he knew two race car drivers. T.K. was cool.
He treated him, Silas, like a real person, not just some
kid that didn't know anything. Speaking of T.K., Silas
was wondering. He had never seen his Mom with
another man before. She got all googly- eyed when T.K.
came around. Her face looked different, softer sort of,
or something.

He wasn't sure. He could tell she liked him a lot.
Silas liked him too. He was a good guy, and if it made
his Mom happy, he was easy with it. He wondered if
they would see T.K. when they got back home.

He rolled over, and as he did, he felt a slight twinge
of pain in his legs. It was okay. Just the usual stuff.

- O -

T.K. tossed and turned until well after three in the morning. He was sore, but that wasn't what was keeping him awake. It was the tight ball of adrenaline in his stomach. Time after time, he replayed the scenario in his mind. Starting last wasn't going to be easy. He had the whole pack in front of him. What if the car wasn't right? It might not even be raceable. What if Paolo got the setup wrong? What if the pit crew wasn't up to their usual standards? What if, what if…Finally, he dropped off to sleep and was sleeping soundly when the alarm went off. He came awake slowly, then rolled over to hit the snooze button and drifted back to sleep. Ten minutes later his phone rang. The ringing set the ball of adrenaline dribbling in his stomach once again.

"I'm cooking breakfast. If you want some, come on over. You can help me persuade Silas to eat something."

"Uh yeah, what time is it? …Give me a few minutes."

"T.K. Look, I'm sorry to wake you up, but something happened last night, and I think you should know about it."

No, he couldn't do this now, not this morning. He couldn't put anything else on his plate. Whatever it was would have to wait until after the race.

"Look Sarah, I don't mean to be rude, but this is a very important day. If it is real serious, I can come right over, but if it isn't…well, I can either move up in the points or be out of the race completely. Today is make or break and I need to concentrate. I have my work in front of me. I just can't cope with anything else right now. Let me meet you after the race, okay?"

"Sure, no problem." He could hear the hurt in her voice.

- O -

Alicia was up early. She had already had her shower, and washed her hair. She was sitting at the little table in the room in her robe going over some last minute things. It would be a busy morning with sponsor appearances and all the other details that needed to be attended to before the race. They called her the chief-shepherd. She worked with Carol, making sure everybody got to where they were supposed to be. Then during the race she would sit on the pit box and keep track of timing and scoring, and do her best to answer any questions Paolo might have in regard to who pitted where and how much fuel and …She smiled to herself as she thought about last night.

That big dummy. Asking her to marry him in front of all those people. What could she say? No. No, she couldn't say that. It was what she wanted more than anything. She loved him so much. He was such a romantic, and he wasn't afraid to voice what he was feeling. That was for sure.

They went to the coffee shop next to the hotel after the concert. Doug took off and went to bed. Paolo was so funny. He insisted on sitting beside her at the table instead of sitting across. He held her hand the whole time they talked, and kept kissing her hair. He seemed like a little boy that had received the most special gift for Christmas ever. He was just full of wonder and appreciation. She liked that. She loved it, in fact. He listened intently to every word that she said. That was a new thing. In the past, he had often blown her off like a little sister. At least that was what she thought.

Apparently, it wasn't so.

They had a million details to work out for the wedding and all that…but not today. Today was business. It was his first time on the "box" as a crew chief and there was a ton of responsibility riding on his shoulders. She knew better. She knew he needed to focus to do the job right. There was plenty of time. Two more races and the season was over. Quite frankly, she was glad.

The daily grind was a bit overwhelming. It was a short off-season, but at least they could spend it together. She looked at her phone to see the time. Yeah, he was probably already up and meeting with Bear. She noticed that she had a new text message. It was from Paolo and had been sent early this morning. It said simply "I love you."

- O -

Paolo was shoveling food down as he listened intently to Bear. Bear was eating sparingly. A poached egg and some wheat toast. Everybody knew that Bear had a delicate stomach, particularly on race day. He'd greeted Paolo warmly and congratulated him briefly on his engagement to Alicia and then the rest of the conversation was all business. He spoke and Paolo listened. The victory was going to be in the details, and there were tons of them.

"We both have to pay attention to track temperature. If the sun comes out, it could loosen up quit a bit. Texas traditionally gets loose toward the latter part of the race, but then if it stays cool, the cars are going to get tight. I think T.K. will get faster as the race progresses.

At least he has in the past. I have a hunch Orly is going to be fast out of the box. He's got that look in his eye this weekend. He told me he wanted a bonus point for leading and another one for leading the most laps, and he wants the three bonus points for winning. Wanted to be in clean air most of the day if he could."

Bear took a sip of coffee. "What is your driver thinking?"

"Me and T.K. talked a bunch yesterday. I would like him to lay in the back for the first few laps and pick off the odd car now and then. Kind of let the dust settle, then as things progress, start going for it. Let the race come to us. I'm trying to get him to use his head and save some of his stuff for the last third of the race. I think he's listening, but you know ...the heat of battle and all that. It'll be hard to tell."

Paolo mopped up the last bit of gravy on his plate and looked at his watch. "To be honest with you, Bear, I'm not sure what he is thinking. I am just going to do my best to keep the wheels on the thing and give him whatever he asks for." He took a final swig of coffee.

"We gotta go, Bear. The garage opens in a few minutes. I want to go over the checklist again. You sure that is the best carb jet to run today?"

Bear picked up the tab as they headed to the checkout. "Yeah, I'm certain of it. History and today's weather report. It will give us the best mileage without sacrificing any power."

"Okay, I trust you. See you at the driver's meeting."

- *O* -

"Hey Mama, how you feeling this morning?" Orly asked as Hildy came out of the bedroom.

"Kinda urpy, but I'll be all right. I am nervous as a cat...what is it that Coburn said, a cat with a long tail in a room full of rocking chairs." Hildy flopped into a chair. "I'm not usually nervous but today I am. How come, I wonder?"

"Just 'cuz, that's why. Might be a good sign. Maybe we'll win today and take the point lead."

"How are you feeling, Racer Man?"

"Actually, I'm feeling pretty good. The soreness is gone out of my hands. They look a lot better. My leg is doing better, too." This last comment was a lie. Orly's leg was still red and raw and oozing in a couple of places where it had been burned. "I think I'm good to go. I'm ready."

"I'm glad. Yuck, Orly what is that smell?"

"Oh, I cooked some bacon and eggs, and I think I got the pan too hot and burned the bacon a little. Do you want me to make some for you?'

Hildy turned a pale shade of green as she hopped up and hustled to the bathroom, fighting another bout of morning sickness.

"Guess not." Orly said as he opened a couple of windows.

- O -

NASCAR opened the garage at 8:00 AM sharp. Ten minutes later, it was a seething ocean of activity. Every car was the focus of attention. Crew chiefs were talking with car chiefs. Car chiefs were passing out orders.

Nearly everybody was checking some sort of checklist on a clipboard as they worked under, inside, and over the cars. Everything that could be checked was double checked and then checked again. In the midst of the activity, the media folks were trying to get last minute interviews with the harried crew chiefs.

It was way too early for the drivers. Most of them knew better and simply stayed out of the way to let the crews do their jobs. After the cars were checked, double checked, triple checked, then they were pushed to the tech area for the final mandatory trip through the "room of doom". Once they were cleared for competition, they were pushed to the gas pumps, filled with fuel and pushed out to the pit lane to their designated starting spot. Then they were covered…and it was pretty much done.

The activity didn't cease, however. Things got even busier as the "over the wall" pit crews off the charter plane arrived. The war wagons and crash carts were coming together in the pit lane as the crews set up behind their pit boxes.

The days of a couple gas cans and a rollaway toolbox were long gone. It was the digital electronic age. Satellite dishes were cranked up and the cable feeds were checked. On board monitors were dialed in and the computer hookups were tested. Every crew had a place for everything and everything was in its place.

During the race, if something was needed, it would be needed in a hurry, and it was important to know exactly where it would be. Things were always in the same place no matter the track. Air hoses were uncoiled and recoiled and the fittings checked then rechecked.

The two hundred pound psi air guns were lubed and tested. Not once, but several times by the tire changers. Each tire changer was responsible for his own gun and he treated it accordingly. It had to work perfectly for the thirteen-second pit stops. The tire man was sitting on tires, patiently gluing lug nuts on every wheel with silicone glue affectionately called "gorilla snot". After he finished with the five lugs on a wheel, he placed a round iron plate over them to hold them in place while they dried. It was an important, delicate job.

If a nut fell off during a tire change, it could cost a driver positions on the track or even mandate another trip through the pits to put it back on. Once the glue was dry, the tire man carefully stacked the tires in sets of four. Each was marked with chalk. LF, LR, RF, RR. Serial numbers on each tire were carefully notated and matched. The teams owned the wheels, but Goodyear only leased the tires.

Tires were important and matching them together to get the best performance was considered one of the finer arts of a tire guy. The air pressure on each one was carefully and meticulously checked. The tires were filled with a nitrogen mix, and the balance was such that a pound or even a half-pound variation could affect the handling of a car. They would go through six to ten sets of tires, depending on circumstances. At over four hundred dollars a tire, they had to be perfect.

The fuel man was checking his scale and then making sure the check valves and nozzles were perfect on the fuel cans. How much fuel was put into the car was determined by weight. Immediately after a fuel stop, the fueler placed the eleven-gallon can on the scale, and the weight was notated on the computer, then sent to the crew chief. Mileage was important. It could mean the difference between winning and losing.

Things got more frenzied as the tour groups started coming through, making it even more difficult for the crews to do their jobs. Tons of people with the coveted credentials wandered here and there, hoping to get a glimpse of a driver or perhaps an autograph before the race started. The crew guys were professionals. They were used to the crush of people. Somehow organization triumphed over chaos, and things began to come together.

- *O* -

Driver's meetings were mandatory for crew chiefs and drivers. They had to sign in to make sure their attendance was recorded. They were not open to the general public or to the media. Team owners could attend at their own discretion. Others might attend, but it was strictly by "invitation only." It was a time for the competition director to go over the rules, such as the mandated 45 mph pit road speed at Texas, plus many other particulars. It was also a time when drivers or crew chiefs could ask questions or get clarification about a particular issue.

Bear pulled some strings and Silas was allowed to attend. They wheeled his chair in the room and lined him up against the back wall. T.K., Paolo, Orly and Bear were sitting just in front of him. He sat quietly with his autograph book clutched to his chest, listening intently. He did not notice the helmet that was circulating through the room.

Several dignitaries spoke and the NASCAR officials did their thing. Finally, the meeting was reaching its conclusion when Dr. Miller was asked to step up to the microphone. He said a few words in greeting, then made this statement:

"As you all know, courage comes in many forms. This morning I would like to introduce you to a young man who is one of the most courageous that I know. He fights a daily battle, almost minute by minute against a very tough, debilitating foe. Through it all, he has demonstrated an attitude of grace and forbearance. He is our guest this weekend and I want to thank all of you for making his time with us so very special." He was handed the white helmet.

"Silas Biggs, we are privileged to present you with this helmet as a memory of your time here at Texas Motor Speedway. It has been signed by every driver and every crew chief participating in the race today."

Everyone stood then turned as they applauded Silas in the back of the room. Silas painfully pushed himself out of his wheel chair and stood acknowledging the group. *Wow!* he thought to himself.

As the room emptied out, several stopped by to pat him on the back, as he clutched the helmet in his lap. He couldn't stop smiling.

- *O* -

Sarah stood next to Alicia as they waited to file into the building for the Chapel service. She debated about saying anything then finally screwed up her courage and spoke. "I guess I really did the wrong thing."

"What did you do?"

"I know you heard about last night and Williams and all. I think everybody has heard about it except T.K. So this morning, I invited him over for breakfast with Silas and myself and told him I had something to tell him. At first he was coming, and then he just sort of blew me off and said we could talk after the race." Sarah fished in her purse for a Kleenex. She wiped her eyes. "I don't understand."

Alicia put her arm around Sarah's shoulder. "Let me ask you a question. Have you ever been to a race, or do you know any race car drivers?"

"No, I don't know anything about this business at all."

"Okay, imagine this. These guys are going off to battle. Like, I mean war. It takes everything they have to do what they do. I've seen them come out of the car just totally exhausted. I've seen them not be able to get out of the car after the race. They had to be helped out. T.K. and Orly are both in the Chase, and they both could win it, or they could have a rotten day and end up in such a hole, they are out of the running. That is the only thing on their minds right now."

Alicia took a breath. "Sarah, don't take it personally. Where are you going to be during the race?"

"I think I am supposed to be next to Silas. On Orly's box."

"Listen. We have an extra seat. Would Silas be okay by himself? During the race, Hildy will be right next to him."

"Yes, I suppose so."

"Then come and watch the race from our box...
you will have a better idea of what I mean."

"Okay, if you think it's okay."

The garage area Chapel Service was open to anybody in the garage. It usually took place right after the
driver's meeting in the same room. A few of the drivers
and crew chiefs hung around to attend, and a lot of
the crew made it a habit. Most of the Orly Mann guys
attended.

Paolo was surprised when T.K. didn't take off. He
hadn't been interested much in Chapel in the past,
but today he hung around like he was going to stay.
Nobody said anything to him. He was joking with
Silas, and admiring the helmet with him when Sarah
and Alicia walked in. He smiled at Sarah and stepped
back as Silas excitedly showed her the helmet. She was
dutifully impressed. Then he took her hand and they
sat down together.

"Hey Beautiful." Paolo said as he sat down next to
Alicia.

"Hey yourself. Are you nervous?"

"Well, I wasn't until you said something. I don't
think nervous is the right word. Terrified might be a
better description." Paolo squeezed her hand. "At least
I got you, Babe. If it all falls apart, I could go work in
a junkyard or hot dog stand or something, and maybe
we could make it."

"You will do just fine, Big Guy."

The Chaplain did a good job running the service.
The music was upbeat. The prayer time was refreshing
and to the point. His message was simple. He spoke with
the authority of God's word. And it boiled down to the

fact that God loves us. He provides for us. Therefore, act accordingly.

It struck a chord with Sarah, and she went over the events of last night. God had indeed certainly intervened. Hopefully, Willie was out of the picture, at least for a while, and T.K. wouldn't have to worry about him. Then it dawned on her that maybe God was speaking to her own heart in regard to T.K. Maybe she just needed to stop pushing the river and let it flow by itself. God was in control.

- O -

It was time. The pre-race driver introductions would happen in just a few minutes. Orly and T.K. were headed to the mobile stage, walking side by side. Orly's driver's suit was a bright yellow with splashes of orange and purple and the Speed King logo. It matched the color of his car.

T.K. looked over. "Man, you are colorful today."

"Yeah, I know. They keep changing the design. Looks good, though. At least they can find me in a crowd."

"Hey Orly, I'm thinking that maybe I should, well you know, maybe pursue things with Sarah a little bit. I really like her." They both stopped to sign a few autographs as various fans stuck things in front of them.

Orly leaned over as they continued on their way. "You are a grown man. Do what you think is best, but you might want to think about the differences in your lifestyle. You are a gypsy going from here to there. She isn't used to that. Just saying, you know."

"Yeah, I hear you. I've been thinking about that."

"Hey, have a good day. Do your best to keep the shiny side up," Orly said as they separated for introductions.

"Yeah, you too."

The introductions were over. Dr. Miller had offered the invocation. A major pop artist hammered her way through the National Anthem, and at the appropriate moment, the F16's made their flyover. The collected excitement was so thick it could almost be seen.

Then the signal came down the pit lane for the drivers to get in their cars.

T.K. took a look up the line for the last time: forty-two cars ahead of him. he thought to himself, . He climbed in the car. Paolo reached in and helped him straighten his belts. "We can do this, you know. You are that good."

"Thanks, man. We'll see what happens."

Paolo snapped the window net into place.

Orly's car was second in line. He threw his right leg into the car. Grabbed the roof and the pillar post and slipped into the car, dragging his left leg behind him. It hurt, but at least he wouldn't have to do that again until the end of the race. It was good to get in the cockpit. He hunkered down and worked his back into the seat. Hildy stuck her head in the window and kissed him. "I love you... Go fast, Papa."

He smiled at her. "You bet." Then she disappeared.

Bear kneeled down and looked into the car. "You got a plan?"

"Yup, I think so, Bear."

"Okey-dokey, then." He put his hand on Orly's

shoulder.

"Lord, keep us all safe, and help us to do this thing in a way that brings glory to your name. Amen." Then he snapped the window net and stepped back.

Chapter Thirteen

"If you can get that big beast under the hood wide open, she'll take you in the right direction in a hurry."

Clint Bowyer, NASCAR driver.

"Gentlemen, start your engines!" The call went out, and forty-three cars came alive in the pit lane. Doug's voice came through the form fitted earpieces. "Afternoon there, Mr. Kittridge. This is a radio check. Are we good to go?"

"Ten four, gotcha Doug."

"You guys got me?" Paolo said.

"Roger that."

Alicia adjusted the volume on her headset and handed a headset to Sarah.

The pack formed up behind the pace car and went rumbling down the front straight. Sarah watched wide-eyed. The crowd was coming to its collective feet. All of a sudden, she realized that there were thousands and thousands of people in the grandstands. Many of them were looking across the racetrack right at them.

Because he was last in qualifying, T.K. was at the

very end of the pit lane. In fact, his was the last pit box. Orly, on the other hand, was pitted close to the front. The pole sitter was sitting in the very first box with nothing but racetrack in front of him. Bear picked the next box that had an open space in front of it to keep Orly from getting boxed in. Sarah looked up the lane. She hoped Silas was doing okay.

The starter was fiddling with the flags on his perch above the track. He finally pulled the green flag and held it down beside his leg.

The pace car held a constant speed that was consistent with the mandated pit road speed. This allowed the drivers to set the telltale on their tachs. Then the pace car began to pick up speed. The momentum started to build as everyone got lined up. The seventeen car sitting on the pole elected to start on the inside. That was fine with Orly. If he could hold his line on the outside with cold tires, it would give him a good run for the lead.

The pace car came off turn four as the noise level began to rise, drowning out the voice of the crowd. The pace car dove for the safety of the pit lane as the noise climbed the octave scale to a crescendo of thunder. The starter watched. Left hand out with his fingers in a "hold 'em" pattern, and then suddenly he whipped out the green flag and the race was on. Forty-three drivers mashed down on the accelerators, unleashing tremendous buckets of horsepower.

Orly eased into the gas, careful not to spin the tires as he shifted into fourth gear. He could see the seventeen car beside him in his peripheral vision.

Jimmy's calm voice was in his ear. "Inside, inside, inside, you're pulling him, inside, got him by half, inside, inside, clear by one! You got him. Choose your line."

Orly came off turn two leading as he thundered down the backstretch. He crossed the start/finish line as Bear said, "Bingo, one point."

Sarah was not prepared for the wave of sound that practically knocked her out of her seat. It sounded so… *violent*, she thought to herself. It was incredibly intimidating. She watched the cars flash by, searching for T.K. She missed him as he flashed by.

T.K. had wasted no time. As he crossed the start/finish line, he dove to the inside, forcing his way through the slower cars. He sailed into the first corner four wide and then drifted up to the wall as he dove off turn two.

Doug's voice was in his ear. "Clear. Go for it. You got it, inside."

At this stage, T.K. was driving on pure instinct. Paolo said nothing on the radio. He was dividing his time between the track and the video feed in front of him.

Orly was comfortable, at least for the moment. The Speed King Chevy was running like a top. He was liking the clean air on the car, and it felt like he could put it anywhere he wanted. Jimmy spoke in his ear: "plus three. Plus three."

Already in the first ten laps, he had a three second lead.

Silas was goggle eyed. He was trying to look everywhere at once. The crew had made some adjustments, so his wheel chair would fit on the pit box. It was neat being up a little higher and being able to see everything that was going on. He had a headset on his head over his Orly Mann hat. It was a trifle too big, but he wasn't about to adjust it. He was sitting behind Bear, which was an experience because Bear never stood still, so he was constantly wiggling, trying to get a better view. Hildy was sitting beside him, and she too was wearing a headset. She tapped his leg, and showed him how to change the channel so they could talk together. The outside noise made it impossible to carry on a regular conversation.

"You doing okay? Just push the button to talk."

Silas pushed his button. "Yeah I'm doing great. Orly is really going fast. He is leading, Hildy!"

"Yes, I know, but don't get too excited. We have a long way to go. This race is 334 laps long. If you want to know who is in what place, you can just look over there at the scoring pylon or check out the big screen over there. Or you can check out the laptop that has the NASCAR scoring input. Or you can watch the race right here on the network video feed."

"Roger that." Silas said.

Hildy smiled as she shifted back to Orly's channel.

- *O* -

"Inside, inside, you're clear. That puts us in 28th. Nice job." Doug's voice was cool and calm in T.K.'s ear.

"Ten-four. Paolo I'm good to go. I'm down in the track, and at the moment, I can stick it anywhere. Good job guys. This thing is a rocket ship today." He was good to go and going he was. Now he was picking cars off pretty much one at a time as the fast pace strung the pack out.

"Be patient, T.K. We are going to pit in about ten laps. You're running equal speeds with the leader."

"Ten-four. Who's leading?"

"Thirty-seven car."

Orly was leading. That was cool. "Ten-four."

- *O* -

Bear was down off the box, huddling up with Orly's pit crew. They were called the Thunderfoot Ballet Company, which was a name given to them by the media because they were incredibly fast with their choreographed pit stops. It looked very much like this was going to be a green flag stop. It could be critical. They were ready. Bear could tell just by looking at them. The only one missing was Paolo. He had been the jack man for the team, but now that was impossible. Gary, his backup, was good, though. They wouldn't lose anything with him. He climbed back up on the box.

Bear was paying close attention. Orly's times were just starting to fall off some. Fourth through tenth or thereabouts were planning to pit this lap or already had come in. They could see that they couldn't catch Orly. Might as well come in for fresh tires, a few adjustments, and see if they could reel him in. He made a few calculations in his head. The pit window was between fifty and fifty-five laps, depending on mileage. He would know for certain after this fuel stop and he could run the numbers. He would also find out how the tires were doing. Goodyear had a decent compound and it so far was holding up through the weekend. It seemed like a good time to come in. So far, Orly had led every lap.

Bear pushed his talk button. "Pit next time. Going with four." He gave a quick nod to the two NASCAR officials dressed in their white fire suits assigned to their box. Every pit box had two officials that checked things like lug nuts and equipment infractions. One stood at each end of the box to check all four corners of the car. It was common courtesy to let them know when you were pitting so they could protect themselves. Things could get hairy on the pit lane with stressed race cars and overstressed drivers. They were ready. More importantly, the Thunderfoot Ballet Company was ready.

Orly clicked the mic twice. He made a brilliant exit off turn four and sailed into the pit lane, braking hard.

"Watch your speed, watch it, watch it." Jimmy said in his ear.

Bear counted him in as the pole went over the wall with the yellow and purple Speed King logo. "Here we are, three, two, one. Perfect." Bear said as Orly slid into the box and the crew swarmed the car.

The crew went to work. Right side tires flew off, then fresh rubber was slammed on. The tire changers sprinted around the car with the carriers in tandem and put fresh rubber on the left side. The gasman worked the second can of fuel into the tank.

The front tire changer reached out and gave the grille a swipe as Bear gave the command. "Go, go, go. Outside, stay outside." He looked over at Hildy.

"Twelve nine. Not bad."

Bear nodded. Then he watched as one official listened intently with his hand pressed against the earpiece, then motioned to Bear. Bear put his head down,

"Too fast entering. Have to do a drive through."

Bear nodded. There was no use arguing. The pit lane was loaded with sensors that picked up a signal from the race car's transponder. It was all done electronically nowadays. It came up on the computer, and if a car exceeded the mandated speed, it flashed red.

"Bad news, Orly. Speeding on entry. Have to do a drive through."

"My fault. I was pushing pretty hard. Sorry guys." Orly didn't waste any time or effort berating himself. Still plenty of time.

In the meantime, T.K. was flying. His pit stop was flawless and actually gained him several spots. Paolo only made a couple of minor pressure adjustments in the tires.

Paolo came down off the box to take a long look at the rubber that came off the car, and for the moment, he was happy. T.K. was pushing the car as hard as he possibly could and the right rear was showing it, but nothing dangerous. T.K. continued to run consistent laps as fast, if not faster, than the leader of the race. By the eighty-fifth lap, he had cracked the top ten and was sitting in ninth.

Orly wasn't finding it quite as easy to move up through the field. His car liked the clean air and was fast out front, but unfortunately, it was not nearly so quick back in the pack. He seemed mired back in the field.

"I've got a pretty bad push, Bear. Makes it really hard to get by some of these guys. Besides, there are a lot of loose cannons in the mix. I don't want to get caught up in somebody's lack of talent."

That was a polite way of saying that some of the boys were driving just a tad bit over their heads.

"Ten-four driver. Do what you can, and as soon as we get a chance, we will fix it."

Orly's mic clicked twice.

The chance came on lap 97 when the first caution came out. It was nothing major, just some debris on the exit of turn two. Looked like a cooling hose, but it could still do some damage if somebody ran over it. It opened the pit window for nearly everybody.

Paolo saw the flag first and gave the universal sign for caution, which was waving a pointed forefinger in a circle. It was a perfect time to come in.

"What do you need, T.K.?"

"Loosen me up just a tad. I'm just starting to get a little tight. Not too much though." T.K. flipped his visor up as the field idled behind the pace car and wiped his forehead. If they ripped off a good pit stop, he would be in this thing.

When the pits opened, practically the whole field came down the pit lane. Cars came down the road two and sometimes three abreast. Sarah wasn't prepared for the frantic activity.

Air guns were screaming, motors were thundering and tire smoke filled the air as the pit crews went about their work. Near misses were common. Tire changers and carriers were working at full speed. Every tenth of a second was precious. If you could pass your competitor in the pits, then you sure wouldn't have to pass him on the track.

Because his pit box was on the end, T.K. came sliding in first. The Blue Saber team did their job in spectacular fashion, and had him back out in a flash.

"Help me, Doug." It was the crew chief's job to exit

the car from the pit box. T.K. couldn't see much to the side. He had to rely on Paolo's call but Paolo couldn't see that far down the pit lane.

"Got it....go, go, go, T.K. Outside all the way to the grass."

T.K. exited the box in a blast of tire smoke.

Orly had an easier time. He found his box, no sweat. The Ballet Company did their thing. Bear made a small track bar adjustment and adjusted some air pressure. Because he had an open spot in front of him, they had Orly back in the mix in record time. As a result, he picked up several spots on the field.

Silas was enthralled. Hildy smiled at him.

"Don't worry, Buddy. He will make it up. He has a good car today. I bet you a nickel he's in the top five in twenty laps. What do you think?"

Silas nodded his head. He thought so too.

- *O* -

Experience shows that cautions breed cautions. What that means is that a caution flag bunches the field. Everybody essentially pits at the same time, and then the cars form up behind the pace car.

A number of guys are on new, cold tires that don't grip as well until they warm up and the pressures build. Everybody is eager also to take advantage of the situation, and the cars are running extremely close together. Because the cars develop over 800 horsepower, it is easy to spin the tires and lose traction as the green flag flies. One mistake and several innocent bystanders could reap the havoc.

- *O* -

When the dust settled and the field formed up, T.K. found himself on the outside of the fourth row in the eighth spot. Orly was back in the ninth row.

The starter watched the field carefully as they came off the fourth turn. He was satisfied and whipped the green flag from behind his leg. The car on the inside of the front row got a great start and jumped into the lead. The outside car fell into place behind him as the pack thundered into turn one.

By the time the cars hit the back chute, Orly had picked up four spots and T.K. moved up two. The pack stayed bunched as they built speed down the back chute heading for turn three. Everybody was cool until the second place car had something let go, and the car kissed the wall. As he ricocheted off the wall, he was immediately punted by the car behind him and the melee was on. Tire smoke filled the air as several cars piled into each other, spilling a lifeblood of oil and coolant and scattering parts across the track.

Both Doug and Jimmy went into high gear as they tried to get their drivers through the ensuing mess.

When the melee started, Orly was already committed to a move to the inside and the bottom of the racetrack. "Stay low, stay low...They're wrecking all around you. Back out easy, stay low." Orly dropped as low as he could, trying to miss several spinning cars. He dropped two tires into the grass, and that was all it took as he went sliding sideways through the infield. Twice the car bounced into the air, and he thought it was going over. He held the wheel lightly as he slid across the painted logos on the grass. It is a known fact that grass, particularly if it is damp, does nothing to scrub off speed. In fact in some cases, it seems like it does just the opposite. The Speed King Chevy seemed to pick up speed as Orly slowly pirouetted in two lazy circles. Finally he gathered it up and got it pointed straight.

"Watch the splitter!" Bear said as Orly slowed and headed back up to the racing surface. The splitter was the piece below the front grille. It was instrumental in providing the down force needed to keep the front end on the ground. It was made out of a one-piece fiber compound that was incredibly tough, but if it broke or was damaged, it would take a long time to repair.

"Howzit look Jimmy?"

T.K. in the meantime had also just made an aggressive move to the low side of the track when the chaos started. He found himself sliding sideways to the inside as somebody barely tapped him in the rear bumper. At the same time, he just caught a blur of something bouncing down the track, then *blam!* He nailed it. The racetrack looked blocked as he downshifted. He saw the opportunity and dove down the pit lane, trying to keep the car straight. He blasted by his own pit box at a 150 plus, trying to scrub off speed.

Doug yelled in his ear. "Good move. Back it down, back it down."

NASCAR was okay for "a move of avoidance" down the pit lane if a driver did everything he could to prudently slow the car. T.K. did just that, narrowly missing a car that was bouncing violently through the grass totally out of control. It was headed straight for him. T.K. swerved as the car slid backwards behind him and kissed the pit wall next to T.K.'s pit stall.

Paolo saw the car coming and said calmly "Get off the wall. Here he comes. Look out." *Bam!* The car hit the wall. Everybody on the pit box except Paolo jumped as the NASCAR officials and Blue Saber team scattered.

Sarah let out a little scream as she grabbed her seat with both hands.

There was a little puff of fire as a fuel line ruptured, spilling a small amount of gas on the ground. They just made a stop, so Paolo knew the car was chock full of high octane. But the fuel cell did its job and kept most everything inside, just like it was designed to do.

"Somebody get an extinguisher and get that out before we have more trouble." Paolo shifted focus. "You got any damage, T.K.? How does he look, Doug?"

"I'm not sure. I think I may have run over something. I heard a heck of a bang. Maybe a piece of brake rotor. I don't know, something heavy. Look it over good."

"I don't see any damage from up here." Doug was studying the Blue Saber car through his binoculars. "We have time. It's going to take awhile to clean up this mess. We have four cars that are finished. They won't be able to get them fixed for a long while. Three of them are Chase cars and one of them was ahead of us in points. If we can keep the wheels on, we might move up." Doug paused for a minute.

"Hold on. Yeah, NASCAR is red flagging the race while they get the mess cleaned up. Going to stop you up in turn one."

"Roger that."

"Park it on the banking up next to the wall in case

it won't start," Paolo said. Stock cars were notoriously hard to crank after they got hot. If it wouldn't catch, then T.K. could roll off the 24-degree banking to get a bump start. Everybody in the field had the same idea. It was against the rules for anybody to do anything to a car under the red flag. That didn't keep crews from getting their tools and replacement parts together so they could leap into action the moment the competition resumed.

Orly flipped the channel on his radio so he could talk to T.K. direct.

"Hey Man, how's it going?"

"Doing okay so far. Dodged that one by a hair. Got tapped and found myself heading down the pit lane. How about you, Orly?"

"Yeah, me too. Took a little excursion across the grass. Messed up the logos pretty good. Think the groundskeeper isn't going to be too happy."

"Did you get the splitter?"

"I don't think so, miracle of miracles, but they can't tell 'til I pit."

"You want me to get out and take a look?"

Orly laughed. Getting out of the car on the track during a red flag stop was immediate disqualification. "You damaged?"

"I think I ran over a brake rotor or something. Took out the right rear crush panel, I think. Where you running?"

"Not sure, tenth or twelfth or something. Where are you?"

"How did you get behind me? Last I saw, you were pulling the field by a bunch. Me? I think I am fifth or sixth, or maybe better. I don't know either."

"I broke the law on the first stop and got cited for speeding. Had to go to the back. Can't get the thing to handle quite as good in traffic."

"Bummer. Well, good luck, We'll see how it plays out."

"Yeah, you too." Orly looked down at his left leg. It was really throbbing, and it felt wet inside his driver's suit. *The burn has probably opened up*, Orly thought to himself. His hands were hurting as well, though not as much. He thought about peeling his gauntlets off, but he was afraid he wouldn't be able to get them back on. *Ah well, just have to live with it. Not going to quit now.*

- O -

The break in the action was a blessing for Sarah. She'd really been terrified when that race car came sliding right toward them. It hit the wall with a grinding thump barely ten feet away. It was at that point that she realized this auto-racing thing was not for her. It was incredibly noisy and so...well, violent. It seemed pointless.

She turned to Alicia. "Do you like this?"

"What, you mean racing?"

"Yes, I mean all the noise and things going on and the danger. It seems so dangerous. People could really get hurt. It just doesn't make a lot of sense to me. Why would somebody do this?"

"People do it for a lot of different reasons. Paolo does it for the challenge and the competition, I think. Doug does it because he has always done it and loves it. It is his heritage, his roots, I guess. I'm not sure what motivates T.K., but there is a lot of insecurity and desire to prove himself there. Gosh, Sarah I don't know. I do it because I like the excitement and travel and seeing and meeting new people. Besides, it pays well."

"I don't think it's for me." Sarah stood up and headed to the ladder off the box. She turned and said over her shoulder "I'm going down to check on Silas."

Sarah stepped out into the crush of people milling around behind the pit boxes and headed up the road toward Orly's box.

These people just don't understand, she thought to herself. *I live on the edge of danger every day. The most precious possession in the world could be taken from me at any moment. Silas' days are numbered. No sense in denying it.*

The thought filled her with dread. That was why she found it so hard to rationalize people risking their lives when they didn't have to. That's what made it seem pointless, at least to her. T.K. was a great guy, but it could just never work between them. She fished in her purse for a tissue. She blew her nose and wiped her eyes, as she walked with her head down.

Sarah stood and looked up at Silas on the box. "Hey Mommo, how you doing? Isn't this cool? Are you having a good time?" Silas was bubbling over with excitement. "I think Orly is still going to win. Bear and me have been calling a good race. T.K. is doing good, too. You watch, Mom, this is going to be great."

Hildy leaned down from the box. "You want to come up here, Sarah? We have room."

"No, I'll just stay down here. Is he being a good boy?"

"Yes, he is a wonderful boy."

Silas leaned over and spoke in Hildy's ear. "She still thinks I am boy. I'm getting to be a man."

"Of course you are, but you have to remember, all Moms think that about their children. You'll always be a boy in her eyes."

Sarah crossed the walkway behind the pit stalls and took a perch on a stack of tires. She couldn't see any of the track from there, which was fine with her.

- O -

Finally the command came to fire them back up. In the meantime, the official word came down from timing and scoring. T.K. was sitting sixth and Orly was in eleventh. They followed the pace car for a lap until the pits opened for business, and then it was game on.

Orly's crew put on four fresh tires and gassed the car. One tire carrier went to work clearing the sod off the splitter.

"Any brackets broke?" Bear asked him over the radio.

"No, don't see any. Not even bent. Splitter itself is beat up some, but no damage. Everything looks good."

"Turn him loose."

- O -

T.K.'s crew did the same thing, but they took a little longer checking the car for damage. Apparently the piece went under the car and knocked a chunk out of the right rear quarter panel and bent the crush panel. The crush panel was the piece that covered the rear wheel and sealed off the body of the car. It helped with the aero, but more importantly, it also kept the exhaust gasses from filling the inside of the cockpit. Back in the day, a driver could get very sick from carbon monoxide poisoning by the end of a race. Nowadays, drivers had a breathing system that not only cooled the air, keeping the driver comfortable, but filtered it as well. Air was pulled into a box, filtered and fed down from the top of the helmet. It was a vast improvement. T.K.'s crew went to work with the bear bond and the damage was soon fixed.

"Shouldn't bother you any," Paolo said.

"Roger that."

- *O* -

Both cars gave up a little track position with the long pit stops, but it couldn't be helped. T.K. was now back in twelfth, and Orly was back in the twenties somewhere. The field fell into place behind the pace car.

Bear leaned over to Hildy. "All right, where we sitting? I saw the 99 car go in the garage, but I haven't seen him come out yet."

Hildy looked at her screen. She was prepared for the question. "We started with Orly 7 points behind the 99 car. He's going to take a huge hit, and already has lost ten laps. The third place car in the points is currently running first and he could take the points lead if he wins, keeping Orly in second. If Orly wins…Ah Bear, there are fifteen different scenarios that could play out right now. T.K. stands to improve the most. If he wins, he could be right in the mix."

Bear nodded. "We need to win this race."

The pack came down and took the green flag once again. This time everybody kept things sane and was strung out by turn three.

T.K.'s voice came over the radio with a touch of anxiety. "Got a vibration. Are you sure all the wheels are tight?"

Paolo looked down at both tire changers. They both gave him a thumbs up. "That is a ten-four. Do you need to come in?"

"Not yet. But when I do, I need you to loosen me up. Maybe take a little wedge out of it."

"Run it a while. It will come to you." At this point, Paolo wasn't too concerned about the vibration. Could be any number of things. That brake rotor or whatever it was could have nicked the driveshaft or something. It might just be rubber buildup on the tires from the yellow flag laps, which would go away as the tires got hot. The crew said the wheels were tight with all the lugs on. He had to take their word for it. In the meantime, vibration or not, T.K. was working his way toward the front.

Orly was slicing and dicing like a surgeon. The adjustments Bear made to the car were working well. Orly was able to pass on the inside as well as the outside. He too was working his way toward the front.

Chapter Fourteen

"My purpose in life was to run 100 percent. Maybe it cost me some races but nobody ever hired me to ride."

Buddy Baker

Orly eased his foot down hard as he exited turn four. The eight hundred horsepower turned the Speed King Chevrolet into a guided missile as he whistled through the tri-oval. He was fast. He knew that. Right now this thing was a rocket ship, and he was liking it.

He set the car up, putting his focus on the entrance to turn one. He hit his marks perfectly, breathed the throttle for a second at the apex of the corner, then matted the gas. The car just started to slide on exit and rode up to the wall. Orly gently caught it, and without lifting, pointed it down the back chute. He could see the eighth place car about six car lengths in front of him. The guy was all over the seventh and sixth place cars. He was pushing hard as well, as he looked over his shoulder.

"You're catching him big time. Hit your marks. He

knows you're coming," Jimmy said. "Everybody has traffic coming. Got three lappers ahead of those guys. Should catch 'em in turn one. Be ready."

Orly clicked his mic twice.

Bear looked up at the scoring pylon. Ninety laps left. This latter section of the race was all green flag so far. If that trend continued, they could finish this thing out in two stops. Odds were it wouldn't. There was just too much at stake. Almost every single driver out there was giving it all that he had. Under this kind of pressure, somebody was going to screw up, or something break, or a tire go bad and there would be another if not several yellows before this thing was over.

- O -

Paolo stood on his pit box with his foot on the rail. As Bear would say, he was wound as tight as a dollar watch. He looked calm on the outside, but inside he was catching butterflies with a rolling pin. T.K. was running third and had been harassing the second place car for several laps. The guy was blocking. T.K. was going to run out of patience here in a minute and do something maybe a little bit foolish. When T.K. went high, the guy moved up to block. When T.K. dove down to the inside, the guy moved down, forcing T.K. to change his line. Paolo could hear the calming tone of Doug as he spoke.

"Be patient, T.K. Be patient, Dude. He's going to make a mistake. Pick your spot. It's just you and him. The leader isn't getting away, and fourth place is out of the picture for now."

Paolo watched as T.K. ran the car up to the wall through turn four and used a late apex to pull down behind the guy. Then, ever so slightly, he ducked to the inside, pulling the air off the guy's spoiler. It was just enough to make the lead car twitch, then T.K. made his move to the inside. He tucked his right front fender up next to the left rear quarter panel, side drafting the guy. The bubble of air from T.K.'s car was just enough to slow the guy down, and bingo, just like that, T.K. was into second place.

"Clear, nice move." Doug said as T.K. pulled away.

Man that guy can drive, Paolo thought to himself. It was a testimony to Paolo's humility that he gave no thought to the fact that he was calling an excellent race and keeping T.K. in this thing.

"Vibration is back. Seems to be getting stronger. Could be a wheel weight, I dunno."

"Roger that. We're in the window to finish out with two stops…whoa, yellow is out…looks like Orly…no, he is okay." Paolo looked at the pylon. Fifty-nine to go. "Bring it in as soon as we open for business."

- O -

Orly wasn't the cause for the caution, but he was nearly in the mix. Somebody got into a back marker and both cars spun. Orly had to tiptoe his way through the tire smoke, and in the process, flat spotted his own rubber. It was okay. It was time to pit anyway. This is the break everyone was looking for.

Bear had his head down making calculations. The best they could expect on a run was fifty-two or maybe fifty-three laps. After that, they would be out of fuel. The caution came out with 59 laps to go. It had been two laps since it came out, so now they were down to 57 left. The pit lane would open next time around, and that would make it 56. Two laps more before the green, figuring two yellow laps equals one green flag lap in terms of mileage, making it very, very close. Still too far, even if Orly could save some fuel. But then there was an option if they had another yellow and could save some fuel that way.

In the meantime, Paolo was doing exactly the same thing. T.K.'s driving style wasn't conducive to saving fuel. It didn't make sense to him. If you were going to run a race, then you might as well do it flat out. Period. Paolo knew from experience that Orly could be the master at saving fuel if he had to. If anybody had a chance at finishing this thing without any more stops it would be him. T.K....not so sure. The scenario didn't fit his style.

Silas was paying close attention. He was in this thing. In the course of the afternoon, he decided that he wasn't going to be a driver. Instead he was going to be a crew chief, just like Bear. He watched intently as Bear made his calculations. Then he leaned over to Hildy.

"Is Bear going to try to stretch the fuel and not come in again?"

Hildy looked back at him and shook her head. "Boy, you're pretty smart for a kid."

"I know how to pay attention. My Mom says I'm a good 'study'. I don't know exactly what that means, but I watch people a lot."

"Well in answer to your question, we will see.

Whatever he decides to do will give Orly the best shot. I think they were thinking two tires only, to get some track position, until Orly spun. Now he needs four."

Silas nodded his head wisely. Yes, that is what he would have done. Just putting on two tires would have saved some time in the pits and got him out sooner.

Both pit stops were flawless. T.K. held his position and would restart in second, outside on the front row. The Ballet Company did a spectacular job and got Orly out in fifth. Bear was effusive in his praise. "Good job, guys. Great job." Orly would start on the inside of the third row.

T.K. wanted Paolo to loosen the car a little more. Paolo was okay with that, but not as much as T.K. wanted. Of course, he didn't tell him. He simply had the tire man drop the pressure in the right front tire a tad more. He was very happy with that decision when he took a look at the right rear tire. It was wearing pretty good, but had just started to chunk. That explained the vibration. Telling T.K. to back off, especially at this stage of the race, would be a waste of time. Better to just watch the race and see what happens.

Orly was in pain. Not just little twinges of pain but deep searing, "my goodness this really hurts" pain. His leg seemed to be bleeding, although he couldn't tell how much. The g-force in the corner was pushing it against the seat and the fabric of his suit had rubbed the bandage off. His hands were absolutely throbbing. They were swollen, particularly the left one, but so far they still worked. He could grip the wheel. Fifty some odd laps left. *I can do this*, he thought. Orly would have to. He shifted gears in his head and put all his focus on the restart.

When the green came out, T.K. snatched the lead. After the race, the lead car driver said that T.K. jumped the start. But the camera replay would show that he didn't. Orly got bottled up, but on the next lap, he went three wide through the dogleg to move into third. Second place got his momentum back and set off after T.K. He pulled out to a nice two-second lead in the clean air, but then the second place car started reeling him in. The laps were melting down, one by one.

Orly was hanging in third, biding his time. He wasn't using everything the car had, at least not just yet. Just enough to stay out in front of fourth, fifth and sixth, which were bunched behind him.

With thirty laps to go, the second place car was on T.K. Twice the guy had tried to get a run on him, but T.K. fought him off. The crowd was on its feet. This was getting good. In the meantime, Orly was lurking in third, just hanging, and waiting to see how it would play out in front of him.

"He is getting ready to make another run. He has been cooling his tires for a couple of laps. Think he might dive to the inside." Doug sounded like he was watching a chess match.

"Roger." T.K. sounded just as cool.

The second place car made his move. He came high off turn four and tried to dive to the inside. The slight bump in the track upset his balance and put him on the edge of control. Using every bit of driving talent he possessed, he fought the car, still intent on making the pass for the lead. For race car drivers, there often comes a time when talent is overruled by the laws of physics.

As he pulled down beside T.K., his car slid up ever so gently to kiss the left rear corner of T.K.'s car. The contact put T.K. into a full throttle wiggle through the tri-oval. He managed to keep the car straight without scrubbing off too much speed.

The second place car was toast. The contact knocked him out of control and he spun, pounding the wall backwards in a cloud of smoke and grinding sheet metal.

"YELLOW OUT!"

Orly was through the mess before the pieces had time to scatter across the track. With 19 laps to go, the Orly Mann racing Team was now first and second.

Bear looked down at Hildy. "How many cars on the lead lap?"

"Twenty one."

Bear surveyed the track. It would take them at least five laps to clean up the track and drop the green. That would leave them with fourteen laps of racing left. If he brought Orly in for fuel, he would lose valuable track position. He also knew that T.K. pitted the same time as Orly. That meant he had about the same amount of fuel left. Probably a little less.

"Save me as much gas as you can, driver."

"How close are we, Bear?"

"Never you mind. Just drive the wheels off the thing. We will make it. Save me some fuel on these yellows and hold your position."

Orly's mic clicked twice.

- *O* -

The media crew was waiting for just this moment. Bear found himself with a microphone stuck in front of his face and a camera looking down his ear hole.

"So Henry, also known as Bear, what are you going to do? Any team orders here? You are the co-owner of the Orly Mann Team. Are you going to tell T.K. Kittridge to back off? Orly is leading in the points and a win would be a pretty good boost. Are you coming in for fuel? You must be pretty marginal."

"These guys are race car drivers. You don't tell them a whole lot. They drive and I just try to give them the best I got. Stop for fuel? You know better, Bob. I'm not going to tell you and the whole world. You'll just have to wait and see."

- O -

Paolo was faced with a dilemma. Run out of fuel and take a big hit in the points or bring T.K. in, be safe, and lose valuable track position and any opportunity to win the race.

"How many on the lead lap Doug?"

Doug was anticipating the question. "Twenty one."

Paolo looked over at Alicia to confirm. She nodded her head.

"Save every drop you can, T.K....every drop on these caution laps." Paolo folded his arms then pushed his talk button. "I think we can make it, and it's our only chance to pull off a win. If you want to come in for a splash and go, we can do that and salvage as many points as we can out of this, or you can stay out and we can gamble on finishing. The only thing that would kill us is a green white checker, and if that happens, then we come in. What do you want to do?"

"Let's go for it."

At least the TV reporter waited until Paolo was done talking with T.K., But as soon as Paolo was done, he stuck the mic in his face. "Are you going to stop, Crew Chief? You have to be right on the edge."

"Don't know yet. I think we'll probably do what the thirty seven car does."

"There you have it folks. Paolo Pelegrini, the young crew chief for the Blue Saber team is calling his first race and has elected to follow his boss. Sounds like a good call to us."

Paolo winked at Alicia. She smiled and nodded her head. Of course T.K. would go for it. *Does a Bear live in the woods*, as Bear would say. Alicia knew that Paolo was just as much a gambler.

The clean up took one lap longer than Bear figured. In the meantime, the pit lane opened but there were few takers. T.K. stayed out just using enough fuel to maintain reasonable speed behind the pace car. He was shutting the thing off as he let his momentum take him high on the banking of the corners and coasting down. Orly was doing exactly the same thing.

"Hey Hoss, is that you back there?"

"Yup. Right behind you."

"You got enough push juice to finish this thing?"

"Don't know, hope so. How about you?"

"I dunno. Guess we'll find out. I'm going to beat you, you know."

Orly smiled behind his shield. "Uh huh, that is if you don't run out of gas or I pass you, or we wreck or something."

Bear's voice came across the radio.

"All right, let's do this thing right."

The lights went out on the pace car, which meant that the green was coming next time by. Bear was pleased when the lights came back on. That meant that the track was not quite right, so they would run one more lap under yellow. *This is going to be the difference*, Bear thought to himself. Two yellow laps equal one green. Maybe just one more yellow lap for insurance. It was not to be.

Once again, the pace car scurried for the safety of the pit lane as the pack built momentum for the start.

Sarah could hear the thunder building. She looked up at the pylon and saw the #11 at the top with the #37 just below it. T.K. was leading, eight laps to go. Orly in second. She thought about standing up and finding a place to watch but thought again and stayed where she was.

T.K. timed it perfectly, but so did Orly. There was no tire spin from these guys. Just blinding acceleration as they thundered neck and neck through the tri-oval heading into turn one. The rest of the pack dropped quickly, left in the dust by the thoroughbreds.

Some drivers like to lead. Some like to follow. All of them like to win. Both Orly and T.K. could do either one, but when push came to shove they wanted the lead. Orly was known to say "The view is a lot better when you have a clear track in front of you. Sort of like the lead dog on a sled team."

It was strange for Doug spotting T.K. with Orly on his bumper. For almost his entire career, he had been part of Orly's team. Now he was trying to beat him. Jimmy on the other hand had no problem. His only responsibility was to see if anybody was closing on them from the back. Quite the contrary, T.K. and Orly continued to dump the field. It was basically a two-car race.

If there is one thing a professional race car driver must be able to do, it is to focus. Orly was so focused, he could count the rivets on T.K.'s bumper at 200 miles an hour. His brain was like a mega computer as he researched the various strategies he might use to get by this kid. He could flat out bump him out of the way. Just tap him a smidgeon and run him up the track out of the groove. No. He wouldn't do that. If Orly was going to beat him, he would do it fair. He would race him clean. He might crowd him some to get him loose, but he wouldn't touch him if he could keep from it.

T.K., on the other hand, was just trying to get every ounce of speed he could wring out of the Blue Saber car. For two solid laps, he never lifted his foot off the floor, knowing full well that Orly was doing exactly the same thing. Both of them had switched electrical boxes during the last caution period. What this did was take the rev limiter off the motor, allowing them to run it as tight as they possibly could, wringing every ounce of power it had. If it blew, it blew. So be it.

With four laps to go, T.K. came off turn four slightly airborne over the bump, sliding right up to the wall. He had to lift ever so slightly. Orly was on him like a hawk on a piece of meat. Orly tucked inside him, crowding T.K. up the track. Inch by inch, he gained the advantage. Finally, the side draft worked, and he gradually pulled ahead to take the lead into turn one. Now T.K.

was the aggressor.

The mega crowd at the Speedway was going absolutely crazy. They were certainly getting their money's worth today. Fans were screaming, pumping their fists and pounding each other on the back, urging the two cars on. The team up in the booth was falling all over themselves trying to find superlatives to describe the level of professional expertise that was unfolding in front of them.

Bear was off the pit box and down on the pit wall. He had to move. He couldn't stand still and watch this unfold. *Don't take each other out*, was all he was thinking. Paolo, on the other hand, was standing as still as a statue with just his head turning as he watched the cars flash by, then he focused on the big screen at the end of the pit lane until they came down the banking through turn three and into his vision once again.

Alicia was watching the network feed on the center counsel. Hildy didn't try to stand up. She knew her knees were too weak to support her. She felt sick to her stomach. She too was watching the network feed. Silas had struggled to his feet and was whooping and hollering and pumping his fist like everyone else.

With two laps to go, nobody was thinking about fuel until the third place car dropped down to the apron and coasted into the pit lane. Then the seventh place car followed him. Now it was a guess as to who had enough and who didn't. Several crew chiefs had everything crossed they could cross.

In the meantime, Orly felt it coming. He knew T.K. would give it one last shot. He could feel T.K. setting him up as he eased into turn three as smoothly as he could.

"He's a-comin'." Jimmy said calmly.

T.K. tried the crossover, diving to the inside as they came off turn four. Orly was already committed to his own line. They flashed across the start/finish line as the starter waved the white flag. This was it.

They jockeyed for position as they clawed up the banking in turn one. T.K. was on the inside. They came off two into the backstretch side by side for the last time with both engines screaming in agony. The side draft pulled both cars together, and they touched just ever so slightly at over 200 miles an hour.

It was apparent that neither man was going to lift. Both cars wiggled as the drivers fought for and regained control. Orly rode into the corner high then cheated down as low as he could, searching for the apex of the corner. T.K. was doing everything possible to hold the lower line. They powered through the corner side by side with neither driver having the advantage.

Then at the exit of the corner, they touched again, hanging together for a millisecond before coming apart. Fifty yards further, *bang!* They slammed together again, but this time with violence. The impact knocked the valve stem off of T.K.'s right front tire and as he came down on the inner liner, he lost control. The two cars locked together, spun backwards and slid across the finish line together in a massive cloud of smoke and debris.

The flagman was waving the checkered flag while fishing for the yellow. The cars then separated, and slid in opposite directions with T.K. going down low to the inside, spinning through the grass and harmlessly into the infield. In the meantime, Orly slid backwards up against the wall in a shower of sparks and grinding sheet metal, gradually coming to a stop.

The frantic flagman was waving two yellows and the checker as the pack thundered down. Fortunately everybody was still in the game and nobody hit anybody else.

Orly sat in the Speed King Chevy, trying to catch his breath. The last impact into the wall about did him in. He felt like his leg was going to split open like an overripe watermelon. He could hear both Jimmy and Bear trying to talk to him. But he couldn't understand what they were saying. He tried the starter switch. Nothing. He was stuck here up against the wall until they moved the car so they could get him out. No way he could climb out of this thing.

Finally a track medical worker slithered over the car and managed to get the window net down.

"You okay?"

"Left leg. Going to have to pull me out. Who won?"

"You did. They just showed the video. The back of your car crossed the line before his. You beat him by a the length of a deck lid."

- *O* -

They finally got Orly out of the car. He waved off the ambulance and headed to the Winner's Circle in a golf cart. The crowd was paying him tribute with a standing ovation. T. K. stood waiting for him. He would have the trauma center check his leg out after the victory celebration for the winner. Somehow it didn't hurt quite as much right now.

T.K. hopped up beside him on the cart to the delight of the crowd. He gently patted his back. "How you doing?

"What is it Coburn said? Feel like I been rode hard and put away wet."

"Yeah, I know what you mean. I didn't think I was tore up 'til just now. I couldn't get out of the car. Man, I'm sore from Friday and today, too."

"Who says race car drivers aren't athletes?"

"For a fact. Hey Orly, you beat me fair and square. Maybe someday when I grow up, I might be as good as you." He started to hop off the cart. "See you in the media center afterward."

Kid you have no idea how good you really are, thought Orly to himself.

"No, come with me. We'll celebrate together with both teams. We deserve it."

- O -

Bear sat down on the pit wall totally exhausted. He finally relaxed when they got Orly out of the car. He offered a quiet prayer of thanks. Dr. Miller came up and sat down beside him. "You must be just flat worn out Henry, my friend. They are saying that it was the closest finish in the history of the track. Also the first one in which the first and second place cars finished backwards."

"You know Roger, this just don't get any easier the older I get."

"Well, it looked to me like Paolo did a pretty good

job. You know, maybe you ought to start thinking about the future."

"Yeah, that's a thought. You going to Phoenix next week?"

"Oh yes, they've asked me to come. Besides, I wouldn't miss it." Miller put his arm around Bear's shoulders. "Thanks Lord for today, this weekend and all that has taken place. We hope it brings glory to your name, Lord Jesus."

Dr. Miller stood up. "You better get going. They'll be looking for you in the Winner's Circle. Looks like both your teams are there."

The celebration in the Winner's Circle was chaotic. Everybody was still whooping and hugging and dancing around. The soda pop was flying, making everything sticky but nobody cared. This was a major team victory and it was treated accordingly. Bear couldn't have been more proud.

Orly shot the six guns, which were a part of the winner's tradition at Texas, and put on the hat. He gave his interviews, thanking his team and most of all, his sponsors. Then he put his arm around T.K. and said "Folks let me tell you something. This kid can drive. What a race huh?"

Silas had the time of his life in the celebration. Afterward they had to power wash his wheel chair to clean all the soda pop and sticky stuff off everything. They even let him hold the six guns that are traditionally awarded to the winner. They took his picture in the ten-gallon hat next to the trophy, and he was included in all the team pictures. It was great fun. Then R.W. Coburn showed up with a great big old silver belt buckle and presented it to him. Engraved on it were these words:

Winning Crew Chief Assistant.
Silas Biggs
Texas Motor Speedway
Sponsored by TxARM

Everybody took his picture holding it up. A copy of that picture hangs on Dr. Miller's wall.

- *O* -

It took T.K. awhile to get disentangled from the media obligations, but as soon as he did, he set out in search of Sarah. He found her back in the motor coach packing up.

"Can I come in?" he said over the intercom.

"Sure, come in. Silas is in the tub getting that sticky stuff off him and out of his hair."

T.K. came into the coach. He hadn't taken time to change and he was still in his grimy driver's suit.

"Sarah, I'm sorry about this morning. I didn't mean to be so selfish. Listen, I heard what you did last night for me. The risk you took. I had no idea! I wouldn't have let that slime ball get anywhere close to you. I was pretty angry when Coburn told me about it, but after I thought about it, I realized you did it for me. Thank you."

"Yes I did, T.K. I thought you deserved better. It's done now and hopefully he won't bother anybody for a while."

"Thank you. Listen, Sarah, I was wondering…Well,

I was wondering if you and Silas would like to come to Phoenix next weekend. I could put you in a coach. Fly you there and back. It is just a short hop. It would be fun."

"No T.K., you don't understand. Silas looks fine tonight, but I can almost guarantee you that by tomorrow he will be exhausted and more than likely will spend a few days in bed. I'm praying that he doesn't develop a fever before we can get home and back into our routine. This weekend has been fantastic, and I just can't thank everyone enough for making it so special for him and me." Sarah started to cry. "I just can't drag him around. He hasn't got the strength for it."

T.K. crossed the room and took her in his arms. "Sarah, I want to see you."

She pulled back. "I know you do, T.K., and I would like that, but we just live in a different world than you do. Silas is in the midst of a war that he can't win. I have to do everything possible to keep him strong. You have to understand that."

"He also has a right to live, Sarah."

It was at that point that Silas came hobbling out of the bathroom in an oversize robe. "Hey T.K. you almost did it! Wow, that was exciting."

"Thanks, Silas. We gave it a shot, but Orly just had too much. Hey, I just dropped by to say so long. I'm flying out of here in a little while. Got to take care of some business then get ready for next week. It has been great fun getting to know you and your Mom. You guys are good people. I hope I see you again soon." T.K. dropped down on one knee and gave Silas a gentle hug.

Then he stood up and said to Sarah "I understand. I

understand a lot more than you think I do. Thanks for everything." Then he was gone.

- *O* -

Once you hit highway 287, it's a direct route from the Denton area to Amarillo. The highway shoots straight across the cotton fields and the flat prairie. Maybe fifteen miles outside of the little town of Childress, there's a rest stop. Parked in that rest stop was an abandoned RV with Arizona dealer license plates. The owner was nowhere to be found. The RV sat in the rest stop for the prescribed legal limit until it was dutifully towed to the storage yard to await its fate.

Epilogue

"When you are finished, then you are done."
Henry "Bear" Erickson

Bear sat in his office looking down on the deserted shop. The black dog sat patiently with his head on Bear's knee waiting for a scratch behind the ears. The shop was quiet for once, but that was to be expected this time of year. It was the Christmas holiday break. Most everyone was spending time with family and friends, and trying to recover from a very wild season.

Orly won the Championship but not by much. T.K. nearly pulled it off with a win at Phoenix, but Orly won the last race of the year at Homestead, sealing the deal. It really was a fantastic finish, and Bear couldn't have been more satisfied. He had made up his mind that he would turn the Orly Mann team over to Paolo next year, but they still weren't certain who would be driving.

Orly was retiring. Bear wasn't surprised. The baby was due in the middle of April. Bear wasn't exactly sure, but he thought they were doing the holidays out in the Napa Valley. They liked it there. Perhaps they would

301

put T.K. in the Speed King car and find a driver for the Blue Saber Team. It was yet to be decided.

Paolo and Alicia were on the West Coast enjoying themselves and were deeply immersed in wedding plans. Looked like the first or second week of January. That was a no-brainer.

Bear leaned back in his chair and re-read the beautiful Christmas card and the note inside.

Dear Henry,

Thank you once again for the great time at Texas Motor Speedway. There is no way to express my gratitude. You were all so very kind to us, just wonderful. Dr. Miller and the TxArm people were a blessing beyond belief. Silas talks about it nearly every day.

Silas is not doing well. He has had several bad episodes and they have sapped his strength. Dr. Eilersen is deeply concerned and in his kind way, has tried to prepare me for a possible bad outcome. I am taking it one day at a time and trying to do my best to live life with Silas. We are simply trusting God.

We do see T.K. on a regular basis, and he is coming to see us this Christmas. Silas is excited, as am I. He bought Silas a cell phone, and I understand that they text each other all the time. T.K. is a very kind man. He and Orly have made such a difference in Silas' life.

Thank you again, Henry. May the Lord Bless you and keep you.

In His Peace,
Sarah Biggs.

Bear laid the card down and absently scratched the dog. Then he looked down. "Well my friend, what's it going to be for us? I think I got a nice, big ole sweet bone for you at home. Let's get out of here and go put our feet up. What you say?"

CPSIA information can be obtained at www.ICGtesting.com
Printed in the USA
LVOW040145310312

275436LV00001B/4/P